THE
EULOGIST

THE
EULOGIST

JEFFREY B. BURTON

THE PERMANENT PRESS
Sag Harbor, NY 11963

For information, address:
   The Permanent Press
   4170 Noyac Road
   Sag Harbor, NY 11963
   www.thepermanentpress.com

Library of Congress Cataloging-in-Publication Data
   Burton, Jeffrey B., author.
      The eulogist / Jeffrey B. Burton.
      Sag Harbor, NY : The Permanent Press, [2017]
      ISBN 978-1-57962-502-3
         1. Serial murder investigation—Fiction. 2. Suspense fiction.
      3. Mystery fiction.

   PS3602.U76977 E95 2017
   813'.6—dc23   2017024218

Printed in the United States of America

For my daughter, Maddie.

Here rests his head upon the lap of earth
A youth to fortune and to fame unknown.
Fair Science frowned not on his humble birth,
And Melancholy marked him for her own.

—THOMAS GRAY, "Elegy Written in a
Country Churchyard"

PROLOGUE

"How does one take measure of a man? What tailor tape to assess a love of family? What surveyor wheel to gauge the depth of friendship? What scale to weigh his deeds?"

The orator paused to take a breath. "It is with weighted hearts that we gather here today to bid farewell to a dearly loved public servant, a man who placed every fiber of his being—his very soul—into helping others. A man considered by even the most jaded cynic to be a guiding light in an oft dark night. We want not to mourn or grieve today, as there shall be ample time for sorrow, but rather to share memories, and to commemorate, celebrate, an extraordinary life . . . extraordinarily well lived."

The orator paused to peer over a set of designer spectacles at an audience of one—a gray-haired man sitting silently, listening with a fierce intensity, in the armchair before the eulogist.

"Please indulge me in some remembrances of our mutual friend and forgive me if I get a bit misty-eyed. His was a charitable spirit that rose from the most

9

humble of beginnings in the marshes of Big Lick in the heart of the Blue Ridge Mountains, but he went on to soar to truly remarkable heights in the nation's capital. He came from working the railways of the Blue Ridge to chairing the United States Senate Committee on Agriculture, Nutrition, and Forestry. Yes, indeed, his was truly an amazing journey, and one that began a mere fifty-six years ago this past March. The late Senator Taylor Brockman—"

The solitary witness began to tremble in his chair. An unintelligible sound rose from deep within his throat—a series of moans, a grunt, and then a whimper—all struggling to escape, but the words failed in their flight for freedom most likely due to the wide strip of duct tape covering his mouth. More strips bound his wrists, abdomen, and ankles, anchoring him to the armchair.

"The late Senator Taylor Brockman," the orator resumed after the witness had settled down, "devoted family man that he was, leaves behind a loving wife, Elaine, and though Senator and Mrs. Brockman had no children of their own, the couple doted on their niece and nephew, Traci and Richard, of whom they could not have been prouder." The orator stopped for a moment of silent reflection before resuming. "It must also be noted how the church played no small role in Senator Brockman's life; sculpting him from early on into the generous and loving soul that all here would be proud to call our friend. A deeply religious man, and, as a fixture of Saint Peter's on Capitol Hill, the senator will be sorely missed at Sunday Mass."

Again the witness began to struggle in his chair, this time rocking back and forth, hard, then harder, but the chair was heavy and his limbs bound tight. The orator brought a forefinger to lips, then took it away and gently whispered, "Please, you're being disrespectful."

After a minute the struggle trickled down to minor quivering, like a terrified puppy, and then nothing at all. The witness began to breathe heavily through his nose.

A second minute passed before the orator continued. "Though the senator was fearless in his politics, he never let partisan rancor get the best of him. He was modest in victory, good-natured in defeat. Those on the other side of the aisle would be the first to admit that once debate had ended for the day, Senator Brockman would be there with an outstretched hand, a broad smile, and an open heart. Political differences set aside, the senator had nary an enemy." The orator thought for a second and then ventured off script, "Well—nearly none."

The witness sat motionless, eyes straight ahead; a single tear rolled down his moist face, past his nose, and onto the duct tape.

"Always optimistic about the future, there were, unfortunately, undertakings near and dear to Senator Brockman that remain unfinished. There were serious budget matters to address, there were the citizens of the Commonwealth of Virginia that he'd sworn to protect, there was his relentless work on behalf of our wounded warriors—the senator would be embarrassed for my even having mentioned that. But that is now all in the past, his past, and, as

Senator Brockman himself was fond of saying, 'The past is no place to dwell.'

"Yes, it hurts to think that this good man is gone, when there was more on the senator's plate for him to complete, more endeavors to bring to fruition, more lives to better;" the orator placed the eulogy on the senator's cherrywood desk and reached for the small satchel that had been waiting there, "but such is the tragedy of an untimely death, such is the tragedy of a life *cut* short."

PART ONE

GATHERING MEMORIES

CHAPTER 1

Day 1

Special Agent Drew Cady edged through the gathering of reporters and badged his way past the police barricade that had been set in place to keep the news media from roaming freely about the normally tranquil street in the predawn light of Woodley Park. If Cady hadn't gotten that sinking feeling when his ex-boss Roland Jund, the newly minted director of CID—the FBI's Criminal Investigative Division—had called to switch locations of where the two were meeting for breakfast from Lincoln's Waffle Shop on Tenth Street to a residential address in one of the swankier districts of DC, he certainly got one hunting for an open parking spot in a neighborhood now bustling with official activity. Cady took in the scene as he squeezed past the barricade. News vans, squad cars from the Metropolitan Police Department, flashing police lights, a couple of ambulances, some government sedans, glaring headlights, the buzz of police radios, cameras rolling, snapshots clicking, officers and plainclothes buzzing about like bees around a hive, the symphony of a dozen urgent conversations.

And outside the front door of the three-story brownstone which seemed to be the central focus—in the heart of the mix—stood Director Roland Jund, who watched Cady as he approached.

All this and the sun had yet to rise.

"Absolutely not," Cady said as he shook Jund's extended hand. Waffles and a side of murder were never a good mix.

"But Liz is up there," Jund said, ushering Cady out from the limelight and to a darkened boulevard across the street from the brownstone. "Don't you want to say 'Hi' to Liz?"

Liz was Special Agent Elizabeth Preston—CID Director Roland Jund's right hand at the bureau. Liz was the person who made the trains run on time and, without whom, Cady figured Jund would still be an AD, an assistant director of CID, had Jund a bureau job at all. Cady would walk through fire for Agent Preston. For Roland Jund? Not so much.

"I'm meeting Liz for dinner tomorrow at Filomena." Filomena Ristorante was an Italian eatery in Georgetown.

"And you didn't invite me?" Jund frowned like a kindergartner forced to surrender his pack of Crayolas.

"You were going to buy me an early breakfast this morning, and then you detoured me here," Cady said and pointed down the street where the expanding herd of reporters was being held at bay. "They don't look like waiters."

Cady had worked as a CID agent for Jund for the better part of a decade. Throughout that time he'd been shot at, stabbed, and knocked to a pulp. As a result of one particularly trying case, he'd had six separate surgeries on his right hand, which, on a good day, worked at 40 percent. Cady had fallen in love with a resort owner in northern Minnesota, Terri Ingram, gotten married, and had been able to pull off a midcareer rebellion—leaving CID—and, instead of tracking violent felons, Cady now pursued white collar criminals or "white collar pussies" as Director Jund deemed them.

It was the last day in July and Cady was in Washington, DC, as the FBI liaison for the Medicare Fraud Strike Force out of Minneapolis, which, along with official representatives from similar groups sprinkled about the country, had come to the nation's capital to testify before the United States Senate Committee on Finance. Cady was essentially attending as a gopher, on hand to reply to any statistical queries on which the Minneapolis field office had tracked in regard to their attempts at recovering the mountain of cash scammed by felons committing healthcare fraud—doctors penning needless prescriptions in return for kickbacks, patients leasing out their Medicare numbers, fake physical-therapy claims, phony DME charges for nonexistent durable medical equipment, bogus invoices for unused drugs, mythical MRI and MRA tests—a seemingly endless buffet of phantom billing schemes set up by Medicare cheats to bilk the already overmatched federal program.

More essentially, Cady saw it as a free trip to DC, and it provided Cady an opportunity to visit old colleagues at the J. Edgar Hoover Building, the headquarters of the Federal Bureau of Investigation. But now, at the crack of daybreak in Woodley Park, he stood before his ex-boss and listened as Jund did

his best to coax, wheedle, cajole and tap-dance Cady
into taking a gander at what, based upon the flock
of uniforms stationed about the entranceway of the
upscale brownstone across the street from where
Jund and Cady stood quibbling, appeared to be the
site of DC's most recent homicide.

Cady marveled at how Jund had once been able
to play him like a cheap toy out of a kid's meal box.
But those days were gone.

"Not my problem," Cady replied.

During his time in CID Cady had successfully
plodded through a handful of onerous cases and—as
a result, Cady figured—Director Jund had an overin-
flated notion of Cady's investigative abilities. Either
that or the director was too lazy to mentor new
personnel.

"I don't see what harm can come from us going
inside."

"No offense, sir, but Terri believes you caused
the dinosaurs to go extinct and Atlantis to fall into
the sea."

Jund frowned again, that same kindergartner now
being informed by the principal that his parents had
been called. Cady noted that with his ascension to
director of CID, Jund's line of dark suits also appeared
to have ascended. He now stuffed his barrel chest
into Brioni and Hugo Boss instead of off-the-rack
two-for-one deals from the Men's Wearhouse.

At nearly six foot one, Cady loomed over Jund—
not that it had any effect on his old boss. Cady had
dark brown hair—medium cut per Terri's input—with
a few gray strands recently added to the palette.
He had a halfway pleasant-looking face, but, having

bounced back from a shattered jaw and busted nose, Cady was thankful he didn't scare small children.

"Don't get me wrong. Terri finds you charming, Roland, but remains convinced you're the Antichrist."

"She gives me too much credit," Jund replied. "I hardly believe going inside for a quick look will drop the seven plagues upon us."

"Terri feels that my working for you again would tempt the fates. According to her, it would be, 'Hubris with a smackdown by Nemesis,' unquote."

"Lit major, was she?"

"I'm sorry, Roland, but you know I no longer work these cases."

Jund shook his head. "I'm not asking you to give up that cushy gig of yours, and I'm certainly not asking you to come back to CID, god forbid—we wouldn't take you back. It's just a damned shame that you happen to be here in town the first time a sitting United States senator has been assassinated since Robert Francis Kennedy, and you won't so much as cross the road to piss on a fire."

Cady stared at Jund a long second, and then turned toward the brownstone.

"A dead senator's in there?"

CHAPTER 2

"Hey, Liz."

Agent Preston was on the second floor landing of the brownstone talking to a shaved head that Cady pegged as an ME—medical examiner. Instead of the expected smile or nod, Cady got rolled eyes as Preston began fishing about in a side pocket. She took out a twenty-dollar bill and handed it over to Director Jund.

"What's that about?" Cady asked.

"He bet he could get you in here, Drew," Preston replied. "I said no way. Turns out he knows you better than I do."

"That's a scary thought."

Jund smirked as though he'd had a big night in Vegas.

Cady had known Liz Preston for north of a decade. Their relationship had evolved from the strained discomfort of colleagues pursuing different methods of investigation—age-old questions of ends and means—to one of trust and reliance before, somewhere along the line, evolving into friendship.

Cady hadn't seen Liz Preston since he and Terri had tied the knot. In the interim, Preston'd had her hair trimmed medium short and, evidently, stopped the coloring as it was now more salt than pepper. And she looked exhausted. Cady knew Liz logged ungodly hours at CID—a life he no longer missed— and he imagined that the frantic wake-up call she'd undoubtedly received several hours earlier hadn't helped matters.

Preston finished with the ME. "As long as you're here, Drew, there's something you need to see."

"A thin blade, razor sharp, perhaps a scalpel twenty-two or longer." The ME's name was Quenan. Quenan was with the bureau. In addition, a physician from DC's OCME—Office of the Chief Medical Examiner—who'd been early to the scene drifted around the periphery, doing his best not to look angered that his initial work might be getting second-guessed. Senator Taylor Brockman had been duct-taped to an armchair. The late senator was clothed in plaid pajamas, his head lolled forward and it appeared as though he were fixating on his own death wound— the blood from a single lesion had streamed down his chest, flooding over patches of tape, before settling in his lap. Quenan used a tweezers to pull aside the pajama top. "The blade entered below his left nipple, between the fifth and sixth ribs. The blade sliced through the costal cartilage like a hot knife through butter. One thrust, straight to the heart." ME Quenan glanced from Agent Preston to Agent Cady and then looked hard at Director Jund. "The UNSUB knew exactly what he was doing."

Cady knew about stab wounds, and what Cady knew would make him opt for death by gunshot any day of the week. The main purpose of the rib cage is to protect the vital organs of the chest cavity, primarily the heart and lungs. Most stabbing deaths result in the victim bleeding to death from multiple arterial wounds as a deep pierce directly into the heart is quite rare. Unlike the slasher films—where it appears effortless for the man in the hockey mask to impale the screaming coed to the kitchen cabinet with the carving knife—in real life the rib cage and shoulder blades stop the death thrusts until the perpetrator eventually figures out that he'd have better luck with the soft tissue of the neck or going upward under the rib cage from the abdomen.

A nasty way to die. However, per ME Quenan, their UNSUB—unknown subject—knew exactly what he was doing, with almost surgical precision. And that meant one thing to Cady.

Their man had done it before.

"The home security system indicates that the senator used his keypad password to disarm the system when he arrived last night at 7:02."

"So Senator Brockman was seen leaving Dirksen at roughly half past six o'clock last night and arrived here at 7:02." Cady digested aloud what Agent Preston had recited from her notes. Dirksen was the Dirksen Senate Office Building which housed Brockman's office. "He enters through the garage door where he parked his LS, punches in the code so he can move about the house, but still leaves the sensors active in case someone kicks in a door or breaks a window. Right?"

"Correct," Preston replied.

"But there were no busted windows or kicked-in doors. And no alarm went off?"

"Correct," Preston repeated.

"So potentially," Cady said, glancing about for Jund—but the CID director was now MIA, had likely hightailed it out of there to go eat the breakfast that he had promised to buy Cady—"the UNSUB had gotten in earlier and was lying in wait."

Preston shook her head. "The senator went for a late walk last night and got back at eleven."

"How do we know this?"

"We've got a record of him returning home, by the front door this time, at 11:04 P.M."

"And how do we know this?"

Preston consulted her notes. "There's a motion-activated security camera trained on the front entry. It's at the second-floor level to keep thieves from knocking it out. It takes digital pictures of visitors, delivery men, whatnot."

"Show me."

Unlike the bald ME, the agent from the FBI Laboratory had a tennis-ball buzz cut—there was still potential. The agent's name was Merrill. The three stood in the front entryway as he tilted a palm-sized app toward Cady and Preston. Merrill first back-arrowed them through a half dozen or more shots of Senator Brockman's executive assistant, a young redhead named Thornton Moss, out front pressing the doorbell, checking his watch, re-ringing, then knocking, looking up, and, finally, working his cell phone. Moss had been pointed out when Cady first entered the brownstone. Late twenties with crimson hair in a cowlick, the aide still sat on brown leather in the living room, staring straight ahead, his complexion whiter than the wall paint. The photographic portfolio of young senate aide Moss that Merrill displayed had been time stamped throughout the course of an eight-minute interval, beginning at 12:40 A.M.

Agent Merrill then displayed the single portrait of Senator Brockman and said, "Only took a quick snap so the senator must have had his key ready and was inside within a second. With motion units like these, if there's a FedEx guy fumbling with a dolly and packages, you get enough proofs for a wedding album."

"When was the senator clocked leaving for his walk?" Cady asked.

"He's not," Merrill replied. "No pics out the front door from earlier in the evening. The sliding glass door in back has a similar digital unit, but that also indicates no activity. Which means he left through the garage."

"But then he'd have to carry the clicker from his Lexus to shut the garage door."

Merrill shrugged. "The battery on my car remote ran out once and I spent a week hitting the button by the house door and then running like hell to beat the door coming down and jump over the sensors. He could have done that."

Cady nodded, figuring that fell within the infinite realm of human nature. He focused on the picture of the senator returning from his nighttime stroll. "His head's at an awkward angle, Liz. Not a natural posture. So all we get is thick gray hair, part of an ear lobe, a portion of his suit"—Cady had earlier walked through the late senator's walk-in closet and seen nothing on the wooden hangers besides gray wool suits—"and down at the bottom there we see the tip of a pointed-toe shoe or boot."

Cady twisted his head at what appeared to be a similar awkward angle for several seconds and shrugged.

"Talk to me, Drew."

Cady pointed at the senator's hair and looked at Preston. "Is that a rug? Did Brockman wear a toupee?"

"Mine started falling out in my early twenties." ME Quenan hunched over Brockman and ran a comb through the senator's hair, examining the follicles. "It hit me harder than 9/11. I wasn't married at the time and realized I'd have to get by on my sparkling personality."

"It's real, right?" Cady asked.

"No rug, no plugs," Quenan said, standing. "That's the senator's real hair."

"Tay's hair was his most authentic feature," a voice spoke from the brownstone's office doorway.

The agents followed the voice to a forty-some-thing redhead, a woman in heels and a black dress and who appeared more suited to attend an opera than identify a body. An officer from the front foyer stood by her side.

Senator Brockman's wife had arrived.

CHAPTER 3

"I took the house on Chesapeake Bay, and Tay lived here," Elaine Brockman said. "Our marriage had become one of . . . convenience."

Cady smelled mints—Certs or tic tacs—and figured Mrs. Brockman had had a bump or three on her flight to DC after having been notified of her husband's death. Up close her makeup contrasted with her formal attire and looked as if it had been applied by rote. Her eyes were red and she clung to a saturated Kleenex one sneeze away from biodegrading.

"A marriage of convenience?" Agent Preston asked, gently probing.

"Wouldn't be the only one in this town," Elaine Brockman replied. "Campaigns, major events, photo ops, Christmas cards—count me in. Otherwise, well, his office kept me in the loop."

Cady remembered reading an article in the *Washington Post* a year or two back detailing the country's wealthiest legislators. Senator Taylor Brockman had been near the top of the list, not so much from his taxpayer-funded stipend, but because he'd married the single remaining heiress to the Newell Suites Hotel Company, LLC, the parent company of the world-renowned chain of Newell Suites Hotels. And the heiress stood before him now—Elaine Newell Brockman.

"But you called his aide to check on him last night, right?" Cady asked.

"Our Chesapeake house looks like the set of *Falcon Crest* and needs a major facelift if we ever hope to sell. Tay caught wind of the upcoming renovation costs and left some snarkiness on the answering machine for me. I heard the message late last evening and it became imperative that I tell Tay to 'shove it' before his head hit the pillow. I couldn't get him on his cell or the landline and he wasn't returning my text messages, so I started worrying about his diabetes and called Thornton to go check on him. I thought he might be having a diabetic attack."

"Has he had attacks before?"

Mrs. Brockman nodded. "That's what led to his diagnosis last year. Tay lost weight, which is good, and he's on meds and has an insulin pen, but, I didn't trust him to monitor his glucose levels. Quite frankly, Tay wasn't happy that he now had to bother with all that bullshit."

"Would you know if the senator worked on a draft of his own obituary? Perhaps after the diabetes came into play?"

"It was diabetes, not incurable cancer. Why do you ask?"

"A draft of Senator Brockman's obituary, or, more accurately, a eulogy written for him, is sitting on top of his desk."

"Let me see it."

"We'll get you a copy once they're done in here," Cady said, nodding toward the forensic activity continuing in the senator's den. "It's full of praise for the senator."

"I could see Tay tinkering with an obit on his PC, highlighting accomplishments he'd like to be remembered for, but not a *eulogy*. Eulogies are prepared by others, right—a family member or friend?"

The agents both nodded. Then Preston began— delicately, tactfully—following another line of inquiry: "Could your husband have brought a *visitor* home last night?"

"By visitor you mean another woman?"

Preston nodded again.

Widow Brockman shrugged. "I imagine Viagra may have bought him a new lease on life. We had one rule: Be Discreet. Tay knew damn well I'd never be a Silda Spitzer and stand by him at a podium." She glanced across the room at a photographer snapping close-up pictures of her dead husband and brought the dying Kleenex up to an eye. "Whatever his personal flaws, Tay didn't deserve this."

Preston gave Mrs. Brockman a moment to compose herself and then in a warm, imitation social-worker voice asked, "Is there anyone you'd like for us to call? Family members."

"His parents are dead and I couldn't—" She stopped midsentence. "We didn't have children."

"Do you have any idea who could have done this to your husband?"

Brockman shook her head.

"Anyone who harbored ill will against him?" Cady asked. "Recent death threats?"

Brockman shook her head again. "Just the usual partisan pissiness. If you believe the polls, more than half of Virginia hated his guts. You should check with Thornton on any death threats."

"How tall was your husband?" Cady asked.

"Six four. Maybe six three with age."

"Did he wear boots?"

"Cowboy boots now and again on the campaign trail. It is Virginia after all and he made a point of getting close to his opponents, knowing they'd look like dwarfs next to him in the newspaper photos."

"Did he wear them in Washington?"

Brockman shook her head. "Tay was more city slicker than clodhopper."

"Would the senator go for walks late at night?"

"How late?"

"Eleven . . . thereabouts."

She thought for a second. "It's not impossible, but not likely. Even before the diabetes, he had a treadmill put in the bedroom." Her eyes focused on Cady. "Why are you asking these questions?"

"Just trying to establish a timeline, when the senator was last seen."

Mrs. Brockman nodded her understanding. Cady glanced at a portrait in a gold wood frame that hung in the hallway at the top of the staircase. It was likely taken after Taylor Brockman first won election to the senate, as a younger Mrs. Brockman sat in an armchair while a more youthful Senator Brockman stood behind her in one of his trademark gray suits, white shirt, and red tie. Both looked somber, perhaps instructed to look serious by the photographer. The senator had a hand on each of Mrs. Brockman's shoulders. Cady saw a gold wedding ring on the senator's left hand, and a silver ring on the corresponding finger of the senator's right hand.

"We'll also need you to go through the house and make a list of anything that you notice is missing."

"You think this was a burglary?"

Cady shrugged and pointed at the portrait. "He's not wearing that silver ring on his right hand."

"Oh, Christ, that thing," Brockman said. "Tay had that made when he got elected. It's sterling silver with the senate seal on top. Other senators gave him a lot of shit about it. I'm sure he tossed it years ago."

There was a mild commotion from below, and then a female voice, tentative, "Elaine? Elaine, are you up there?"

Mrs. Brockman glanced toward the stairway leading down to the brownstone's first level. "That's my chief of staff."

"Since I'm Elaine's only staff member, you could consider me her chief of staff, but I'm really her social secretary," Dorie Searles said in response to brief introductions.

"Don't believe her. Dorie's a lifesaver—seriously— a counselor at Betty Ford, where we met. And where I stole her from."

Unlike Mrs. Brockman's formality of apparel, Dorie Searles looked like she'd escaped a fire in the middle of the night—tennis shoes and gray sweats, brown hair ponytailed back with a scrunchie, not a drop of makeup—however, a pair of black Burberry eyeglasses added a hint of bookishness. Inches taller than the senator's wife, Searles enshrouded a passive Brockman in her arms, a mama grizzly embracing her cub, and whispered, "I am so sorry, sweetheart. I am so sorry."

Cady wondered if Searles had caught a whiff of Elaine Brockman's minty breath. He checked his watch for the third time in the last minute. He was still late. And not just for breakfast. He was officially tardy for the start of the Finance Committee hearing, which had begun in a room in the Hart Senate Office Building on Constitution Avenue several minutes earlier.

He had joined the senator's wife as she headed down the stairs and made her way to the entrance hall of her husband's DC home. Searles had gotten past the barricade, dropped Mrs. Brockman in front of the brownstone, and then went in quest of an elusive parking spot. Deemed nonessential at a secured crime scene, Searles had not been allowed in, and had been fussing with one of the officers in the entryway as to whether he would grant her fair notice if a truck were dispatched to Woodley Park to tow away her Passat. She wasn't having much luck when Cady and Mrs. Brockman came downstairs to join her followed moments later by Agent Preston.

With a quick nod and a wave Cady headed out toward the street. He took the long way around the police barricade in order to avoid reporters and cameras. The gaggle of news trucks kept in check had grown and Cady didn't require clairvoyant powers to know what the scoop of the day—and possibly the month—was going to be. Agent Preston paced beside him, stride for stride.

"You're talking toupees and boots," Preston said. "What did you see in that picture, Drew?"

"I'll tell you what I didn't see in the house. I didn't see any boots in the senator's walk-in closet, bedroom, entryway, or anywhere else for that matter."

"And?"

"The senator was a tall man. The person in that picture wanted his image to look like the senator for the two seconds of exposure on the front stoop, to throw off any neighbors who might be about."

"You're thinking that's not Senator Brockman in the picture."

"The hair looks like it could be a wig and his head's at an unnatural incline as though he's intentionally shielding his face from the security camera," Cady replied, taking out his car keys. "No, Liz, I don't think that's Senator Brockman in the picture. I think it's his killer."

CHAPTER 4

"There was a pardon scandal."

Cady was exhausted. After the early morning look-see at Senator Brockman's residence in Woodley Park, it had been a long day of sitting. It took all of his discipline to keep from being lulled comatose as self-important voices droned eternally on the state of Medicare in America. Cady stayed conscious mostly by shuffling through his ten-inch stack of fraud statistics in case a senator fell out of love with himself or herself long enough to ask a pertinent question. Cady was sipping a Heineken in the Avenue Café Bar & Grill of the DC Holiday Inn where he was lodged and awaiting a cut of medium rare when his cell phone had buzzed. It was Liz Preston and she dove right into the case.

"Taylor Brockman's opponent tried to milk it back during his first senate run, but Brockman did a heartfelt and it faded away."

"A heartfelt?" Cady said.

"He did an interview with a sympathetic news anchor in Virginia, and talked about how the kid he pardoned in one of his last acts as governor had nearly done a year in prison when what he really needed was a chemical dependency program. He spoke about how much he believed in second chances."

"The kid came from money, right?"

"Oh, yes," Preston said. "The kid's name is Thaddeus Jay Aadalen."

Cady thought for a second. "I'm drawing a blank, Liz."

"Aadalen Pharmaceuticals. Smaller than Pfizer, bigger than Bristol-Myers."

Cady took another taste of Heineken. "Let me guess, the kid's family kicked big money into Brockman's coffer?"

"Not directly—no quid pro quo exchange, but you know how that plays out."

Cady did. Set up a PAC—Political Action Committee—to dodge FECA, the Federal Elections Campaign Act, bundle contributions, soft money, 527 groups, amid other less savory avenues.

"What did the kid do?"

"Thaddeus Jay Aadalen—or TJ as he was known to family and friends—went to the University of Virginia where he majored in bad grades and frat parties. The university was on the verge of giving him the boot when Aadalen was in a single car accident that involved a death." There was a pause and Cady could hear Preston flip through her notes. "The car he was a passenger in, a Toyota MR2, flipped off the road for no apparent reason. The driver, a younger friend of Aadalen's, went through the windshield and was pronounced dead at the scene. Aadalen was banged up pretty badly and flown to a nearby hospital. Meanwhile the state police discovered a leather satchel inside the car. Inside the satchel was an assortment of goodies: club drugs like MDMA—ecstasy or Molly—and Special K, which is ketamine; a number of opiates and benzos; a dozen bags of cannabis, also Spice, which is synthetic cannabis; a number of stimulants too—you know, amphetamines, Adderall; and a bottle of Vicodin tossed in for good measure."

"In other words, a large enough stash to peg him with trafficking. What did the kid get?"

"Fourteen years at Haynesville. It was a severe sentence as the judge took the death of the driver into consideration. The pathologist performed a forensic toxicology test and was able to detect benzoylecgonine, the marker for cocaine, in the driver's blood. The driver was also amped up on amphetamines and should never have been behind the wheel of the MR2. Aadalen initially claimed that the drug case belonged to his dead friend, Drew, but only Aadalen's fingerprints were found on the paraphernalia."

"What a stand-up guy."

"His defense shifted gears, claimed young Aadalen never dealt drugs, and that it was a party kit he shared with friends. That's probably close to the truth, considering his family's wealth, but a moot point. They had him on possession of narcotics and controlled dangerous substances with intent to distribute—whether for sale or as party favors—and the Virginia prosecutor threw the book at him."

"If you're thinking the senator was a vengeance kill," Cady said, watching his waitress head his way with a steaming rib eye, "start sifting through family and friends of the dead driver, see what pops up."

"You at the hotel?"

"Yes," Cady said and mouthed *thank you* at the waitress.

"I can be there in three minutes."

"I'm just about to eat, Liz. And you don't need me to ferret through—"

"TJ Aadalen is dead," Preston interrupted. "He was murdered last week."

Cady thought for a second. "The timing is coincidental, but if Brockman pardoned Aadalen back when he was the governor of Virginia, that's—what?—a decade back? It's a pretty thin link."

"It's not only the pardon that links them, Drew. It's the cause of Aadalen's death," Preston replied. "A single stab wound to his heart."

CHAPTER 5

"We got a call about a slumper." Captain Tony Pecha of the Baltimore Police Department's Homicide Section sat behind his desk sipping coffee from a Ravens mug. Pecha looked to be fifty and appeared to have spent the bulk of his half century getting windburn.

Cady'd had the waitress box his meal, charge his room, and toss a wad of napkins in his direction as he left for Liz Preston's waiting car. On the ride to Baltimore, he'd eaten the steak and baked potato with his fingers as though they were slices of pizza. His technique wouldn't earn him any seal of approval from the Emily Post Institute of etiquette, but Cady wasn't proud. Preston had glanced his way a time or two, but withheld judgment.

"You know about slumpers, right?" the captain asked.

Both agents nodded. A "slumper" was a call into the police department to report a body slumped over the wheel of a car when no other information was known. Often the driver turns out to be someone not in the fittest of conditions, a person who's suffered a heart attack or seizure, a passed-out drunk, someone asleep in the car, or, sadly, someone who slid behind the wheel of the vehicle, shut the door, and quietly passed away.

"So we sent a squad car and an ambulance, only we didn't find a slumper. We found a murder victim." Pecha nudged a file across his desk toward Agent Preston with one finger. "Here's a copy of the file, highlights to include: Thaddeus Jay Aadalen lived in a basement efficiency shithole in Coppin Heights; Thaddeus Jay was estranged from his family after years of shaking them down for table scraps; young Thaddeus Jay, as you're no doubt aware, pulled a prison hitch in Virginia until he won the pardon lottery back when Taylor Brockman was Virginia's governor. By the way, I was perturbed by your call as it meant missing dinner, but if this is tied to Senator Brockman's death, I'm willing to stay all night."

"Thank you." Agent Preston opened the Aadalen file and began paging through it.

"Other highlights include Aadalen's rather dismal curriculum vitae of shoplifting, panhandling, selling grass, a handful of vacations in detox for being under the influence of this or that in public; and, most recently, our boy ventured into prostitution. Mind you, most of these transgressions came after his parents said *no mas*."

"Aadalen was a prostitute?" Cady asked.

Captain Pecha nodded. "He'd been picked up for tricking twice by male undercover officers. Aadalen spent his life chasing the next high. That's not cheap. His family finally had gotten wise and cut him off the tit. Read the interview with his parents and you'll get the feeling that he was not so subtly giving them the middle finger, making them turn a dark hue of purple if anyone asks about him at Thanksgiving dinner. The kid got along for a while by maxing out his credit cards and fucking over childhood chums for loans that would never be repaid." Pecha pointed at the file. "His apartment painted a bleak picture of low-rent rock and blow. The guy's halcyon days of designer drugs were long gone. We found ten-dollar packets of heroin—cut with chalk and talcum powder—a couple of well-used crack pipes, an eight ball of meth, even some evidence that Thaddeus was huffing spray paint. A downward spiral."

Preston looked up from the file. "He was stabbed to death in his sports car?"

"A beat-to-shit Porsche Boxster. His parents had bought it new for him in high school for remembering to flush or something. You know," Pecha said, "rich people—farting through silk. Anyway, Thaddeus incurred one stab wound to his heart with a hell of a sharp knife. Pretty slick. His pants were undone and he'd bled all over his . . . junk. He was parked off Charles Street, so our thought was he'd been cruising Mount Vernon and picked up the wrong john."

"Who called it in?" Preston asked.

"A couple walking home from a bar. Their names are in the file, they waited for us to arrive, and we have no reason to doubt their story. And they didn't see anyone exit the vehicle. We did a door to door, but nobody saw anything, heard anything. It was dark and nobody recalled any yelling or screaming. No loud noises."

"So your initial thought was that Aadalen found a *customer*, picked him up, parked down a secluded street for a tryst, but instead an altercation ensues— over money or whatever—and the trick stabbed him in the heart." Preston summarized while placing check marks in the margins of her notes.

"That seemed the most likely scenario," Captain Pecha said. "That is, until you called."

"I don't care if you're a meth head or Mahatma Gandhi," Detective Danfifer said, "you don't treat a Porsche like it's a Yugo."

Captain Pecha had assigned the squat, dark-haired detective to escort Agents Cady and Preston to the Baltimore Vehicle Impound Facility, where Aadalen's Porsche had been brought by BPD for criminal investigation. Before being towed, digital photos had been taken, pictures of the deceased sitting behind the wheel, pictures of the exterior from each side, and then additional shots of the interior from the front driver's area to the glove box to the trunk shelf. Cady and Preston had flipped through the pictures on the short ride to the impound lot.

"Based on how he shitted up the Boxster, Aadalen deserved getting stabbed," Detective Danfifer said.

"I wonder why he hadn't converted it to cash for drugs," Cady replied as they walked down a back row of impounded cars before reaching Aadalen's Boxster. It was a sporty two door with an exterior shade, as the detective informed them, of Orient Red. "Maybe some kind of psychological tie-in to his childhood."

"I don't think these scumbags do tie-ins to child-hood." Danfifer pointed at the car. "The engine still roars, but Aadalen would have needed fifteen grand in body and interior work to sell it for twenty. The only reason it didn't get jacked is that no self-respect-ing car thief would be caught dead in it."

The Baltimore detective was correct. The Box-ster mirrored its owner: beat up by life, dinged by decades of bad decisions, bald tires, chipped paint, a cracked windshield, and more dents and bruises than a bumper car at a county fair. Cady figured any money paid on insurance claims more likely worked its way into Aadalen's bloodstream than into car repairs. The interior followed suit: burn marks pep-pered the leather upholstery—possibly from ciga-rettes or more mind-altering substances, a rip here, a soil there, a knob or two missing off the dashboard, the driver's seat stained black with Aadalen's blood on top of years of less-definable discolorations.

"Plus," Danfifer continued, "the kid was using it to give head for cash."

Cady looked in the driver's window, while Preston walked around to the passenger's side. "Doesn't seem like there's enough space for much maneuvering."

Detective Danfifer shrugged. "How much room do you need for a blow job?"

Cady nodded at the Baltimore detective's wisdom as Preston slipped on a pair of latex gloves. Cady opened the driver's door, knelt down, and looked at how some blood had made its way onto the floor. He then watched as Preston popped open the glove box and removed the Boxster's owner's manual as well as a brown booklet envelope stuffed thick with maintenance plan receipts and tune-up invoices from better days—back when it was under warranty by the dealership, and then under warranty by Aadalen's parents. It appeared as though the kid folded and wedged any paperwork from the Porsche dealership into the envelope for vehicle archaeologists. Aadalen likely never gave them a second thought as long as daddy footed the bills. Preston flipped through the owner's manual and then began pulling invoices out of the envelope, auditing them one by one. Knowing Liz, Cady figured they'd be tucked neatly back in chronological order.

Cady asked for the car inventory from Danfifer and began walking through the list: jumper cables, half a snow brush, and—under the driver's seat—a crack pipe and an empty bottle of Vicodin prescribed for someone other than Aadalen. Cady pointed that out to the detective.

"That prescription is for the father of one of Aadalen's old grade school chums. The guy told me Aadalen stopped by last year to see if his old classmate was around, which made zero sense as the guy's son is now a controller at some firm in Miami and had stopped hanging with Aadalen by high school. The guy lets Aadalen know that his son's in Florida, but suddenly Aadalen starts asking if he can use the restroom and jogs upstairs. The father officially has the heebie-jeebies, is ready to dial 911, but Aadalen comes down, thanks him profusely, and heads out."

"He raided the medicine cabinet."

The detective nodded. "You know these poppers—that's what they do. Turns out the old guy had had back surgery, got that prescription, but weaned himself off immediately. Forgot he even had the stuff until I contacted him."

"Drew." Agent Preston sounded as though she'd seen a snake. "You need to look at this."

CHAPTER 6

Young Master Aadalen had demons—he fought
them incessantly—but . . . in the end . . .
Thaddeus Jay Aadalen lost his war with
addiction. Hearts today shatter as memories
of a younger and unbound TJ—a boy of
cherub cheeks, infinite energy, and an eternal
willingness to please—swirl about the room
like the first flakes of snow in a winter breeze,
reminding us of a quatrain from the poet
Thomas Gray:
   Here rests his head upon the lap of earth
   A youth to fortune and to fame unknown.
Fair Science frowned not on his humble birth,
   And Melancholy marked him for her own.

"A suicide note?" Detective Danfifer asked.

"A eulogy," Agent Preston replied.

"And that page was stuffed in there?" Danfifer's eyes darted from the page Preston held toward the booklet envelope of invoices she'd placed on the hood of the car. "I flipped through that entire goddamned packet, even shook it upside down in case pills or powder fell out."

"I had to unfold it before I noticed the typing," Preston said.

"Aw, shit," Danfifer verbally kicked his own ass.

"What would you have made of it last week?" Cady asked, cutting the detective some slack. "A written exercise they made Aadalen do in treatment to get him thinking of his own mortality, to change the path he was on? Something he took seriously for a day or two before shoving it in the glove compartment?"

The detective appeared as though he wanted to stomp another dent into Aadalen's Boxster, but instead said, "I know the kid grew up in private schools, but I just don't see him writing that note. Using words like 'cherub' and 'quatrain.'"

Cady turned to Agent Preston. "It seems a bit short for a eulogy, Liz."

"You know the piece being referenced?" Preston asked. "That poem from Thomas Gray?"

Cady nodded.

"It's titled 'Elegy Written in a Country Churchyard.'"

"I've got your back."

"You've got my back?" Cady spoke into his cell phone. It was nearly midnight and he stood outside Captain Pecha's office at Baltimore PD.

"On the Finance Committee," Director Jund replied. "Agent Erik Markes will be sitting in for you tomorrow."

"Agent Markes?"

"Yes, and don't worry about it; Markes is smarter than you."

"Thanks for the vote of confidence, but the only reason I'm in DC is for those committee meetings."

"And that's why I've got you covered. Look, Liz filled me in on Boy Aadalen. You two are making incredible progress, and I think you should be with her to interview his parents in Richmond."

"Oh, Christ."

"You'll be in beddy-bye in an hour and change. Hell, you can even sleep in and be in Richmond by eleven."

It felt as though a Julian year had passed since his morning meeting with the director. "This is not what I agreed to."

"Just one more day, Drew," Jund replied. "Trust me."

CHAPTER 7

Day 2

Leahy examined his hairline under the harsh florescent lights above the restroom's sink—glowering tubes that made you look like something out of a 1940s horror movie, but at least the wolfman had a head of hair. Leahy had been balding since ninth grade, which placed a profound limit on his social opportunities, but the thinning had gone into remission in his late twenties, so now he was stuck in the middle, perpetually looking like some wretched chemo patient. He'd blown chunks of his paycheck on Rogaine and Propecia, shampoo thickeners, growth vitamins, and a dozen snake oils—to little or no effect. And every morning he arranged the loyal scraps in a manner that might look somewhat appealing were he 106, and then he shellacked it down with hair spray as the wind had long since become his mortal enemy.

"Shit or get off the pot," Leahy mumbled as he edged a couple of stray strands upward with a forefinger.

Leahy often mumbled to himself. A habit that had nearly gotten him pummeled at a Nationals game when the drunk swaying in the concession line in front of him took forever figuring out the correct change for the vendor and yet somehow—miraculously—heard Leahy mumbling "Fartskull" below his breath. Just Leahy's luck to irritate an inebriated brute who was able to discern sound with the sensibility of a cave bat. Fortunately security guards had arrived amidst Leahy's various denials and apologies. As security interceded, the drunk was made to produce both his ticket stub and driver's license. Leahy made a point of memorizing the bully's name. That night, after the game—and after ten minutes of work on his basement PC—Leahy had rearranged the terms of the drunk's home mortgage.

Good luck with your foreclosure, Fartskull, Leahy had chuckled to himself.

Leahy plodded back to his desk, eyes on the floorboards to avoid pointless salutations by the tribe of tree-dwelling primates classified as his coworkers. He shook his head, unable to believe he had to spend his days with this chattering gaggle of clichés. The Isle of Misfit Toys, this craphole. A Greek chorus of *me and my dad built computers and wrote programs together when I was a kid.* Fuck you and your daddy and your bullshit home-written programs, Leahy thought every time he heard one of them reminisce. Leahy never knew his own father, but understood why Leahy Sr. had flown the coop at the first opportunity—he'd have done the same. Mommy Leahy Dearest was a birdbrain. Time came to a standstill in her company, ten minutes stretched to eternity, and during each of her soliloquies on other family members, the new pastor at church, the singers on reality TV shows, Leahy wanted to gnaw through his wrist, not to escape like a captured animal, but to end it once and for all.

Yet here he was, day after day, stuck in the sandbox with this bunch of supernerds. It was an insult, like when his mother would force him to play with his moron cousins in the backyard. It was tantamount to forcing Einstein to run a daycare for hydrocephaloids. Here he was, the "Star Child" from *2001: A Space Odyssey*—he should be soaring about the galaxy, yet here he was, day after day, anchored to earth by these hominids.

What a fucking waste.

As he approached his workstation, Leahy noticed that someone had tossed a blue folder atop his desk. Blue folders typically contained birthday cards for each staff member to sign and pass around the office so that the birthday boy or girl would have a card waiting for him or her on the special day. On Leahy's birthday, a card would be waiting for him on his desk, leaning against his coffee cup.

Leahy fed his birthday cards into the shredder unopened.

Funny that no one ever handed the blue folders directly to Leahy when he was at his desk. Much like today, they'd magically appear after he dropped a deuce or came back from lunch. And, quite frankly, Leahy figured, lacking contact was probably best for all involved.

Today's blue folder was different. It contained a sympathy card. Lynn's father had just passed away. Leahy's burning question was—who the hell was

Lynn? The one with the buck teeth and big tits? Or the one with the pink hair extensions?

Leahy grabbed a black marker and scribbled: *Sorry 'bout the dead dad* and then his name. Three strides later he plunked the blue folder on Wenstead's desk. No words were exchanged.

At his cube again he plunked down in front of his four computer monitors, glanced quickly at his programs, and then turned his attention to the morning paper. Some asshole senator had gotten himself killed and the media was all over it, reveling in it, like dogs rolling in their own fecal matter. Leahy couldn't care less. In fact he thought of politicians the way most people think of attorneys and adjusted the jokes accordingly. What do you call a hundred dead members of congress at the bottom of the ocean? A damned good start.

Ha!

The front page of the *Washington Post* had some pictures of Senator Brockman, one an obvious portrait, and another with his wife—who, as it so happened, turned out to be the bitch that owns all them hoity-toity hotels. There wasn't much hard news outside of Brockman having been whacked in his Woodley Park residence and later found by one of his aides. The cops were keeping tight-lipped about the details, so Leahy figured he may do some *browsing* to get up-to-date on what the pigs were really looking at.

He flipped the *Post* to page two, which contained a montage of pictures taken outside the late senator's building, up to and including a late-morning shot of the senator's body bag being hauled out.

Although the meat truck had backed up to the senator's garage, some photojournalist Jimmy-Olsen-wannabe was able to zoom in at a diagonal angle and digitalize the moment forever. The other pictures were padding—useless shots outside the residence, police mingling about the entryway, an ambulance that wasn't needed, squad cars, figures milling about the darkness, and . . .

"No fucking way," Leahy mumbled, and then realized he'd spoken aloud. He could feel Wenstead staring at him from a neighboring cube. He flipped his middle finger without so much as looking up. Leahy figured that amongst Wenstead's assorted duties, keeping an eye on Leahy topped the list.

Near the margin of one predawn snapshot were two figures. There was enough light spilling from the entranceway and from whatever exposure young Jimmy Olsen had the aperture of his Nikon shutter set at to reveal Roland Jund—the recently appointed director of the FBI's Criminal Investigative Division. But the other figure, half hidden in the shadows as though intentionally avoiding the media, had a familiar look and was the person whom Leahy was really interested in. He leaned forward, tapped his keyboard, and brought up the online version of the *Washington Post*. He surfed through the story, which contained even more pictures. And there was a snapshot of the two silhouettes in the margin, but this time he got a clearer glimpse of the other man's profile.

"No fucking way," Leahy muttered again, not giving two shits about Wenstead.

Whenever breaking news captured Leahy's curiosity, he'd grant the report five or ten minutes of off-the-books contemplation—culling through a few less-than-licit channels—in order to get at what that dead radio broadcaster used to refer to as *The Rest of the Story*. And on more than one occasion, Special Agent Drew Cady *was* the rest of the story. Director Jund had brought the agent into the senator's murder investigation. With Agent Cady onboard, this case might just get interesting.

Leahy decided he'd definitely be doing some extracurricular browsing.

CHAPTER 8

"He was no longer our happy little puppy dog." Cathrin Aadalen dabbed at the corner of her eye with a Kleenex before it retreated into the folds of her skirt.

Marcus and Cathrin Aadalen lived on a 200-acre spread in Goochland County—the Piedmont Plateau region of central Virginia—a short caravan east to Richmond or northwest to Charlottesville. On the paved road that wound itself toward Aadalen manor, the agents had to intercom their way past a daunting set of wrought-iron gates. Once past the gates, Cady counted three men in blue uniforms walking German shepherds along the outer perimeter. Someone appeared to be taking the senator's premature demise seriously. Their mansion—Liz had mentioned Georgian Revival as she parked her Prius in the front circle—sat on a bluff overlooking the James River.

"TJ got the looks while his older brother, our first son, Colin, got 'the brawn,' as Marcus likes to say." Mrs. Aadalen sat on the sofa facing them, her husband nodding next to her.

The two agents had been led from a large foyer down a lengthy marble corridor and into the library by a man wearing a dour expression and black tuxedo. The room was big enough to train elephants for Barnum and Bailey. Cady and Preston sat on a leather sofa facing the Aadalens, a black walnut coffee table holding today's *Wall Street Journal* stood between them.

Cady had commandeered Agent Preston's notebook on the ride to Goochland County in order to bone up on the Aadalen family business. Aadalen Pharmaceuticals had been founded by William and George Aadalen in Richmond, Virginia—the city from which the brothers hailed—in 1908 as a manufacturer of fine chemicals. Today Aadalen Pharmaceuticals was a research-based company with 64,000 employees worldwide and assets totaling $62 billion and change. As the founders' descendants, the Aadalen clan retained 52 percent of the company's shares. As such, they had a controlling interest. As such, they remained heavily vested in the strategic direction and daily business operations of Aadalen Pharmaceuticals. As such—outside of a two-year stint in the early 1950s due to an unexpected illness—there had always been an Aadalen, by either name or marriage, at the helm in the company's century-plus empire.

"It's not maternal of me to express these thoughts," Mrs. Aadalen continued, "but TJ had these blue eyes and brown locks and a youthful demeanor that made you forget his latest transgression, that made you forgive the meetings with the school administrators, the other parents, the attorneys, and, ultimately, the police because, at heart, he was this happy little puppy dog that just needed to be loved, needed to learn to go outside and to not chew the furniture. But, in later years, TJ was no more the happy little puppy dog, but this grizzled, hardened mutt piddling on the Chinese rug, begging to be fed, begging for us to bail him out of his latest arrest or—"

"Fucked-cup," Mr. Aadalen blurted, interrupting his wife.

"My husband has been known to use profanity, of which I disapprove," Mrs. Aadalen chastised. "Unfortunately his apraxia has him making inconsistent sound substitutions, but I suspect you get the drift."

Marcus Aadalen had suffered a cerebrovascular incident—a stroke—in February and, though he'd been making a remarkable recovery, Mrs. Aadalen assured them, he continued work with a speech therapist for the mild apraxia issues he had when speaking out loud. As a result, Mrs. Aadalen had carried out the lion's share of the conversation. Cady was amazed at how swiftly she was able to translate a mangled phrase or a touch of the arm by her husband of forty-something years.

"Once the puppy dog was gone, it was no longer possible to ignore how pathetic my son had become. TJ was this rail-thin presence—unkempt, clammy, jittery eyes—he made everyone nervous . . . everyone except Colin, who wanted to snap his neck and had been after us to kick him to the curb for years." Cathrin Aadalen reflected for a second. "But that's nearly impossible for a parent to do, wouldn't you agree?"

Both agents nodded.

"It was last fall when you decided to go the tough love route?" Preston asked, moving a pen in her notebook.

"Yes."

Mrs. Aadalen was striking for a woman in her midsixties—slim, hair a salon brown, no indication of cosmetic procedures. Cady appreciated her genuineness. Her son was dead, and it was a time for family mourning, but Cady figured the actual grieving process for those who loved Thaddeus Jay Aadalen had occurred some years earlier. Yet here she was, laying herself bare, voicing her motherly guilt over her relief that the nightmare of dysfunction she had birthed had finally come to an end.

Mr. Aadalen, by contrast, looked every inch of his sixty-five voyages around the sun—white hair cut short, face a crumpled road map of wrong turns and switchbacks, and a minor spray of saliva bubbles whenever he attempted a word or phrase. Marcus Aadalen, as CEO, had been the corporate face of Aadalen Pharmaceuticals for several decades.

Those days were done.

Marcus wore a gray cardigan with elbow patches over a white T-shirt and a pair of dress trousers. Cady figured it was easy attire for a recuperating stroke victim to slip in and out of while still projecting an image of refinement. Likely due to his near muteness, the former CEO was difficult to read. And though the senior Aadalen nodded and shook his head in all the right places and at all the right moments, Cady got the sense that, unlike his wife, he wouldn't be too choked up with pangs of guilt over the fact that a sharp thorn had forever been removed from his side.

"And that was the first time your son had to fend for himself?" Preston confirmed. "Pay his own bills?"

"Crr-ed-it cards," Mr. Aadalen enunciated slowly, and then leaned back in victory.

"We weren't on the ball at first and TJ took cash off some cards before we canceled them," Mrs. Aadalen said, confirming what Captain Pecha had told Cady and Preston. "We'd enabled our son in one way or another since he was a kid, allowing him to limp along in this destructive *lifestyle* that he'd established for himself. We twisted TJ's arm on numerous occasions to get him into treatment. Inpatient. Outpatient. Promises, Crossroads, Betty Ford. Meetings, sponsors. But our son never shook his addiction. The cycle of dependency continued. TJ would relapse."

Mr. Aadalen reached out and tapped his wife's forearm.

"My husband doesn't like it when I use the word *relapse*. Relapse implies a period of sobriety, of seriousness and self-reflection. It implies that our son had cleaned up his act for however short a duration of time. That was never once the case. TJ was never serious about cleaning up his act, about staying sober. Finally we decided to use tough love in order to let our son hit rock bottom." A tear made its way down her nose and Mrs. Aadalen again pulled the tissue from a hidden pocket and dabbed at her face. "And I guess he finally hit rock bottom."

"How well did you know Senator Taylor Brockman?" Cady asked.

"We've known Taylor Brockman for decades. We ran in similar circles. I would say we were friendly acquaintances if you know what I mean," Mrs. Aadalen said. "But you're here about the senator's death, so perhaps we can skip the dance and cut to the pardon since that dreadful thing's back in the news." She pointed at the *Wall Street Journal* on the coffee table.

"One of Brockman's last acts as governor of Virginia was to free your son from prison," Cady said. "An act that met with some controversy."

"There was a minor flare-up when it occurred— the Richmond papers were all over it and the AP picked it up—and then it was used as a campaign issue against Taylor when he ran for the senate. Even Mr. Sandin appeared in an ad for the Republicans."

Cady nodded his recollection from the police file. Karl Sandin was the father of the other boy who had been in the car crash with young Thaddeus Jay Aadalen back when both were students at the University of Virginia. Karl Sandin's son was Evan Sandin, the boy who had skipped class to spend the day doing lines of cocaine with TJ Aadalen. The boy who had left the scene of the accident in a body bag.

"There were allegations of a conspiracy to sell that pardon."

"Bull-fuck," Mr. Aadalen said in a mist of spittle.

Mrs. Aadalen shrugged, and then used a fresh Kleenex to wipe the white bubbles from the corners of her spouse's lips. She said, "Yes, we spent much time, effort, and financial resources to get Taylor Brockman elected to the United States Senate, but everything we did was within the law—well, perhaps not the *spirit* of the law—but that would be a conversation for you to have with our attorneys."

Cady leaned forward. "Any reason to believe after all these years that Karl Sandin could be involved in the death of your son or of Senator Brockman?"

"If Mr. Sandin could snap his fingers and send TJ and Taylor and Marcus and myself straight to hell, I've no doubt we'd be there in a New York second. We tried connecting with him after the accident, at the time of his son's funeral, and were told—quite unpleasantly and publicly—what we could *sexually* do to ourselves. He thinks of TJ as the pusher who killed his only child, he thinks of Taylor Brockman as the political scum that got TJ out of prison. And he thinks that Marcus and I were criminal enablers as parents." Mrs. Aadalen stopped to place a fistful of Kleenex on the coffee table. "Would that I could disagree with Mr. Sandin's assessment."

Cady went the direct path. "Did Karl Sandin kill your son?"

A smile worked its way across Mrs. Aadalen's lips. "I doubt it. Mr. Sandin is a broken man, living a broken life. I know the police are looking at him. I know that he lives alone in a Lynchburg trailer park, but I don't see how he could have known TJ was in Baltimore, much less find TJ in that appalling neighborhood. And the thought of Mr. Sandin killing Senator Brockman is laughable."

Cady glanced over at Liz Preston, who caught his eye and opened her leather organizer.

"A note was found in the glove compartment of your son's Porsche." Agent Preston placed a photocopy on the table in front of the Aadalens. "Does this message mean anything to you?"

Cathrin Aadalen finished first, drew a dry tissue from her hidden pocket, and began dabbing at her eyes. Mr. Aadalen used a forefinger to highlight the typed words as he slowly read from left to right. When he finished, he looked up at the investigators and shrugged.

"Our son's funeral was yesterday. Only the family came—only the family was invited. The pastor talked a little about life and about personal struggle," Mrs. Aadalen said. "Quite frankly, I rather he'd have read that note."

"Could this have been written by your son?" Preston probed.

Mrs. Aadalen shook her head. "Years ago, maybe. TJ wasn't illiterate. But the person he'd become, this thing he'd evolved into . . ."

"Who do you think killed your boy?" Cady asked.

Marcus Aadalen returned the volley this time, looking Cady straight in the eye. "Thug drillers."

Cady didn't need Mrs. Aadalen to translate Mr. Aadalen's latest struggle with apraxia. It was clear what the convalescing billionaire meant to say.

Drug dealers.

CHAPTER 9

"**I**f I knew who killed Senator Shyster or that fucking human toilet, I'd never tell you. And if I got seated on the killer's jury, I'd hang the verdict." An unshaven Karl Sandin, wearing faded blue jeans and a black T-shirt, sat opposite Cady and Preston on a picnic table under the awning of his trailer home in a remote corner of the Forest Lane Mobile Home Park in Lynchburg, Virginia, as the agents had not been invited inside to chat. "You're wasting your time talking to me."

"I appreciate your honesty," Cady said and shuffled through the papers of Sandin's previous interview with Baltimore's Detective Danfifer. "In the interest of just ruling you out, is there anyone who can account for your whereabouts two nights ago?"

"Yeah, me," Sandin replied. "This is such bullshit, same as when Danfifer came by to quiz me about the junkie. The only good that came from Danfifer was I found out mommy and daddy had cut him off, so the turd had to blow fags for speedball money." Sandin began to speak slowly, as though he were lecturing special needs students. "No, I was not getting blown last week by the little shit chunk who killed my son, nor did I kill the shit chunk. And I sure as hell didn't drive to Washington, DC, the other night and snuff a United States senator, for Christ's sake, no matter how much that fucking fraud deserved it."

"Can anyone place you here that night? Barbeque with the neighbors? A receipt from a store?"

Karl Sandin had taken early retirement the previous spring, at age fifty-eight, after several decades at a metal supply shop off of Lynchburg's Industrial Drive. Before that civilian turn, Cady had noted, Sandin had done four years in the army, an active stint, after he'd graduated from high school. Sandin's story was indeed a sad one as his wife, his high school sweetheart, Jenn Sandin, passed away after a two-year struggle with breast cancer when their son, Evan, was nine. After his retirement, Sandin sold his home in Madison Heights—*too many ghosts,* he'd told Danfifer—and bought the used trailer home at Forest Lane.

"I'm asleep by nine o'clock. Until then, I watch TV and eat popcorn," Sandin said. "Look, if I'd have known that the little junkie and the fraudster were going to get themselves killed, I'd have danced naked in front of the neighbors or at least made some long-distance calls on the landline to rig up an alibi. Thinking about it now, I'd expect my not having an alibi would indicate my innocence."

Five minutes later, as they wrapped up, Liz Preston said, "I'm very sorry about what happened to your son."

Sandin exhaled and spoke for the first time without a hint of hostility. "Evan was a beautiful kid. He took after his mother, a genuinely nice guy. And I swore to Jenn—on her deathbed—that I'd take care of our son, that I'd make sure he was safe. I made her that promise. And I did the best I could as a single parent. Off Evan goes to college—the first in my family—and, yes, I'm worried about him being on his own. What parent wouldn't worry? But I'm sweating the normal shit, the underage drinking and the fake IDs, and I'd talked to him about being careful about that kind of stuff, but I never thought there'd be some snake in the weeds waiting for him. Half a year earlier Evan was working on the high school yearbook and worrying about a couple of zits ruining his prom picture . . . then he's off to UVA where this cokehead asshole starts whispering in his ear about snorting heroin and dropping Ecstasy for Christ's sake. Our little boy never had a chance."

"I place him at five ten, Liz, so a pair of boots and a wig and Sandin becomes the Taylor Brockman imposter in the photo. Sandin also did four active years in the service, so he knows a thing or two about a thing or two," Cady said on the ride back to DC. "He likely has a pot of gold from selling his house and a lifetime of work, so he could also hire a hitter."

"His motive doesn't appear to have softened with time," Preston replied.

"Sounded red hot to me," said Cady. "And he feels righteous—a righteous man and a righteous cause.

No alibi, and from here Sandin could be in either Baltimore or DC in less than four hours."

Preston's eyes turned to Cady, then back to the road. "Is that what you think?"

"Sandin's got means, motive, and opportunity—the holy trinity—and needs to go under the microscope." Cady shrugged. "I don't know. The righteousness may be a facade. I get the sense that Sandin lives in a bucket of self-loathing, and has for years. In his mind he betrayed his dying wife when his son died, but he's smart enough to know that his son was not blameless in the car accident that took his life. I think Sandin lives with ghosts and other volatile notions, and that these thoughts of his, forever percolating, could send him off in all different kinds of directions."

They drove on in silence for several minutes. There'd been a light mist for most of the ride and Preston fidgeted with the intermittent windshield wipers.

"Terri okay with you helping us out on this?"

Cady inhaled, and slowly exhaled.

"Oh, Drew." Preston shot a glance his way. "You didn't tell her?"

"Who said anything about my helping out?" Cady said. "Jund lured me to the murder site under false pretense."

"So Terri thinks you're at the committee hearing today?"

Cady said nothing.

"She doesn't know you've gone AWOL?"

"AWOL?" Cady said. "I was eating steak and thinking happy Medicare thoughts when you showed up and kidnapped me."

Preston risked another glance. "I don't want to wind up in Terri's doghouse."

"Don't worry," Cady said. "I've got that reservation covered."

"I should not have come to you with the link to Aadalen."

Cady waved away her concern. "It's a vacation from the mundane, Liz. Trust me, I pound coffee to keep awake at the hearings, and then sit three hours on a full bladder," Cady said. "This is old home week. I get to thump about with you for a few days. If anything turns up, you and Jund can have at it. If nada, I'm home this time next week helping Terri set up the fish fry."

Preston played again with the windshield wipers and then said, "Jund has never been one to *articulate* his gratitude, Drew, but I guarantee he appreciates your help."

Cady stared at the road ahead. "I'm not doing this for him, Liz."

Preston realized what he meant and risked a final glance. "Thank you."

Cady shrugged and said, "So . . . Roland Jund as director of CID."

"Yes," Preston replied with a nearly imperceptible smile. "Roland Jund as director."

"Do tell?"

"He loves every minute of it though I imagine he could do without the trial by fire of Senator Brockman's death."

"The case is too big to fail."

"Let's hope so for Roland's sake."

Another minute passed, and then Cady said, "He would never have made it this far without your help, Liz."

"He has his virtues, Drew. Don't underestimate him."

"Oh, he's smart all right, politically savvy, and can schmooze till the cows come home, but so can half the people in the DC phone book. What makes him good is that he picks the right people—your name at the top of that list—and then stays the hell out of their way."

"There are several initiatives," Preston replied with a now perceptible smile, "I'm hoping to *help* Roland enact."

Terri had voiced her concern to Cady, how she worried about Liz sailing through life single-handedly. Some years back there'd been a gentleman that Preston had been seeing—Ronald or Donald something—who'd taught history at George Washington U. Cady liked the scholar, would wind up having a beer with him in a deserted corner at this function or that. When the relationship ended, Cady was sorry to see Ron or Don go quietly into the night, but he never said a word to Liz. It wasn't like Cady to pry, and, unlike Terri, he knew Agent Preston already had a significant other in her life . . . the bureau.

Preston's cell buzzed. "Speak of the devil," she said as she tapped speaker.

"When will you two be back in town?" Roland Jund barked over the phone line.

"We're about an hour out, sir," Preston replied.

"Make it sooner."

"What happened?"

"It turns out Senator Brockman *was* having an affair."

"That's hardly earth shattering," Cady said.

"It would be if you knew whom Brockman was having the affair with," Jund said. "He was sleeping with Holocaust Barbie."

"Who the hell is Holocaust Barbie?" asked Cady.

"Tanya Pritchard." Cady pictured Director Jund sitting behind his desk of aged cherry and maple—the broad top of which Cady figured would have saved a dozen or more passengers on the *RMS Titanic*. Jund's office real estate had doubled with his bump up the totem pole. Jund continued, "Senator Duke Pritchard's wife. Part Leona Helmsley, part Eva Braun, and part Godzilla. If there's hell to pay, don't misspell her name on the check."

"Senator Pritchard's a Republican," Preston said.

"Bipartisanship at its finest, Liz," Jund replied. "They were able to dig up older images from that security camera. Turns out Mrs. Pritchard made three late-night visits to Senator Brockman's brownstone in the past two weeks alone."

CHAPTER 10

Day 3

Tanya Pritchard filled her days managing an art gallery in a second-floor space in a faux-industrial warehouse off Florida Avenue that housed a couple of other galleries as well as a Belgian café. Agents Preston and Cady were met in the entrance by an art student-slash-intern who was spending her summer there as a receptionist-slash-curator. The expression on the young woman's face changed from one of blissful good cheer to that of confused fright as she realized that the two agents from the Federal Bureau of Investigation were there—sans appointment—to see Mrs. Pritchard and that the task of informing her boss of the morning's unexpected visitors fell squarely on her shoulders.

Preston was coasting the gallery in her acquire-knowledge mode, lost in thought as she memorized the exhibits in the empty corridor, focused in her learning—much like she'd been the day she'd devoured everything Cady could tell her about American numismatics. Cady was a coin collector; small scale, of course, but he found numismatics an addictive hobby and a pleasant diversion between the rounds of surgery required to rebuild his right hand.

Cady had once erred in sharing his interest with Roland Jund, only to be met with a resounding *Good God! Could there be anything more tedious?* Cady's wife, Terri, had been a good sport about his pastime. She even had pointed at a coin or currency display when he'd first unveiled his wares at her lake home, but after ten minutes of nods and fidgets, Terri had mumbled something about needing to check on the boats. It didn't make a lot of sense as most of the resort guests brought along their own speedboats and auditing the clunky rowboats that came paired with each rental cabin had never been a priority on Terri's daily to-do list.

Liz, on the other hand, had peppered Cady with questions about the slice of history that each piece in his collection represented. As with most topics foreign to her—and what made her a meticulous investigator—Agent Preston thirsted for knowledge, her curiosity a force stronger than gravity. Liz sorted, classified, and filed the numismatics data away in her mind for future reference, and she soaked in all of Cady's responses as though she were cramming for a final exam. Liz had even scored Cady an 1861 Abraham Lincoln ten-dollar demand note from Philadelphia—with limited creases—as a parting gift when he'd taken his gimp hand and left the FBI's Criminal Investigative Division to work with the Medicare Fraud Strike Force in Minneapolis.

Agent Preston's hobby was a bit more exerting than Cady's. Liz was a fifth-degree black belt in karate. Cady had been in attendance at Preston's exam to receive her fourth-degree black belt, an event in which Liz had to take out a number of attackers bearing fake knives and rubber guns. Although the assailants, all black belts themselves, sported face gear and chest pads, and were not, for the purpose of the assessment, expected to go full throttle on those martial artists testing out, Cady was impressed with how quickly Liz had placed the faux assailants on their respective asses.

And he had made a mental note to stay on her good side.

Unlike Agent Preston, Cady didn't prowl about the gallery in a quest for wisdom. Instead he sat in a lobby chair and gawked about the place. This month's art displays, per the poster on the door, included an *eclectic blend of abstract sculpture in expressive three dimensions as well as face jars and other popular trends in ceramic art.* What Cady knew about sculpture you could stack in a thimble and still have room for a peanut. And all he knew about pottery was that Terri had purchased a set of clunky clay bowls that weighed about three pounds apiece and he lived in terror of the morning when he dropped one on a bare foot while searching for Cheerios.

Cady brought up a sports page on his mobile phone and was halfway through an article analyzing the Nationals pitching woes—there'll always be next season—when he began hearing muffled strands of conversation emanating from a back office located down the hallway, from where the intern had headed minutes earlier as though she were walking the plank on a pirate ship. Actually Cady could only distinguish one side of the conversation, muted half words and profanity—heated words of anger that in no way stemmed from the fresh-faced intern who had greeted the agents upon their arrival and had only seemed too eager to please potential fine art aficionados. Pritchard's curses became louder, and with heightened volume also came enhanced cadence and tempo. Cady nearly began nodding in rhythm with Pritchard's string of eff words. There was a thump as though a bowling bowl had been dropped on a desktop and Cady stood when he heard Pritchard call her intern an *idiot.*

Suddenly Pritchard's nickname became apparent.

He looked across the gallery, but Preston was too far away to hear the commotion, deep in thought reading a description of the sculpture in front of her. Cady heard a door slam and then hurried footsteps in the back hallway. He turned the corner to greet the art student.

"Killed the messenger, did she," Cady said.

"You need to make an appointment." The student intern appeared on the verge of either tears or throwing up.

Cady stepped closer and spoke quietly. "Sorry I got you into trouble. Is she always this way?"

The intern wiped a sleeve across moist eyes and nodded. "Lately it's been much worse. I only need to make it until September to get my credits at Georgetown . . . so I keep telling myself."

"What's about to happen is on me, okay?"

The art student looked worried.

"You did your best to stop me," Cady said, "but I was an asshole. I wouldn't take no for an answer and I shoved you aside, okay?"

The art student nodded.

"Liz," Cady called across the gallery. "Pritchard's ready to see us now."

"Sir!" the art student yelled from the lobby as the agents passed the bathrooms and neared the gallery's headquarters at the end of the hallway. "Sir, you can't go down there. Sir!"

Cady admired the student's improv as he reached for the doorknob to Pritchard's office. He caught Preston's look of puzzlement in his periphery as he twisted the knob, flung open the door, marched in as though he were new management, and plopped down in the green couch that stretched along the back wall. Preston hung back in the doorway.

Tanya Pritchard shot up from her desk chair as though goosed. She was five seven in heels and a pink pantsuit, a chemical blonde, flush cheeks, and taking on a little weight as she neared the end of her fourth decade—likely from a surplus of five-star restaurants and the natural effects of gravity. Pritchard could be considered attractive if you found a way to compartmentalize her personality, and she stared at Cady with a scowl out of a B-grade melodrama, circa 1955.

Cady thumbed the exit command a few times to close out of the online newspaper, shook his head, and dropped the phone in his breast pocket, muttering, "I need to get a 4G." He scanned about Pritchard's office, the abstract paintings on the wall that he could never in a million years make sense of, the shiny hardwood floor, the L-shaped office desk, all very tidy. "Nice digs."

Pritchard's face turned deeper shades of crimson, which made for an interesting contrast against her hair. Her eyes never left Cady while an arm raised and pointed at Preston. "Get . . . The . . . Fuck . . . Out . . . Of . . . My . . . Office," Pritchard enunciated every venomous syllable, provided each word with a galaxy of its own in which to exist and prosper.

It took everything Cady had to keep from standing and getting the fuck out of Pritchard's office, such was the undertone of hatred and guaranteed carnage of things to come were Tanya Pritchard's edict not immediately obeyed. But then Cady remembered that this wasn't really his investigation, and what was the worst that they could possibly do to him—banish him to northern Minnesota? Been there, done that.

Instead of fleeing, Cady asked, "Where were you on the evening of July 30th? The night Senator Brockman was murdered."

Pritchard glared at Cady, eyes burning into him with the intensity of a thousand suns. Cady prepared to duck as Pritchard's right hand worked its way dangerously near a weighted tape dispenser.

"I am calling 911," Pritchard said in a low voice that maintained menace, "and will have you both thrown in jail for trespassing."

"Do it." Cady tossed a hand in the air. "Let's see how far that'll take you."

"Mrs. Pritchard," Preston spoke in a calm and diplomatic voice, venturing farther into the office while displaying her badge. "There's no reason for us to get off on the wrong foot. We're part of the investigation into Senator Brockman's death, and we just need a few minutes of your time."

"Why would you want to ask me about that?" Pritchard replied. "I have no information about the senator's death. I would have come forward if I had."

Classic good cop, bad cop. Liz was playing it perfectly and Pritchard had begun to talk, which is exactly what they wanted. Cady chipped in his part and chortled.

"That's enough of that," Preston said sternly, holding up a forefinger to shush her partner, and then turned her attention back to Pritchard. "There are images of you arriving at Senator Brockman's Woodley Park residence taken from his entryway security camera. These images indicate that you came to the senator's home on numerous evenings in the weeks leading up to his death."

"That is correct," Pritchard replied. "I've worked with Senator Brockman on a variety of charity projects over the past few years, and he had volunteered to make a not insubstantial donation to this very art gallery."

"I give to Make-A-Wish," Cady said, "and they've yet to show up at my house at midnight."

Tanya Pritchard glared at Cady. "I will need your name please . . . for the report I promise you I will be filing with the director of the FBI who, as a matter of fact, happens to be a close personal friend of my husband."

Cady worked his wallet out of a pocket, slipped out his card, and dropped it in a face jar sitting atop the side table, likely something lifted from the gallery's ceramic display. What is it about senators and younger wives? Elaine Newell Brockman was about a dozen years younger than her late husband. And Senator Pritchard, easing in on sixty, had nearly twenty years on Tanya Pritchard. Of course Tanya Pritchard was the senator's second spouse—perhaps she'd be considered a trophy wife, if you were immune to her venom, that is.

"As I was saying," Pritchard said, turning her full attention back to Preston, "I worked with Senator Brockman on a variety of charity issues. That's all I have to say. Any additional discussions will be held with my attorney present and your yappy terrier absent."

"Thank you for your time, Mrs. Pritchard. If we have more questions, I will call ahead of time to make arrangements."

Cady stood. Preston headed for the door, but stopped and turned back to face Pritchard. "Congratulations, by the way. How far along are you?"

"Second tri—" Pritchard began but stopped herself.

Cady looked at Tanya Pritchard as though for the first time. He'd been wrong; it wasn't middle age or food that had Pritchard sporting loose outfits. It was the circle of life.

And with that notion came an epiphany.

"Did Taylor Brockman know he was going to be a father?"

Tanya Pritchard sank back down into her chair . . . and began to weep.

CHAPTER 11

"Are addictions ever truly cured?" Dorie Searles pondered Agent Preston's query aloud. "Let me cite myself as an example."

"Oh, Dorie." Elaine Brockman issued a loud sigh. "Not this again."

Cady got the feeling he'd stepped into a frequent topic of debate between the two women. He was seated in the unpretentious waiting room of Dr. Searles's Columbia Heights office, off lower Fourteenth Street, only a short hop from the Metro hub. Mrs. Brockman had a corner chair next to a side table awash in back issues of *Psychology Today*. Agent Preston was looking at a collection of Russian nesting dolls that were sitting unnested—arranged from the largest to smallest characters—each on different levels in a glass display cabinet in the opposite corner of the waiting room. The doctor herself leaned against the receptionist counter—Searles had no receptionist—and had been telling the agents about her work with underprivileged teens that suffered from substance abuse.

"When I was young," Searles fixed her attention on the two agents and continued, "I was a shoplifter. I went from snatching candy to lifting scarves to stealing bracelets from friends when they weren't looking to even digging through my mother's purse after school. Penny ante in retrospect. And humiliating. I was a hardcore kleptomaniac."

"With an emphasis on *maniac*," Brockman teased from the sidelines.

"I was almost seventeen the fourth time my parents were called to come bail me out from store security. I couldn't explain it to them, this overpowering compulsion to steal things I didn't need. This time it was a pair of earrings from Macy's. My parents knew that I would soon be treated as an adult in the eyes of the law, and they got me into counseling. It turned my life around, it really did."

"So you decided to become an addiction therapist yourself?" Preston asked.

"Dorie started in nursing, but ran back to school before she could do any permanent damage," Brockman volunteered.

Searles smiled and said, "There may be an ounce of truth in that. I wouldn't say I found my *calling* or anything grandiose like that, but there's a great need out there and I like to think I can make a difference."

"In my case I have to manage my sobriety, which is unfortunate not only because I love a good Long Island Iced Tea," Brockman said, "but because I dread attending those meetings and group sessions. They take years off my life. The only reason I choose to remain sober is to never have to attend those meetings ever again."

"They're not meant to be a walk in the park," Searles responded. "But that treatment has saved lives—as well you know."

"It's all I can do to stay awake," Widow Brockman said, "though some of the stories . . . oh, my god. Like that man who hitched a ride home from the bar on top of a station wagon. Or that mousy woman whose husband had the family doctor tie her tubes without her knowing."

"Remember, Elaine," Searles cautioned, "that's confidential information. Private. What's said in session, stays in session."

"Lighten up, Dorie. I'm not mentioning any names. For Christ's sake, I don't remember their names, but some of the stories are so far out of whack you just can't make up this stuff. Mouse woman had a real doozy of a husband who got his rocks off by sharing her with his friends. Of course she got pregnant. Of course he danced her into an abortion, and, during the procedure, he had his doctor chum perform a tubal ligation. He had his wife sterilized without her even knowing."

"I didn't lead that one, but you're making me uncomfortable. How would you like it if others spoke of your situation?"

"By comparison I'm a little boring, don't you think? Rich housewife fills long days with vodka and gin. News at eleven."

"My grandmother collected these," Liz Preston interrupted, wanting to change the subject. She was now down to the lowest level of nesting dolls in Searles's display case. "She loved the fairy tale characters."

"Half of those matryoshka dolls are from my mother's collection, which, sadly, I dinged up as a kid. The other half are ones I've picked up here and there over the years," Searles said. "I have another set that I use in therapy sessions. The kids come in nervous and scared, and the dolls act as a sedative and ice breaker."

Cady cared as much about Russian nesting dolls as he did about ceramic face jars. He turned to the senator's widow. "Can we talk privately, Mrs. Brockman? Something has come up."

"Dorie can stay," Brockman said. "I have no secrets."

"Absolutely not," Searles said and headed into her counseling room. "I've got notes to wrap up and phone calls to make."

After Searles shut her office door, Cady said, "During the course of our investigation, it has come to our attention that your husband was seeing another woman."

"Or it was another Tuesday in Washington," Brockman replied. "I already told you our marriage was a Potemkin village."

"This particular woman is three months pregnant with the senator's child."

Brockman's mouth dropped so far Cady spotted gold fillings.

"Dear god," Brockman said. "Tell me she's over eighteen."

Cady nodded.

"Who is she?"

"I'm sorry. It's part of the investigation, but I'm sure you'll find out more than there is to know in a short while."

"Jesus Christ." Brockman looked at Cady, and then at Preston. "Governor DeMarco called. He wants to know if I can fill Tay's seat until next year's election. I was giving it serious thought, but I don't want to walk into all this circus bullshit."

The three sat in awkward silence.

"You can annul a marriage," Brockman said, eventually breaking the quiet, "but can you acquire a posthumous divorce?"

They were back in Agent Preston's office when the call came in. They'd cleared a spot for Cady to set up shop; he had his laptop on a desk the size of a TV tray and was scrutinizing the pictures of the imposter on Senator Brockman's stoop for the tenth time when Preston's phone rang. A double ring, which meant the call came from outside the Hoover Building. Liz had immediately picked up.

"You brought in TJ Aadalen's drug dealer?" Preston said a moment later.

Cady's head perked up.

"No, Detective. Never heard of him." A pause. "No kidding?" A longer pause. "Los Zetas?" Longer still. "Yes, that is good news." One last brief silence. "We'll be there in two hours." Preston clicked end call and stared at Cady. "Unreal."

"What?"

"That was Captain Pecha at Baltimore PD," Preston said. "They got a tip that TJ Aadalen owed his dealer eighty grand."

Cady thought for a second. "A million people have died for much less."

"We'll take my car."

CHAPTER 12

The Canadian shot the deputy US marshal through the insulated pizza delivery bag—twice in the heart. The marshal collapsed backward, a dead fall, and the Canadian stepped over his body and into the safe house, a pint-sized rambler in Wayne County, south of Detroit. The second deputy US marshal had just enough time to stand and register shock, eyes wide and mouth open like a figure in a Munch painting. The Canadian fired through the red bag again, spitting one into the center of the man's forehead. The thick mess clinging to the wall behind the marshal indicated a double-tap was not required.

The Canadian kicked the front door shut with a back heel, flipped away the pizza bag and empty boxes, and swept the room, left to right, with the SIG P226. The silencer served to suppress the sound of the pressure wave from the expanding propellant gases, certainly not a near soundless *whoosh* like in the movies, but reduced the noise by about forty decibels. The two deputy marshals had been watching the evening news, but the Canadian heard something else—music—emanating from the other side of the house, possibly piano jazz, which would fit with the bookkeeper's profile. The Canadian made a quick sweep of the undersized kitchen, and then took a classic isosceles shooting stance, facing the hallway. A left-side hallway door to a guestroom was wide open. The doorway to the right-side hall bathroom also was open. The doorway to the master bedroom at the end of the hall, from which the jazz originated, was closed.

The job had gone flawlessly. The source in Detroit PD had been accurate as to where the US marshals had tucked away the bookkeeper in anticipation of the man's upcoming testimony in two days' time. The bookkeeper's testimony was expected to have a rather arduous and liberty-restricting influence on the lives of several top personnel from the bookkeeper's previous employer. The file the Canadian had been provided on the bookkeeper indicated that the man was a glutton for junk food, especially pizza, an accurate assessment based on the 200 pounds of meat hanging off the bookkeeper's five-five frame. Another note in the bookkeeper's file indicated that he ate even more, if that were possible, when under pressure.

And testifying against the Fracasso Family could certainly be viewed clinically as a stress inducer.

The Canadian tapped into the ordering systems of all four of the popular pizza delivery establishments within a three-mile radius of the US Marshals Witness Security Program safe house and got a hit on the WITSEC house within two days. The Canadian geared up and was at the door in fifteen minutes.

The jazz was dialed down and a voice behind door number three barked, "Is it here yet?"

The Canadian coughed in response.

A second later the door opened. The bookkeeper stared at the Canadian and froze like a deer caught in headlights on a cloudy night. He recognized his worst nightmare—the fate the United States Marshals Service had repeatedly assured him never would occur—had arrived.

The first bullet spit through the bookkeeper's left eye. He stumbled backward in an awkward dance and sunk to the carpeting. The Canadian walked over, bent over the dead bookkeeper, and put another round through the man's other eye, and another through his mouth. And if the *See No Evil, Speak No Evil* message wasn't loud and clear enough for those hard of hearing, the Canadian pressed the tip of the suppressor against the bookkeeper's crotch and pulled the trigger.

While driving away from the safe house, the Canadian passed a Domino's Pizza car heading in the opposite direction.

Now the Canadian sipped Blanton's Gold Edition bourbon and looked out the glass windows at the city of Toronto, a skyline not to be missed. The Canadian lived in a condo on the twenty-second floor of fifty-five stories of glass and steel on University Avenue. The Canadian could have sprung for a corner penthouse on the fifty-fifth floor, but it was best to mix anonymously with the upper class and not stand out. Plus, the Canadian could tolerate twenty-two flights of steps as part of staying in peak condition. But fifty-something? Jesus Christ.

Also, in the Canadian's line of work, there could well come a day where one had to vanish at a second's notice, never to return. So best not to spoil yourself with the penthouse lifestyle.

The flight home from Detroit had been nonstop—uneventful—the end of an exhausting day. The Canadian took another sip of Blanton's Gold and thought about an exit strategy, about getting out of the business. Retirement was a concept the Canadian toyed with in the abstract at the end of every assignment. The Canadian had enough assets stashed away in various nooks and crannies to live out a dozen lifetimes on a tropical beach in Bermuda or the Grand Caymans or the Bahamas, but, candidly, how would that play out?

"Know thyself" was the Ancient Greek motto and, after a week of sex, scuba diving, and sucking down Mai Tais, the Canadian would start climbing the walls.

The Canadian had spent a few hours one night researching what it meant to be hooked on adrenaline, the psychological need—the addiction—to place oneself in panic-button situations. It turns out our adrenal glands secrete copious amounts of adrenaline in times of perceived danger. Adrenaline is related to dopamine, and dopamine is the chemical messenger in the brain that plays a leading role in both addiction and pleasure. An adrenaline high from placing oneself at risk is not unlike the high one gets from speed or cocaine. In addition, perceived danger also causes the hypothalamus and pituitary gland to pump out endorphins—the pleasure-inducing, pain-repressing blend that is reproduced by opiates like heroin. Thrill seekers can become addicted to the risk and thus keep increasing the threat level in order to get the reward they seek.

And that likely explains what I did at the Detroit Metro Airport, the Canadian thought, taking a final sip of bourbon.

Yes, I'm an adrenaline junkie, the Canadian would acknowledge, like a sky diver or rock climber—or like those water sports I'm dim enough to love. Yup, two parts adrenaline junkie and, if I took a long, hard look in the mirror, the Canadian further considered, there likely exists one part personality disorder. That is, a personality disorder marked by antisocial behavior with a complete lack of empathy . . . and remorse.

Of course, if someone wanted you dead so badly that he or she were willing to meet the Canadian's upper six-figure commission, you were probably not Mother Teresa.

While awaiting the flight back to Toronto, the Canadian sat in a back row at an uninhabited gate that listed no air travel for more than an hour. The Canadian took out the well-used iPad, set it to the Detroit airport Wi-Fi network, launched Google Chrome, and then logged into the fake e-mail account. The Canadian was surprised to see a new message saved in the Drafts folder. To have a message waiting mere hours after the completion of the Detroit assignment was unexpected. The Canadian used the assigned number-letter sequence to decode the message that had been placed in the Drafts folder by the Canadian's agent, who lived a world away in the capital of Switzerland. No messages ever were sent to or received from this account, for security purposes, and the Drafts folder served as a safe conduit between the Canadian and the agent in Bern. An agent that, if the Canadian ever seriously decided to leave the life, would be paid a final visit—a first and last face to face—just to clear the deck.

But this message from the agent in Bern brought details regarding a new assignment, intimating it stemmed from a *repeat* customer—a *happy* client. Good to be appreciated, the Canadian reflected, but knew that in the unique niche of this vocation there were probably no more than ten, possibly a dozen, recurring patrons who kept the dance card full.

All it would take would be a few keystrokes in response to set events in motion, beginning with half the commission, sans agent fee, to be deposited in one of the Canadian's numbered bank accounts. The Canadian scanned the terminal, the nearby faces of the other early evening travelers to see if anything appeared out of the norm. After ascertaining all was acceptable . . . the Canadian entered the "go" code.

CHAPTER 13

"Fucker's got Curt Rylander of Rylander Hobbs." Captain Pecha was waiting for them inside Baltimore Police Department's main entrance. Pecha looked annoyed. Evidently Rylander Hobbs was one of the more prestigious law firms in Baltimore, its squadron of defense attorneys a perpetual thorn in the side of the men in blue. "Guess he made good use of his one phone call."

Jorge "George" Hierra owned an upscale Mexican restaurant and lounge, Mucha Lucha, in Harbor East along the northern shoreline of the Patapsco River—the Baltimore Harbor—where Hierra often held court with friends, family, underlings, attractive brunettes, attractive blondes, attractive redheads. As far as the Baltimore Police could tell, he didn't discriminate when it came to affairs of the heart. As Hierra had been a recurring blip on their radar over the past eighteen months, BPD had packed the Mucha Lucha's bar with undercover cops in the hopes that loose lips might sink drug cartels, but to no avail. Mucha Lucha was clean, providing Hierra with the perfect front, and no unsavory business appeared to be discussed at the eatery. Plus, the grilled pepper poppers weren't half bad.

BPD had initially been tipped to Hierra's cartel ties by special agents from the United States Drug Enforcement Administration. The DEA had been kind enough to crack open their file on Jorge Hierra, which detailed his suspected connections to Los Zetas. It painted a lively and complex portrait—a most worrisome depiction—mostly inferential and circumstantial, lacking the requisite meat to put Hierra down for the count. And Cady suspected that Baltimore undercovers were not the only plants wetting their whistles at Hierra's restaurant.

That Hierra was smart went without saying. However, after the dots had been connected between the murders of Senator Brockman and Thaddeus Jay Aadalen, a handful of Baltimore's finest were dispatched to Mucha Lucha, that is, several appreciative undercovers were paid to enjoy the poppers and swig Dos Equis. Only this time—after the news media had linked the two murders, though not yet the manner of death, which, in this world, Cady figured, was just a matter of days—one astute undercover overheard Hierra talking to a table of sycophants about how the dead kid owed him "eighty Gs." Eighty grand being one hell of a motive, they brought Hierra in, where he currently sat with Curt Rylander, senior partner at Rylander Hobbs.

"If I owed Los Zetas eighty grand," Captain Pecha continued, bringing the agents up to date as he led them toward the interrogation room, "they'd come take me right out of this building. But now Rylander's claiming Hierra said 'eighty' as in eighty bucks, not eighty grand."

"Hierra sold to the Aadalen kid?" Cady asked.

Pecha laughed. "Hierra doesn't sell directly to anyone. He's the man behind the curtain. He sets up the distribution channels—Baltimore, other East Coast cities—and brings in the heavy hitters if anyone tries to overlap his market channels."

Los Zetas is thought by the US government to be the most sophisticated and brutal drug trafficking organization operating out of Mexico. Spanish for "The Zs," Los Zetas came into existence in the late 1990s when commandos of the Mexican army began hiring on as the enforcement wing of the Gulf Cartel—then the leading drug cartel in eastern Mexico—but the commando squad broke away to form their own criminal syndicate. There is no official figure as to how many tons of cocaine this empire ships into the United States each and every year, but estimates go as high as 600. Ditto heroin. And how much meth The Zs brought into America was anybody's guess. Not simply content to traffic in illicit drugs, The Zs quickly branched out into kidnapping, money laundering, extortion, human trafficking, suborning officials, and assassination. And unlike Zorro from the old Saturday matinees, Los Zetas peppers the ground with severed heads and assorted body parts, all marked with Zs in full public display, in order to terrorize both rival cartels and government forces. A publicity gimmick that tended to do the trick.

"Why would Hierra advance eighty grand in credit to a street junkie like Aadalen?" Cady asked.

"We figure he thought the kid's family would make good, but then found out differently."

"His claim of eighty bucks is an admission that he knows the murder victim," Preston said. "If it's not a lie, why would Hierra loan Aadalen eighty bucks?"

The captain shrugged. "Typical lawyerly bullshit to muddy the water." Pecha stopped and looked at the agents. "But get this. Rylander states there's someone who can clear this all up with one phone call, and you'll never guess who that someone is."

"Who?"

"The kid's older brother," Pecha said. "Colin Aadalen."

CHAPTER 14

"My client will speak only to the erroneous accusation that's been leveled against him by an eavesdropping police officer sitting two tables away during the peak of a boisterous and deafening happy hour."

Curt Rylander was a bald spot in designer glasses, dark suit, and gold cuff links. He spoke softly, but the firm bearing his surname was more than a big enough stick to cause even the most hard-boiled of prosecuting attorneys to pause at each and every step.

"Your client claims friendship with Colin Aadalen, the older brother of the murder victim and acting CEO of Aadalen Pharmaceuticals?" Cady asked.

Rylander nodded. "My client will speak in a limited manner about his acquaintanceship with Colin Aadalen, but only so far as to defend himself against the erroneous accusation leveled against him by Baltimore PD."

Cady sat at the table facing Jorge "George" Hierra. Liz Preston sat to his left across from Rylander. Captain Pecha set the group up in the interrogation room and then departed. So far Hierra had not so much as raised his head in greetings, his gaze fixated on his hands in front of him, the pose of a manicurist wondering where to begin. Aside from his stationary posture, Hierra looked as though he'd stepped down from the cover of *GQ* magazine, black hair slicked back, clean shaven, starched white shirt, and a high-blue dress suit likely born of pampered sheep. Midthirties. Wiry.

"My office," Rylander continued in a voice that Cady strained to hear, "is in contact with Colin Aadalen, who is currently tied up in a closed-door board assembly of some sort, but who promises to contact Captain Pecha as soon as he can break away and put this unsavory farce to an end."

"We hear TJ Aadalen owed you $80,000," Cady spoke directly to Hierra.

Hierra's head raised, a smirk worming its way across his features. He looked to Rylander, who nodded once.

"I've been here for nearly four hours because that douchebag cop can't hear for shit," Hierra spoke for the first time.

Although Hierra was Latino and—he'd been informed by Pecha—fluent in Spanish, Cady caught no hint of an accent. The East Coast face of Los Zetas spoke in straight English as though he could moonlight imparting weather or traffic reports on local radio.

"The news linked that dead senator to TJ Aadalen per some kind of scandal the senator had covered up in Virginia." Hierra went back to examining his hands. "The Aadalen kid got stabbed to death and I'm guessing the senator did too."

The media knew Thaddeus Jay Aadalen had been stabbed to death, but no specifics as to it having been a singular stab wound to the heart. They knew even less about the senator's demise. Cady gave that about another day.

"I've gotten to know Colin Aadalen, predominantly over the course of the past several months. Some weeks back I passed on *eighty bucks* to his baby brother in order to get him some medicine, maybe a shower and shave, maybe some healthy food. The money was a gift, like charity to the homeless. It was not a loan. The news has been going on nonstop about the senator and the dead junkie, so I was relaying how I knew the kid to my companions over cerveza when that douchebag cop pretended to hear something else."

"So you gave TJ Aadalen money out of your friendship with Colin Aadalen?" Liz Preston asked.

Hierra shrugged and looked at Rylander.

"He did in that charitable instance," Hierra's lawyer said, "but my client initially met Colin Aadalen while mediating a disagreement between TJ Aadalen and a Mexican-American acquaintance of my client."

"What kind of Mexican-American acquaintance?" Cady asked.

"For the purposes of today's erroneous allegations, that's irrelevant, and I'm advising my client not to answer."

Cady had heard the word *erroneous* more times in the past five minutes than in the past ten years. Hierra had yet to be formally charged by a prosecutor so BPD could hold onto him for another sixty-something hours, but Cady got the feeling that the chance of any Baltimore prosecutor charging Hierra with Thaddeus Jay Aadalen's murder was fading away, like dusk to darkness.

"He's just a guy who lives in my neighborhood." Hierra's smirk extended into a smile. "TJ Aadalen owed him some money—consulting fees I believe— and I offered to mediate an arrangement. My acquaintance was agitated about the situation as he has a family to feed. TJ talked up his own family, and swore they'd cover his debt. So a meeting was arranged with his older brother."

"How much did Aadalen owe your friend?"

"Inconsequential. Enough time had passed that the interest had unfortunately outgrown the principal, but we're talking less than $5,000."

"So you stepped in to *broker* this situation?" Cady asked.

"Let's just say it piqued my curiosity as to whether the head of Aadalen Pharmaceuticals would show up to help his baby brother."

"And he did?"

"And he did."

"Was this at your restaurant?" Cady was double-checking Pecha's assertion that *business* was never conducted at Mucha Lucha.

"No," Hierra said, shaking his head. "A pizza place in Park Heights."

"And at the meeting, Colin Aadalen reimbursed your acquaintance," Cady said, "and the two of you hit it off?"

"It was amiable. We talked golf. I even sprung for pizza and beer."

"Did the two of you connect on additional occasions following this meeting?"

"I don't think there's a law against that," Hierra said. "Colin knew about my restaurant, and told me he liked it. I gave him my card and said drinks would be on me if he found himself in the neighborhood. I didn't think I'd ever hear from him again, but he called a week later and we grabbed dinner at Lucha. He insisted on buying the dinner and left a hundred dollar tip."

"Was that the last time you saw Colin Aadalen?"

"No." Hierra's smile once more extended into a broad grin. "Colin and I have connected a half-dozen times, maybe more, mostly for drinks, and we did eighteen at Greystone. Fun time—we're evenly matched."

The Aadalen CEO had not only met with Los Zetas's man on the East Coast in order to pay off his brother's debt, but followed up with drinks and dinner and golf. Not exactly how Cady'd run things were he to wake one day and find himself the head of a Fortune 500 company. Cady was taking a moment to digest this information when the door to the interrogation room opened.

Captain Pecha stood in the doorframe looking as though he'd caught his prom date in a compromising position. He stared at Hierra for a long second, and then said, "You can go."

And with those three words, Captain Pecha turned and left.

"That's all, gentlemen. And Agent Preston," Rylander said, shutting his bifold pad and standing.

"But why the charity money for TJ Aadalen?" Preston paged backward in her notes and looked up. "Why were you giving him eighty dollars for *medicine*?"

"I said, that's all," Rylander responded, his voice no longer hushed.

Hierra raised a palm in his lawyer's direction. "Over-the-counter pain meds, antibiotic cream. New bandages."

"New bandages?" Preston said.

"My acquaintance ran into him a week or two after the pizza meeting. The kid's face was black and blue, and his hand done up in a soft cast."

"This interview is over." Rylander glared at his client. Whatever concerns the senior partner at Rylander Hobbs had about modulating his volume had been tossed out the window. "I'm afraid I must insist."

Hierra began laughing, deep and guttural. Cady shot question marks Preston's way.

"I never touched the kid," Hierra said after his amusement died down. "Wasn't me that kicked his ass."

Cady tried filling in the missing hymn notes. "Colin Aadalen assaulted his younger brother?"

"Oh, yes," Hierra replied, nodding. "After pizza we walked the two of them back to their car—this black SUV—a Mercedes, I think. After shaking hands, Colin asked what would have happened if his brother hadn't paid up. My acquaintance mumbles something about having to rough him up a little, maybe break some fingers—strictly in jest, of course."

"Of course," Cady said. "Then what happened?"

"A split second later Colin drives a roundhouse into the side of the kid's face, and the kid drops like a bag of cement. I thought Colin'd killed him, but he's not finished and a half second later he stamps on the kid's exposed hand. I swear I heard a bone snap." Hierra stared at Cady. "I've seen some things in my life, things that'll stick with me forever . . . as we all no doubt have . . . but this startled the hell out of me. I jumped back. Then Colin looks at us and says, 'Like that?'"

"Jesus."

"I don't think *Jesus* had anything to do with it." Hierra pronounced the revered name *Hey-Zeus*. "Anyway, Colin's chauffeur, who's built like a middle linebacker for the Ravens, jumps out of the SUV, grabs the kid by his belt buckle, and tosses him in back, and they all take off. Not something you see every day. Quite frankly, I'm surprised the kid didn't wind up in a coma because Colin Aadalen unloaded, and he's a big guy," Hierra said. "In fact, he's a rock."

CHAPTER 15

Day 4

The International Headquarters of Aadalen Pharmaceuticals sat on ninety acres on the outskirts of Henrico County, Virginia, a short trek southeast of the Richmond International Airport and a twenty-five-minute drive to downtown Richmond, traffic permitting, which it never was. Aadalen's main campus consisted of a twenty-story rectangle of glass, steel, and cement, with smaller facilities, laboratories, and other outcroppings peppered about the landscape. There was underground parking and private elevators in the main building, mostly for the lucky few who populated the top floor, with biochemists, research scientists, physicians—MDs, PhDs, PharmDs, lab techs, medical-science liaisons, clinical researchers, biostatisticians, patent attorneys, data managers, sales reps, and a hodgepodge of other job titles vying for choice spots in the east, south, and west parking lots. The north parking lot was for visitors only, which is where Preston navigated her Prius.

A security guard brought the two agents up to the executive suite on the twentieth floor where they checked in with the receptionist, who informed them that Colin Aadalen was tied up in a meeting and that there may be a slight delay. Forty minutes later they were still in the reception area. Cady was sorting through a rack of medical journals in search of an elusive *Sports Illustrated* or, hell, at this point, even a *People* magazine, when he heard the commotion.

". . . run it right into the fucking ground!"

Cady dropped a couple issues of *JAMA—The Journal of the American Medical Association*—back into the wall rack and spun around. Two suits and a female in a red jacket, all wearing somber faces, marched like Sherman, only instead of heading to the sea, the short suit in front used an elbow as though it were a battering ram to knock open one of the reception doors.

"We said our piece, and he knows we'll be watching," the woman in red said. "Nothing more we can do."

"We'll see about that," the short suit replied. "We'll see about that."

And as suddenly as they appeared, the trio was gone, off to catch the elevator or perhaps invade a small nation. Cady glanced at Preston, who'd been sitting patiently and reading articles from the *New England Journal of Medicine*. She peered back at Cady over the top of the *Journal*. Moments later came a second flock of suits and dress skirts, this wave more jocular, back slapping, several sipping from flutes of champagne, and one carrying a scone for the road. Within minutes this pack had dissipated and the last man standing turned to face the two agents.

"I do hope the sour grapes weren't too off-putting. I could hear their boorishness from down the hall. Forstner balances his lack of diplomacy with an overabundance of melodrama." The man held out a hand to Cady. "I'm Langdon Trutwin, general counsel for Aadalen Pharmaceuticals."

Trutwin looked dapper in rimless glasses and a dark blue suit, every strand of his silver hair in place, a spry seventy with a Caribbean tan.

"I'm so sorry to have kept you waiting." Trutwin shook Preston's hand with a bow of his head. "The board of directors met to appoint Colin Aadalen as chief executive officer. It was just a formality, really, to make it official—a fait accompli—and should have taken all of five minutes, but Herr Forstner drove it into extra innings. However," Trutwin smiled, "the champagne is a Louis Roederer Cristal. Would you care for a glass?"

The agents shook their heads in unison.

"Of course not," Trutwin said. "Forstner notwith-standing, it's been a glorious morning. Though we have no blood tie, I've known Colin since he was born and I consider him my nephew. Please let me take you to meet our new CEO."

CHAPTER 16

Hierra had been right, Colin Aadalen was a rock. Cady pegged Colin Aadalen at six three and perhaps 230 pounds of solid mass. And his handshake was a boulder to Cady's scissors as Cady offered the new CEO of Aadalen Pharmaceuticals his right hand—his gimp hand—out of habit and Aadalen gripped hold of it like a car crusher turning a limo into a cube. Cady did his best not to wince and had flashbacks to junior-high-school fisticuffs as Aadalen stepped tightly into his proximity, invading his personal space. Cady held his ground, but Liz—who evidently had graduated from recess—smiled and took a half step back when it came her turn at bat.

Aadalen's corner office was immense; the local high school could borrow it if graduation ever got rained out. Aadalen had greeted them at the door and the four crossed several time zones on the way to his desk and chairs. Palatial floor-to-ceiling windows allowed the chief executive officer to watch over his fiefdom. Attorney Trutwin forged ahead, producing a wooden coaster from thin air, and placing it under a half-filled flute of champagne on top of Aadalen's solid oak desk. Trutwin picked up the bottle of Louis Roederer, noticed it was empty, glanced quickly at Aadalen, then shrugged and placed the empty bottle in a black wastepaper basket at the side of Aadalen's desk.

Cady'd bet a month's pay that Aadalen spent his nights and possibly lunch hours at a gym, perhaps some cardio but mostly pumping iron. Probably bench-pressed 350 on a slow day. He thought of Aadalen's fist smashing into the side of his drug-addled brother's face and, like Hierra, marveled at how TJ Aadalen had survived the blow. Colin Aadalen had thick brown hair that complemented a thick nose and a jutting chin that looked like bedrock. Aadalen carried with him the air of a man that got his way—in one manner or another.

"It's not every day we receive a visit from the FBI, but I know why you're here," Counsel Trutwin said once everyone was seated, himself on a leather couch, Cady and Preston on expensive uprights in front of Aadalen's desk, and Colin Aadalen, arms crossed, leaning back on his executive throne. "I'd been having such a wonderful week too. My nephew's officially becoming CEO, his father's therapy is coming along better than we had hoped at this stage, we're riding the crest of a blockbuster drug that's going to revolutionize the way Alzheimer's disease is treated, but—of much more importance—the purple flowers on my heart-leaved asters are coming in like never before, I've not screwed up the white turtleheads or the lizard's tails as I feared, and the magnolia and tulip blooms are brilliant," Trutwin said, smiling. "This is Virginia after all."

"Uncle Lang's house opens for public tour during Richmond's garden week," Colin Aadalen informed the room.

"Don't make me turn red like my winterberries," Trutwin replied and then turned to Agent Preston. "Gardeners can always spot one another and I'm going to say that you garden."

"I do," Liz replied. "Not on your scale, but I make do."

"We must compare notes sometime." Trutwin turned to appraise Cady. "I'm going to say that gardening may not be on your list of specialties."

"I water things," Cady said, "if instructed."

"Of course you do," Trutwin said, "of course. Anyway, I don't mean to sidetrack the conversation, but I've also spent time this week plotting my retirement—this coming January—where I plan to utilize my green thumb on a fulltime basis. And possibly even open a flower shop. As I said it's been a wonderful week, one in which I've spent much of the days humming a dearly loved Disney song from my childhood—'Zip-a-Dee-Doo-Dah.'"

"I've heard Uncle Lang." Aadalen looked at Cady and Preston. "Lawyers should refrain from singing."

"Guilty as charged," Trutwin said and then took a second to focus his thoughts. "Unfortunately my sense of wonder, awe, and being in Zen with the universe came crashing down upon my ears last night when my nephew phoned to inform me that, incredulous as it sounds since Colin himself lobbied a full decade to deal with TJ's addiction issues by utilizing tough love sanctions, he met with—I don't know what those of you in law enforcement would call him—*Baltimore's drug kingpin* in order to bail out TJ's debt."

"That's exactly why I was sheepish about bringing it to your attention," Aadalen said, looking at Trutwin. "TJ shows up at my house in April with his whiny-beggy-baby bullshit that we all know so well, only this time he was scared as hell. I believed his story, not only because I'm the last guy he'd ever come to for help, but because it was what we've all secretly feared—TJ screwing over a drug dealer. He thought they were going to kill him. So I decided to bail him out—for mom's sake—and I didn't bring it up because of the living hell that mom and dad have been going through since dad's stroke, but I made it clear to TJ that I had to be there in person to pay just to make sure he wasn't bullshitting me."

"You put yourself in a dangerous situation. If something happened to you, it would destroy your parents," Trutwin added. "It would destroy me."

"I had a security guard with me, it was daytime at a public place, and remember," Aadalen said, "I was *giving* them money, Uncle Lang, not trying to take it from them."

"It was reckless. It was foolish. And I can only imagine the hay that Forstner would have made with the other board members had he been privy to this . . . *incident*."

"I know."

"Do you?" Trutwin asked.

Aadalen nodded his head.

Cady wished more interviews went this way. It was like watching TV and he wished for popcorn and a large Coke as the two leaders of Aadalen Pharmaceuticals were covering several of the topics he'd planned on bringing up. He glanced over at Preston and was surprised to find her scribbling in her trusty notebook. He felt guilty about not cracking open his briefcase.

"But you continued to socialize with this—and I get heartburn saying these words out loud—*drug lord*." Trutwin had talked himself red in the face. "Christ on a crutch."

"A couple of drinks, Uncle Lang. It's not as though I gave him my letter jacket."

"I have trouble wrapping my mind around why you socialized with the man?"

"I could say that I wanted to confirm they weren't selling to TJ anymore, but I assure you they were clear on that point." Aadalen thought for a second. "Maybe because we're on two sides of the same coin—light and dark, fire and water—the yin to our yang." Aadalen scratched at a cheek. "I don't know . . . two worlds meeting."

"Listen to yourself, Colin, just imagine if you had to testify against the man."

Aadalen laughed. "I'm too fond of my head to testify against someone like Hierra. Plus I have nothing to testify about."

Trutwin shook his head again. "Then you alibi the man against charges that he killed your brother."

"Hierra didn't kill TJ. He had no reason to. Trust me; these guys don't do anything without a reason. And you can be damn sure Hierra didn't pass TJ eighty grand in heroin."

Not having popcorn to eat, Cady chose to earn his paycheck. "Who do you think killed your brother?"

Both men looked at Cady as though they'd forgotten he was in the room.

Then Aadalen spoke, "The police have talked about him selling himself which, frankly, is fucking disgusting. So, hell, I don't know. A pimp whose territory he infringed upon? A john? Other street people? Or did old Karl Sandin finally get around to taking care of business?"

"Figuratively, TJ headed down that road when he started snorting designer drugs in junior high. In my mind that's what really killed him," Trutwin said. "Literally, I have no idea. With everything I've read in the news, Karl Sandin's the only link I can think of between TJ and Senator Brockman."

"Was the senator stabbed in the heart like my brother?"

"I'm sorry," Liz said, reverting to boilerplate, "but we're not at liberty to discuss details of the senator's case."

"I wish Brockman had never pardoned my brother. Maybe a lengthy stint in prison would have turned TJ around."

"Hindsight is always twenty-twenty," Trutwin said. "At the time of the pardon we thought TJ'd hit rock bottom and needed a lifeline."

Colin Aadalen looked at the agents. "I'm ten years older, so I didn't grow up with TJ. He was a good kid until he turned thirteen, but a complete fuckup ever since. I was finishing my undergrad by then, so I wasn't at home, but I heard every single story of the shit that TJ got himself into, fucking this up here, fucking that up over there. Then, when TJ was in his twenties, I saw firsthand how he couldn't keep his shit together long enough to make it through a single holiday meal. We couldn't have Christmas dinner with any semblance of tranquility, not with the strange way he'd rattle on, his red eyes—his vacant stare, the shakes, sometimes vomit, you name it. He aged my parents. Aged them. And I don't give a damn what the doctors say, my father's stroke is all on TJ. And if I were to be honest with you, I certainly didn't want TJ murdered, but I'm not broken-hearted he's gone. Not one goddamned bit."

The room digested that in silence.

"Look," Trutwin said, returning to his calm demeanor, "after Colin called last night, I spent an hour with a defense attorney friend of mine, an old law school chum. His take is that Colin did nothing illegal. That he spent a few thousand dollars of his own money, out of his own pocket, to pay off his brother's debt, to get TJ out of a jam, to protect the kid. Now, do I question my nephew's judgment? Absolutely I do. But he found himself in an atypical situation and did the best he could. Colin did nothing illegal."

Cady nodded along with Preston, but got the feeling that Colin Aadalen had held a little back from his general counsel regarding the extent to which he socialized with Hierra and may have truncated the piece about what he did to Brother Aadalen's face and hand at the end of the Baltimore meeting.

"Do you have any final questions?" Trutwin asked.

Cady began to stand, but Preston shuffled through her notes.

"You mentioned earlier that you're 'riding the crest of a blockbuster drug,'" Preston said. "What's a blockbuster drug?"

Langdon Trutwin's eyes widened. "It's a popular drug that generates sales in the billions of dollars a year and—who knows—maybe even does some good. Think statins for cholesterol, think Viagra," Trutwin said. "In the pharmaceutical industry . . . it's the Holy Grail."

"What do you think?" Preston asked as they merged onto I-95.

"Two things," Cady said. "First, we came to see Colin Aadalen, but Trutwin did 90 percent of the talking. If Terri and I ever need a general counsel for her resort, I'm picking him."

"He was smooth."

"I'm sure they rehearsed, which, if you have a general counsel, is, of course, what they would do. And, nonverbally, Colin Aadalen seems to enjoy throwing his weight around."

"I saw that. You weren't happy."

"Not so much his physicality, but after you bail your kid brother out of a deal with the devil, are you really going to start hanging out in hell?"

Preston said, "I don't think Trutwin realizes the true magnitude of his nephew's *acquaintanceship* with Hierra."

"Probably not."

"What was the second thing?"

"Huh?"

"You said two things."

"Oh, yeah," Cady said. "I could garden if I wanted to."

CHAPTER 17

Leahy tossed the *Washington Post* aside.

A glance revealed nothing new in the paper except some fartskull in a wingsuit had recently BASE-jumped himself into the great hereafter. Evidently Birdman had misgauged whatever these gliding idiots need to gauge and smeared himself against the side of an unforgiving cliff. Leahy hoped someone had captured the event on film and spit it up on YouTube. Already friends and family members of the dumb bugger were mumbling about how he went out doing what he loved. What complete bullshit. Yup, Birdman wasn't interested in another six decades of eating blueberry pancakes—but at least he went out doing what he loved. Leahy would bet everything he owned that in those final seconds, as Birdman realized there was no escape from the advancing cliff face, that his final thought was certainly not—*well, at least I'm doing what I love.*

Same goes for all the other Darwin Award winners who have strengthened the collective gene pool by removing themselves from it. From the weekend parachuters who plummet to their deaths, often filmed by awaiting family members, to race car drivers who check out in fiery balls of twisted metal, ditto dumbass surfers losing limbs and lives to starving sharks or scuba freaks getting shish kabobed by enraged stingrays, ditto mountain climbing numbnuts shedding their mortal coils in an avalanche of snow and loose rock.

But at least they checked out doing what they loved . . .

Fucking dipshits.

Leahy stared at some data on one of his middle monitors, tapped in a command, and sat back. The biggest thing about dime-store crackers—with their social engineering and spear phishing and malware and their remote administration tool software, RAT software, and keyloggers and exploiting network vulnerabilities and on and on and on—was that they went through all of this tedious bullshit breaking into computer systems to fuck up data or steal. A bunch of sophomoric thieves breaking into a company's database to grab credit card numbers.

Boring.

Crackers were the mean-spirited, small-minded hackers. Hackers, on the other hand, were more benign, breaking into systems out of an innate sense of curiosity and wonder and blah, blah, blah. Black hats . . . white hats . . . all retards. Leahy didn't consider himself either a hacker or a cracker.

Leahy was the Star Child tethered to earth by an endless chain of Lilliputians.

A second later Leahy looked at the middle monitor again. He'd been running a program of his own devise that searched out patterns . . . that searched out *drama*. There'd been some items of interest, but no smoking gun. He'd been tweaking the program's parameters for the last half hour to no real effect, but now a financial query brought several Microsoft Excel documents to the forefront. One Excel spreadsheet contained interesting numbers, but was ambiguous for not including a title or header or anything to help place the figures into context. The separate sheets along the bottom were labeled per a four-digit alphanumeric code; the first two characters of each sheet indicated a quarter on a fiscal calendar—Q1, Q2, Q3, Q4—with the final two digits indicating the associated year. Unfortunately the figures in no way correlated to any tax records from the corresponding fiscal quarters. It was likely a list of payouts, similar to the ones that Leahy had seen on his other *official* projects.

But it was a background query running on Leahy's other monitor—a search of peripheral elements to add a framework of understanding to his recent unearthings—that very nearly caused him to spit-take his coffee like in some crappy sitcom. Leahy's first reaction was *Holy Shit*. His second reaction was *Fucking Awesome*.

His third reaction was . . . how can I get this to Cady?

CHAPTER 18

The Canadian flew into JFK International using the Johnson passport, and had a ticket in the same name for the flight to Virginia Beach as well as for the rental car to Richmond, but, once there, would utilize a different ID. And after the *assignment* was complete, the Canadian would fly back home using the Andrews passport. The Canadian used a man in Manila—a master artisan of Michelangelo proportions—whose identity documents would convince your own mothers that you were someone else.

The Canadian stretched out and then took another sip of champagne—the perks of flying first class. Although the assignments had to be decoded from the Canadian's booking agent in Bern, and only the name of the assignment was provided along with any additional data that could aid in making the assignment a success, the Canadian was bright enough to put two and two together. Based on an assignment's bio, the Canadian could tell the difference between a drug cartel assignment versus an assignment from one of New York's Five Families or from one of the double dozen other families peppered across the United States—such as the one that sponsored the recently completed Detroit assignment—versus a corporate assignment, that is, corporate espionage taken to the ultimate degree.

The random assignments—where there appeared to be no motive—the Canadian attributed toward the target, at some point in their soon-to-be abbreviated life, having run afoul of someone with money . . . and connections . . . and one hell of a vindictive streak. Many of the random assignments requested a certain amount of bloodletting prior to project completion. The Canadian was not a sadist—however, if the funding had been suitable, on more than one occasion the Canadian had performed some postmortem procedures that would serve to satisfy the most vindictive special requests of clientele.

The Canadian had of late executed four absurdly high-risk assignments in rapid succession—bing, bing, bing, bing. Diving headfirst into this new assignment, which was a twofer no less, would soon raise that figure to six. It not only pushed the envelope—it flirted with disaster. But the adrenaline rush . . . it had to be what Yeager felt breaking the sound barrier. The Canadian would force a lengthy holiday after this assignment set was complete—go dark for six months, well, let's be honest, three. The Canadian took a final sip of champagne, finishing the flute a second before the stewardess began collecting them as the plane began its final descent into JFK.

The current assignment began with a corporate. And as far as the Canadian could connect the dots, it was the same patron that late last year had assigned the Canadian an inconvenient chemist that worked for CDER—the Food and Drug Administration's Center for Drug Evaluation and Research. That assignment had required that the CDER chemist's demise appear accidental, or perhaps a suicide, in order to shut the door on foul play and any subsequent investigation that an outright killing or suspicious disappearance might prompt. Fortunately the bothersome chemist had been through a painful and costly divorce the prior year and, looking not unlike Mr. Magoo, even the Magic 8-Ball would place his future courting prospects as "Outlook not so good."

Suicide also would be easier on the Canadian's back than hoisting Magoo up a ladder and then rolling him off his own roof. Less chance of witnesses as well. Plus, feeling down in the dumps during the holidays was as American as apple pie and baseball. It was well known that mortician labor spiked in late December as depressives the world over almost stood in line to give season's greetings the final full extension of their middle finger. And so the Canadian had slipped into the backyard of the chemist's split-level, careful to avoid clumps of melting snow, pick gunned the back door, and was inside in less than five seconds. The Canadian had a few hours to kill before the chemist returned home from work; enough time to see what items in the house could prove advantageous. The Canadian pulled off the leather driving gloves and slipped into a pair of unpowdered surgical gloves and went to work.

Hours later, the CDER chemist came home, entered the garage door whistling a show tune, plopped a briefcase and mail on the kitchen countertop, and then worked his way toward the hallway restroom to relieve his bladder after a long drive home in rush-hour traffic. The Canadian jumped him from behind, got the chemist in a bloodchoke—compressing a carotid artery—and, in seconds, the FDA employee collapsed into unconsciousness. The next part was poetry in motion—balletic—as time was of the essence. The Canadian set the chemist atop the toilet, wrapped his fingers around the handle of a turkey carving knife, appropriated from a kitchen drawer, and, squeezing the unconscious man's hand about the blade's handle, cut hard through the chemist's left wrist, bone deep, in the same instant the chemist began coming to. At this point the Canadian leapt backward to avoid any pesky spatter, and was in the hallway by the time the carving knife had slipped to the floor.

The CDER chemist blinked his eyes, spotted the knife and blood on the floor between his legs, followed the crimson stream upward, saw his wrist, and screamed. The Canadian had to hand it to the chemist as he immediately gripped his forearm with his right hand, clutching tight, a makeshift tourniquet, attempting to stem the blood flow. The chemist stood, legs trembling, turned, caught sight of the Canadian staring back at him . . . and screamed a second time.

It was a waiting game at this point as the Canadian back stepped toward the kitchen. The chemist, now several whiter shades of pale, staggered from the bathroom, heading toward a landline in the family room. The Canadian cut him off and the man turned around, his face now more a mask of shock than fear, and then stumbled toward the front door.

And he nearly made it.

Over the late afternoon, while scouting the house and sharpening the carving knife, the Canadian discovered an old laptop in the chemist's home office, sitting on a shelf below his printer. The chemist's main PC was password protected, but the laptop was accessible. It didn't appear to have many files on it and the Canadian figured all documents of importance had been transferred. Making certain not to step in the blood trail, the Canadian retrieved the laptop, carried it to the kitchen countertop, and brought up Microsoft Word. Less was more, and using a paperclip the Canadian took a few seconds to tap in the following message.

Without her . . . What's the point?

Yes, the Canadian thought, that particular assignment from the end of last year had gone exceedingly well. No questions or concerns had been raised.

The plane touched down at JFK.

PART TWO

VISITATION

CHAPTER 19

Day 5

"How are the hearings going?" Terri asked over the phone.

Cady knew the question was coming—it was just a matter of time—and he'd been able to dodge the inquiry by bringing her up to date on several of his old colleague-friends that he'd been able to connect with while in DC, although he'd left out the fact that most of the *connections* had been thirty-second chats as he bumped into them in the hallways and byways of the Hoover Building. That, plus he'd also been steering the conversational emphasis away from the Medicare hearings and toward discussions of Sundown Point, Terri's Minnesota resort. Summer was when the lake resort practically minted money, and August was exceptionally busy as her string of fourteen cabins on Bass Lake already had taken a two-plus month beat down due to wave after wave of visiting guests all ready to play hardy on their family vacations, with kids of all ages, sizes, and mental capacities hammering away on her rental units: plumbers were called, torn screens were mended, dock planks replaced . . . a thousand bits and pieces and then a thousand more.

But it was only a matter of time . . . and the time had just arrived.

"Did you hear me?"

"Yes," Cady replied and tried thinking of how best to arrange syllables into the appropriate words so as to limit the coming fallout, but he came up blank.

"Oh, no."

"Terri."

"Oh, no," Terri repeated. "It's that senator's murder, right—Jund's sucked you into that?"

"Terri."

"You know Roland's the portal to hell; every time you're near him it yawns open."

"I'm backseat to Liz on this one. We're only doing interviews and making assessments."

"Your *assessments* always end with me sleeping in a hospital chair."

Cady wished he could tell Terri to stop being so paranoid, but he'd met her on a less-than-pleasant murder case a few years back—the one in which he had lost over 50 percent usage of his right hand. Cady had been dumb enough to dive headfirst into a veritable briar patch of serial killers and lucky enough to come out the other side. Sure enough, he wound up hospitalized with a plethora of operations on the surgical docket. The only silver lining in the case was that, once through the brambles and thickets, Cady found himself going through physical therapy at the Grand Itasca medical center in Grand Rapids while convalescing at Terri's lake house, all of fifteen minutes away in the northern Minnesota town of Cohasset.

She'd been running Sundown Point single-handedly for years, a hard worker and she expected no less from others. Terri was a freckle-faced straight shooter, opinionated, brashly honest, even if Cady suspected he was being lampooned by her periodic rants advocating hanging thieves and rapists from the village square like Christmas ornaments. Then again . . . maybe not. Terri was also easy on the eyes, veering a bit toward the short side—perhaps a hiccup or two over five feet tall—with dirty blonde hair done up in an informal schoolgirl bun and white-cream skin that shrieked of Norwegian ancestry.

There'd been a spark or two at first sight and, well . . . one thing had led to another and before you could mutter Paul Bunyan and Babe the Blue Ox, Cady found his free time swallowed up attaching rental motors to Sundown Point rowboats, making supply runs into town, or riding the mower whenever the grounds were in need of a trim. Even though he griped at each of Terri's assigned chores, it was mostly in jest. This was where Cady was meant to be at this point in his life and he was fortunate, technology being what it was, that he could work with the Medicare Fraud Strike Force from his home office at the resort—he'd dibsed squatter's rights on an upstairs den in Terri's lake house—and only have to spend a day or two in Minneapolis each week.

"Not this time, Terri. You wouldn't believe the moving parts—MPD, Baltimore detectives, practically the entire Washington Field Office, even the Secret Service is poking about. I'm nobody."

"The murder's the only story on CNN and Fox."

"That's why you don't have to worry. The investigation is too big to fail. As for my part, it's like the end of a blockbuster movie where it takes ten minutes for the credits to roll . . . I'm just the third cameraman who brought in donuts one day."

"I just don't get you, G-Man," Terri replied. "You're chasing a killer all over Washington, DC, when you could be home making a baby with me."

Cady opened his mouth to respond, but words caught in his throat.

He'd been married once before, a college sweetheart—Laura—but the demands of a career at the bureau, especially the less-than-savory investigations he was immersed in, gnawed at their marriage like a teething puppy. Cady had been away much of the time—different cases, different cities—but to make matters worse, whenever Cady was home . . . he really wasn't. He was the impenetrable lump on the couch at the end of a day . . . the distant presence at the dinner table . . . the unknowable partner in the bed at night. Laura had been in her fifth month of pregnancy when she'd miscarried. Cady had been in Detroit tracking down rumors of Al-Qaeda connections at one of the Islamic centers—comments by a cleric had raised eyebrows but ultimately were editorial in nature. Cady immediately caught the red-eye home, took weeks off from work, but something had broken—had been years in the breaking—and all the king's horses and all the king's men failed miserably at putting it back together again.

The breakup had torn Cady in half. Laura had gotten remarried not long after the divorce papers had been signed. Some guy who owned a car dealership in Akron. A mutual friend had set them up on a blind date and, evidently, they clicked. Last he'd heard, she was pregnant with their second child. Cady wished her all the best as, lord knows, he'd dragged her through the worst.

Cady also swore that he would never allow history to repeat itself—not with Terri, not ever—which was why he'd put his career at the Criminal Investigative Division in the rearview mirror and stomped hard on the accelerator. Yes, Cady was only too happy to wave sayonara to the unpredictable world of the FBI's Criminal Investigative Division and deal with the far more rational world of white collar criminals involved in Medicare fraud where, when you went to arrest them, they whimpered like toddlers instead of reaching for a concealed straight edge.

"Did you hear me, Drew?" Terri asked softly. "If I remember right, it takes two to summon the stork."

"If you put it that way," Cady said, blinking moisture from his eyes, "I'll be home next week, case solved or not."

"You've got the knuckles, right?"

Cady laughed out loud and waved Preston away when her head perked up from behind her computer.

"Yes, dear."

Terri had presented him with a pair of plastic knuckles shortly after his latest stretch in the hospital. They were in the shape of brass knuckles, but weighed almost nothing on account of being polycarbonates. She'd gotten them off some dubious Internet site and demanded that he carry them in his suit pocket to act as an equalizer for his gimp hand. Cady had grumbled, but Terri had been adamant, sometimes, like today, checking to see if he had them on him like a mother confirming the sliced carrots were in her child's lunch bag. Of course the knuckles had never left his suitcase in his hotel room. Brass knuckles were illegal in most states, certainly DC. And even though plastic knuckles were invisible to X-ray and wouldn't set off a metal detector, the law surrounding them was a tad murkier. But Cady wasn't about to risk looking like an ass going through security for the Senate Committee hearings, even if it would take a pat search to discover them.

Cady felt more secure with his Glock 22 and might someday tell Terri that her gift went underutilized, but, until that day, he didn't dare appear ungracious.

"And be sure to stick next to Liz," Terri continued. "She hasn't pissed off the gods."

"Roger that."

"I watch the news coverage and I keep asking myself why that Senator Brockman's life is so important? Why does he merit all this attention and a full-court press to find his killer? You know why? It's because he's one of *our betters*, and not one of us peons." Terri was a law and order advocate. She felt all murderers, rapists, thieves, and, as far as Cady could tell, politicians should be promptly introduced to a short rope and a tall tree—preferably in the churchyard after Sunday worship for all the towns-folk to see. "Better put me on the suspect list— based on where *our betters* are taking this country—I probably did him in."

"It was Holocaust Barbie!?"

Cady answered his cell phone thinking it was Terri calling back to read him a few more lines from the riot act, but it displayed a DC area code. The voice belonged to Elaine Brockman.

"You found out."

"I assumed anything stuck inside her would melt off."

"Did she tell you?"

"No, I just got off the line with her soon to be ex-husband—Senator Pritchard."

"So she came clean?"

"Indeed she did. At first he was enraged, fuming at me as though it were my fault, as though Tay, the Holocaust, and I had been having a jolly old three-way all this time. He calmed down when he realized he wasn't alone, and that I was the female equivalent of a cuckold."

"How long had he known?"

"About ten minutes before he called me," Brockman replied. "I guess Holocaust told him she's keeping the baby."

Cady thought for a second. "Do you think Senator Pritchard could have known about the affair before today?"

"His anger sounded pretty damned authentic to me," Brockman replied. "But I'll tell you something. If Tay were still alive, I think Pritchard would kill him."

CHAPTER 20

"Duke Pritchard didn't kill anyone." Director Jund spoke to the agents sitting around the conference room table. "I've golfed with the man for twenty years."

"Well then," Cady said, not able to help himself, "glad that's all sorted out."

Jund placed a forefinger in the air. "Pritchard's the chairman of the Foreign Relations Committee and he just returned from a two-week trip to the Middle East." Jund looked down at his legal pad and placed a second finger in the air. "Not only was he out of the country at the time Brockman was hit, but Pritchard is—how should I say this?—on the portly side. Pritchard's definitely not the imposter in the security footage." A third finger went up. "And Pritchard told me that he only found out about the affair yesterday, so why would he kill Brockman in advance of having a motive? That's a pretty big cart to place before the horse." Jund looked at Cady. "But thanks for playing."

Cady ignored the barb and asked, "Pritchard talked to you about the affair?"

"The senator called me for lunch—the man's not an idiot and when his wife fessed up about her extramarital activity, she also informed him about your visit," Jund said, glancing from Cady to Preston, "so he knew we'd be looking at him. We ate fish at Black Salt and Pritchard was fuming; he basically announced to the entire restaurant that he was going to, and I quote, 'divorce that Nazi bitch.' Unquote. Not only did Holocaust Barbie come clean because you two showed up, but because she's starting to show and Duke had gotten himself snipped decades back—after his third son was born with wife number one."

Cady glanced about the conference room table; to the right of Elizabeth Preston sat Special Agent Kent Neely. Neely was young, fairly green, and involved in the investigation due to his background in mortuary science—his family owned a string of funeral parlors across the New England states—and since the UNSUB was shedding eulogies at crime scenes, Neely was tapped as the bureau's resident funeral expert. Next to Agent Neely sat Bryce Drommerhausen, a top profiler snatched from his BAU perch at NCAVC—his Behavioral Analysis Unit at the National Center for the Analysis of Violent Crime—to help the agents get a bead on the UNSUB's motivations. Drommerhausen had submitted the killer's modus operandi into the Violent Criminal Apprehension Program's database for comparison, but, not surprisingly, ViCAP had come up snake eyes—that is, no similar pattern was found.

Next up was Special Agent Lee Quenan, the bureau's medical examiner whom Cady had met that first morning at the Brockmans' Woodley Park residence. Quenan also had pored over the autopsy notes regarding young Thaddeus Jay Aadalen's death in Baltimore, and had previously been discussing the similarities of the killing wounds. Completing the table were special agents Dave Merrill and Maggie Fitzwilliams, the forensic specialists who also had been at the Brockman crime scene. Special Agent Dan Kurtz, likely quite happy not to be there in person, was on speakerphone from Quantico.

Jund turned his attention to Agent Drommerhausen. "Anything you can say to enlighten us, Bryce?"

Drommerhausen took a breath. "The UNSUB is brazen—identical stab wounds, depositing eulogy notes near the bodies—not necessarily what I would do were I to moonlight as a serial killer."

"What do the eulogies tell us?"

"Not much. The Brockman eulogy reads as though it's a draft away from something that could reasonably be delivered at the senator's funeral, that is, if you could get past the dripping sarcasm as well as the insincerity of it having been penned by the senator's assassin. The Aadalen eulogy appears more sincere as it acknowledges Aadalen's addiction, the irony here being that young Aadalen died not from his substance abuse, but from the UNSUB having inserted a blade into his heart. Plus, the Thomas Gray piece doesn't connect. Aadalen was not 'A youth to fortune and to fame unknown'—quite the opposite, in fact—nor did Aadalen have a 'humble birth.' Outside of its popularity, the poem does not fit Aadalen's lot in life."

"Discrepancies like that in poem selections are not uncommon," Agent Neely volunteered. "I'm always amazed when a devoutly religious family selects 'Imagine' by John Lennon to be played during a funeral service for a family member."

"Amazed? Why?" Jund queried.

"The first line of the song is 'Imagine there's no heaven,' which contradicts most funeral sermons. It's a pretty tune, but I don't think the words are given much, if any, thought."

Jund nodded and looked back at Drommerhausen. "Anything else you can tell us?"

"Clearly, much more effort went into the senator's eulogy. Aadalen's eulogy was only a few lines with a cut-and-paste piece of poetry added as filler. Although Aadalen was murdered first, I believe Senator Brockman was the primary target and Aadalen secondary. I also believe the UNSUB is using these eulogies as his personalized calling card. He wanted us to see a connection between the victims in case the identical stab wounds were not powerful enough."

"He's putting an exclamation point on the connection."

"Yes."

Jund looked at the forensic specialists. "What about the paper?"

The forensic agents glanced at each other and it appeared Agent Merrill had picked the short straw. "The paper's a dead end. It's standard copy and print—ninety-two brightness, twenty weight—the kind you could pick up at any office supply store, or at Target or Walmart, wherever. The font is Calibri, size twelve. If you find us a printer, maybe we can match it."

"If I stab to death a United States senator and leave a eulogy as my calling card," Jund replied, "my printer and laptop go immediately into the Potomac."

"But what if the UNSUB's not done?" asked Agent Fitzwilliams.

"Then in a bag in a tree trunk in the boonies."

"The smart move," Cady said, "would be to print it off a thumb drive at a Kinko's or in a public library."

Jund shrugged and turned to Agent Preston. "Tell us about the cartel connection."

"Jorge Hierra, aka George Hierra, is an East Coast drug dealer with ties to one of the more violent of the Mexican drug cartels—Los Zetas."

"Can't we ICE his ass back to Mexico?" Agent Kurtz asked over speakerphone. "A guy like that shouldn't get to play hide and seek in a sanctuary city."

Like Washington, DC, Baltimore was a sanctuary city. Illegal immigrants are protected and police are not allowed to ask about an individual's status. Federal immigration laws are ignored.

Jund shrugged. "Evidently we're not busy enough dealing with our homegrown criminal element so we find the need to import more."

"It's not that," Preston picked the ball back up. "Hierra's got a permanent resident card—a green card—and a team of high-end attorneys to back it up."

"Figures," Kurtz said over the phone line.

"If you buy or sell drugs in bulk in Maryland, more than likely the product worked its way through one of Hierra's pipelines." Preston looked at Cady as she began summing up their meetings with Hierra and Colin Aadalen. "TJ Aadalen ran afoul of one of Hierra's runners to the tune of $5,000, most of that being interest accrued. TJ stalled for time, telling Hierra's crew about his family ties. TJ then ran to older brother, Colin, and begged him to pay off his debt, which Colin did—in a manner—and that's how Colin Aadalen struck up an acquaintanceship with Hierra."

"The CEO of Aadalen Pharmaceuticals is now friends with one of the most-illicit drug dealers on the East Coast?"

"*Friends* may be too strong a word, but they've connected several times for chit chat and drinks and golf since Colin paid off his brother's debt."

"Any Hierra connection to Senator Brockman?"

Preston shook her head. "There may have been recreational drugs in Senator Brockman's distant past—when he was young—but Brockman's drug of choice for the past couple of decades has been Glenlivet with an occasional glass of merlot."

"Brockman chaired the Senate Committee on Agriculture, Nutrition, and Forestry," Cady said. "So unless the committee's recent review of the US Grain Standards Act somehow ran afoul of Los Zetas, there are no dots to connect back to the senator."

"From what you've told us, this older brother Aadalen violently assaulted younger brother Aadalen on at least one occasion. Older Aadalen loathes what younger Aadalen has done to his parents.

Older Aadalen blames his father's stroke on younger Aadalen," Jund said. "We now know that older Aadalen is linked to Jorge Hierra, and Hierra is linked to squads of individuals from Mexico who you'd never want paying you a visit in the dark of night. Those cartel boys were removing heads long before ISIS."

"Colin Aadalen strikes me as an overconfident frat boy. A bully, maybe, but not a fool. I could buy him having one of Hierra's connections take out his younger brother to lance a boil and give the family closure, but killing the senator wouldn't make any sense. And it might open a can of worms that could bring them both down."

"You said Aadalen wished Brockman had never pardoned his brother. That Aadalen felt prison was perhaps the only thing that might have helped younger Aadalen."

"But Brockman only pardoned the kid at the family's request. Colin wouldn't be livid at Brockman for doing what his parents had pushed for," Cady replied and looked directly at Jund. "Cart in front of horse."

Jund sighed. "In the age of carts and horses, it took twelve days to capture John Wilkes Booth. In the age of the Internet and rocket ships, we're five days into this and so far have bubkes. And we're talking in circles."

The room digested that tidbit in silence. Eye contact was avoided.

Cady had worked under Jund for ten long years, back when Jund was a mere FBI assistant director of the Criminal Investigative Division. Jund had an acerbic wit that he used like a blowtorch in times of stress. Cady figured this personality trait helped the director blow off steam and served to keep his underlings on their tiptoes. Attending the meeting reminded Cady why he both loved and hated the head of CID. The polished marble charisma not only allowed Jund to navigate smoothly in the tumultuous waters of the bureau's DC headquarters, but to rise to a position of such power in a relatively short time frame. Cady also had seen Jund's rough edges—coarsened, sharp, sandy, and jagged—where all his Beltway polish had worn thin.

Cady had hoped never to see those edges again.

"In my new position as director of CID, I had hoped there would be a modicum of less stress." Jund tapped his Mont Blanc lightly against his legal pad. "Alas, it's true—those whom the gods wish to destroy, they first make mad. I was here until midnight and when I returned at six this morning, more than twenty messages awaited me . . . including a serious inquiry from 1600 Pennsylvania. And unless Senator Brockman claws his way out of the morgue and screams 'Just Kidding!' on the evening news, it's going to get worse. And worse." Jund tapped his pen harder. "If we hit twelve days, that is, if we exceed the Wilkes Booth ceiling, there will be a yammering for heads to roll—of which mine will be front and center."

Not an utterance was volunteered as Jund searched the faces about the table.

"I am bleeding internally," Jund said. "Any chance of Senator Brockman clawing his way out from the morgue drawer?"

"No, sir," said Agent Neely.

Jund focused his full attention on the youthful agent who had felt an uncontrollable need to answer the director's rhetorical question. Cady guessed it might not be that important for him to memorize the young agent's name, although Cady himself had been caught in the director's glare on countless occasions.

"To the tower with him." Jund dropped his Mont Blanc onto his legal pad. "The king is displeased."

Not a word was said. Not a thing in the room stirred. Seconds stretched into minutes. Jund finally turned to Cady. "We've got to catch this fucker."

CHAPTER 21

Roark Larson's suicide was anything but . . .

"What the hell?" Cady muttered and read the lone sentence in the Additional Comments section a second time. And then a third. He closed out of the summary form to which he'd transferred his notes, thoughts, and ideas—limited as they may be—from the Colin Aadalen interview without saving and then checked the date-modified stamp. 8:26 from two nights earlier. That seemed about right. Cady reopened the document and scrolled down to the form's last section.. . . . and the sentence he never wrote stared back at him.

Roark Larson's suicide was anything but . . .

"Liz, you read my Aadalen report?"

"Yesterday morning," Preston replied, looking up from her PC to Cady's makeshift workstation. "Why?"

"You got it off our shared drive, right?"

"Yeah."

"Did you add to it?"

"No," Preston said. "Why would I? I wrote up my own summary."

"You know anyone named Roark Larson?"

"No."

"Shit."

"Roark Larson died on December 22 last year," Cady said.

"Was it a suicide?" Roland Jund asked.

Cady and Preston sat huddled about Jund's desk, collectively speaking in low voices as though they were being monitored, which, based on the mystery surrounding Cady's tampered-with summary form, might not be far from the truth.

"I only got a chance to Google obituaries before we brought this to you, but Roark Larson's obit states that he 'died unexpectedly,'" Cady replied. "You know my thoughts on the media, right? They'd sell their grandmother for a lead, and if you give them an inch, they'll orchestrate a riot. But the one classy thing they tend to do is downplay suicide, and they use phrases in the obituaries like *died unexpectedly*."

"You two ask around?"

"Yes," said Preston. "We kept it low key, just asking our team. Nobody edited Drew's report."

"I scanned both the document and the shared drive for viruses. No threats were detected, but I think that's meaningless. I had Ben Orbeck from IT come check it out, told him the file had been acting buggy—hanging for chunks of time. He ran some diagnostics and said it was clean. Of course it worked fine for him, so he told me to do something *bold* like rebooting if it ever happened again," Cady said. "Orbeck thinks I'm an idiot."

"I can't imagine why," Jund said. "He didn't bring up the B-word, did he?"

The B-word—breach—was the reason for the emergency ad hoc meeting with Director Jund. It was the reason Cady and Preston had dropped all other tasks as though they were made of molten lava. An intrusion into the Federal Bureau of Investigation's computer network by party or parties unknown tends to elicit that effect.

"No," Cady replied, "but Orbeck didn't have the rest of the story."

Jund rubbed two fingers at each temple. "The Chinese have a thousand specialists on a cyberhacking force in Beijing who wake up every morning with the sole purpose of culling through our government databases. And you can add another thousand Russians in Moscow to that equation as well."

"I can't see the Chinese or the Russians blowing their cover over an interview report with Colin Aadalen," Preston said. "Let's hope it's internal, perhaps an agent in the Cyber Division who got curious and made a connection to Roark Larson."

"What more do we know about Larson?"

"He was a chemist-slash-administrator who worked for the FDA's Center for Drug Evaluation and Research. As far as I can tell, Larson monitored prescription drugs working their way through the approval system."

Jund took a second and then smiled. "If Larson is tied into Aadalen Pharmaceuticals, our hacker may have just solved the case?"

"Our hacker thinks he solved the case," Cady corrected.

"If he did, I hope to god he's internal. I'll buy him a steak before I kick his ass to Lee," Jund replied, referring to the United States penitentiary in Lee County, Virginia. "I need you two to get me everything you can on Roark Larson."

"What about the data breach?" Preston asked.

Cady thought for a second. "I've got an idea."

CHAPTER 22

"He slit his wrist and left a note." Preston had been on the phone with an investigator from the Montgomery County Department of Police for most of the prior hour. "Larson had been through a lengthy divorce and his note referenced not wanting to go on without his wife."

Like Jund, Cady hoped that despite the alarming manner in which it materialized, the Roark Larson tip could lead somewhere—could jumpstart their stalled investigation—but he needed to maintain objectivity, avoid reasoning backward from a desired conclusion. Cady knew the suicide rate among men in the United States is nearly four times that of women, which is an interesting paradox since women have a higher rate of reporting mental health disorders such as depression. Of course, Cady figured, if men collectively refuse to stop the car to ask for directions, you sure as hell can't expect them to confess their debilitating pangs of melancholy to a stranger in a lab coat. Another cause for this disparity would be due to the fact that men attempting suicide tend to use methods that assure death—by shooting or hanging themselves. Women opt for poison, which doesn't cause immediate death and therefore has a substantially higher survival rate. Also surprising is that in recent years middle-aged males have surpassed their younger counterparts and now experience the highest suicide rates. And divorced men are especially vulnerable to suicide ideation as well as to suicide itself.

"What did Larson's note say?"

Preston looked down at her tablet. " 'Without her . . . What's the point?' "

"That's all he wrote?"

Preston nodded.

"They do a handwriting analysis?"

"The note wasn't handwritten. It was typed into Word on his laptop, and the laptop was left open on his kitchen table."

"His laptop?" Cady said. "Jesus, Liz, I think I saw that on a rerun of *Matlock*."

To:	Roland P. Jund
From:	Drew S. Cady
Cc:	Elizabeth J. Preston; Bryce W. Drommerhausen; File
Subject:	Forthcoming arrest of Colin Aadalen in the Thaddeus Aadalen/Senator Brockman murder case

Dear Director Jund,

As discussed in this morning's meeting, video footage from an all-night supermarket on Saint

Paul Street in Baltimore captured images of
Colin Aadalen, CEO of Aadalen Pharmaceuticals,
stepping into a cab at 1:34 on the morning of his
brother's death. Thaddeus Jay Aadalen had been
found stabbed to death in his car, which had
been parked one block south of Charles Street.
The distance covered from the murder scene off
Charles Street to where Colin Aadalen caught
a cab on Saint Paul Street is less than one-half
mile.

Additionally, Special Agent Maggie Fitzwilliams,
forensic specialist working out of Quantico,
informed us this morning that based upon
the curvature of the upper-right cheekbone
and gradient of the forehead, the figure in
the photograph on Senator Brockman's stoop
is indeed Colin Aadalen. Fitzwilliams's lab
ranks the certainty level in the ninety-fourth
percentile.

Behavioral Analyst Bryce Drommerhausen put
together a quick sketch on Colin Aadalen that
merits reflection. This from Drommerhausen:

Colin Aadalen's Cain-like hatred in relation to
his younger brother stretched from Virginia to
Maryland to the nation's capital as he fixated
on Senator Brockman as the vessel that granted
Brother Thaddeus unmerited salvation. Though
Colin's parents lobbied for the then-Governor
Brockman's pardon, Colin was Old Testament
and wanted Thaddeus to pay for his sins

against the family. And once Father Aadalen suffered a debilitating stroke—a stroke for which Colin holds Brother Thaddeus personally responsible—in Colin's mind, both Thaddeus and the senator were dead men walking. I cannot stress enough how the apprehension and arrest of Colin Aadalen must be handled with extreme care. Fratricide as well as plotting and carrying out the murder of a sitting United States senator clearly are not the signs of a healthy mind. In addition, Colin Aadalen lists one of his hobbies on his profile page on Aadalen Pharmaceuticals' website as weightlifting and, based on the disproportionate development of his upper body, Aadalen may be a user of anabolic steroids and/ or human growth hormones, either of which could induce more volatility in his thought process.

Colin Aadalen will be in Washington, DC, tomorrow, spending the morning pressing flesh with members of Congress, that is, he's lobbying for his new Alzheimer's drug. With Bryce's note of caution in mind, I've set up a late afternoon meeting, at 3:30, with Aadalen at Olive Garden, the one across the street from Tysons Corner Center. I will meet him in the parking lot, reach out to shake his hand, and, at that moment, the Metropolitan Police will take Aadalen into custody. Captain Pecha of the Baltimore Police Department's Homicide Section has been notified and will be on scene. We must also keep our eye on Colin Aadalen's chauffeur who is, in fact, Aadalen's bodyguard. The bodyguard came from the Blackwater Agency and, before that, the Navy SEALs. He is devoutly loyal to Colin Aadalen and must be subdued simultaneously with Aadalen's arrest.

Side note: We have received an anonymous tip that Colin Aadalen additionally may have been involved in the death of an FDA inspector named Roark Larson; Larson's death was initially ruled a suicide. Elizabeth Preston is following up on this lead.

CHAPTER 23

Day 6

Holy Shit.

I knew he had FDA blood on his hands, Leahy thought, but to OJ his little brother and that asshat senator—the CEO of Aadalen Pharmaceuticals is like fucking *Dexter*. And if Colin Aadalen is shooting steroids, that shit screws up your mood, twists your behavior. Another junkie, just like his brother.

What a world, what a world.

Leahy reread Cady's memo to Jund and it was all he could do to keep from alerting Colin Aadalen, to refrain from burrowing back into Colin Aadalen's e-mail system and have a message—appearing to come from Barack Obama—pop up on his screen, stating simply: *They Know You Killed Brockman and Little Bro! Run! Run! Run!* A few taps on his keyboard and Leahy could turn this fucker into a nationwide manhunt, but, by and large, he'd rather watch the arrest go down in person.

Leahy realized he'd been laughing out loud when he spotted Wenstead staring at him but he was in too good a mood to shoot his overattentive colleague the bird. It had the makings of a grand day, a field trip was most certainly in order, and Leahy made a command decision to take the afternoon off.

The patio seating at Ruby Tuesday was like scoring box seats at the opera. On the left lay the frontage road and, a short jog beyond that, the Tysons Corner Center shopping mall. But in front of Leahy was the parking lot that the two restaurants shared and then the front entrance to the Olive Garden. Leahy had gotten there at two, sat in his Nissan facing the Olive Garden for ten minutes before deciding that he might look suspicious when the authorities began to scope the area. Besides, catching the upcoming spectacle while sucking down an Amstel would make it all the more enjoyable.

Leahy had eaten most of the plate of cheese fries and ordered a third beer when the idea occurred to him. He took out his iPhone, clicked open the video camera app and swiped zoom with a finger, then centered it on the Olive Garden's front entrance. Perfect. He lowered his hands to the table with the phone still aimed at the Italian restaurant. This would work. He could film the altercation and, with his phone at table level, shrouded by an Amstel bottle or two, the ruins of his appetizer, and the table condiments, no one involved in the skirmish would be any the wiser. Leahy figured that even if there were no fireworks, with the nonstop media barrage about the dead Senator Brockman this and the dead Senator Brockman that, he could get a healthy wad of cash from one of the networks for having filmed the capture of Senator Brockman's killer.

Special Agent Cady arrived at ten past three. Leahy fumbled with the video camera app on his iPhone as he glanced nonchalantly about the area and then toward Tysons Center as though he were fascinated with the architectural structure of that hideous abortion, but was clandestinely filming the agent from the Federal Bureau of Investigation as he stepped over the curb and sat on the bench outside the Olive Garden. Leahy was glad he'd left his car as Cady's attention turned toward the vehicles in the joint parking lot, examining them one by one, which didn't take long as it was a thin crowd this time of day. Cady then scanned the frontage road for a second or two, and then lowered his head and appeared to be in conversation.

He's mic'd up, Leahy thought, now watching Agent Cady from his iPhone at table level. This is going to be great. Cady stood and did a final glance about the area as Leahy casually reached for his Amstel with a left hand. Cady then looked toward Tysons Center, pointed a quick finger toward the side of the Olive Garden, and then turned around and walked into the restaurant. No new vehicles had entered the parking lot, so Leahy stopped filming and set down his phone.

Leahy was giddy. He had to take a leak, but—fuck that—he would go in his pants before he'd miss out on this matinee. He attacked the remaining cheese fries with his fork, and then took another sip of beer. Such feelings of enthusiasm and joy were foreign to Leahy.

Could this be happiness?

Dear God, Leahy prayed to a supreme being that up until this point he'd never given a second thought, please have Aadalen come off the rails when they try to cuff him. And please, please, please God let that Blackwater thug be packing heat. Don't let Cady get hurt, mind you—well, not terribly badly, anyway—cause he's the man. But as far as the Metropolitan Police—well, hell—they're like those security officers on Star Trek . . . who gives a shit?

And while I have you on the line, God, if you do exist, I must compliment you on the advanced security of your network. That's quite a system you have up there, immune to cyber intrusions, social engineering, and viruses; completely resistant to MiMs— man-in-the-middle—or evil maid attacks. You are a programming savant, Sir; the greatest bar none, but if one day, I'm able to crack into your *undiscovered country* and slip you a rootkit—well, hmm—something for me to shoot for.

Leahy nearly jumped from his seat as a throat cleared behind him. He twisted about in his chair and nearly went into cardiac arrest. Special Agent Drew Cady stood there, arms crossed, staring down at him. Next to Cady stood a female agent of about fifty dangling a set of flex cuffs.

"What?" Cady said. "You didn't save me a cheese fry?"

CHAPTER 24

"Certain types of turtles—the North American eastern painted turtle for one—have the ability to breathe through their ass," Leahy said.

Leahy was sitting in a holding cell in the bowels of the Hoover Building. Cady sat across from him. It had not been going well.

"No kidding," Leahy continued. "It's called cloacal breathing."

Cady said nothing.

"Now what you're doing here today is not breathing through your ass, but talking through it."

"Technically," Cady said, standing up, "I typed through my ass when I wrote that memo, but it worked well enough to reel you in." Cady opened the door to leave, but paused for a second. "That true about the turtles?"

"His name is Douglass Anthony Leahy, he's twenty-nine, and he's originally from Scottsbluff, Nebraska." Preston stabbed at her dinner salad while reviewing her notes. "He studied computer science and engineering for a year and a half at the University of Nebraska in Lincoln before dropping out."

The two agents were at a McDonald's on Thirteenth Street, not far from the Hoover Building. Cady was on his second quarter pounder with cheese, something he'd dare not have were Terri in attendance. Liz had disappeared with Leahy's driver's license upon their return to Hoover, while Cady spent face time trying to crack the cracker. Leahy's cheese fries at Ruby Tuesday had been enticing, so Cady'd also ordered large fries with his two burgers, ostensibly to share with Liz, however, his colleague had yet to touch a single fry.

"I was able to get in touch with Leahy's faculty advisor, who remembered Leahy, and said he was, quote," Preston searched her notepad, "'a Mensa-level genius with a computer, and could have taught our staff a thing or two, but had one hell of an attitude problem. He seemed to hate everything human and everything not. Nobody was sorry to see him leave, and I didn't try to talk him out of it.' Unquote."

"Sounds like a real winner. What else?"

"He worked for the Geek Squad in Lincoln while he was going to the university. There's been a lot of turnover since then, but a manager remembered him and provided similar feedback. I guess he made customers nervous, but he worked wonders, so they kept him busy in a back room." Preston stopped for a sip from her bottled water. "Next Leahy shows up in Silicon Valley, living in an apartment in the southern portion of the Bay Area, but I have no work history for him during this period of time."

Cady smiled but said nothing.

"Then early last year Leahy surfaces in Fort Meade, Maryland, and he's getting his paychecks from the Office of Tailored Access Operations."

Cady almost spilled his Coke. "TAO is NSA."

"I knew that would wake you up," Preston said. "TAO gathers cyberwarfare intelligence for the National Security Agency. Leahy now lives in Fort Meade because that's where TAO's headquarters, the Remote Operations Center, or ROC, is located."

"That missing gap in Leahy's background," Cady said. "It got scrubbed."

Preston put down her fork and stared at Cady.

"I'm thinking that Leahy wormed his way into some computer system during those missing years that brought him to the attention of the TAO. It must have been impressive enough for NSA to give the guy an ultimatum: Join us or get buried."

"That's plausible," Preston said. "TAO employs the best of the best to infiltrate computer systems used by foreign entities."

Cady put down his second cheeseburger. He was no longer hungry. "I read a Snowden document that mentioned how TAO uses templates to break into routers, switches, and firewalls from different vendors."

"I didn't take that class," Preston replied.

"Me neither," Cady said. "But I know these folks don't mess around."

"No, they don't," Preston agreed. "Their motto is 'Your data is our data, your equipment is our equipment.'"

The two agents sat quietly, contemplating their next move. It would likely be a long night, and they would have to bring Jund into the picture.

"Liz," Cady said, throwing the remnants of his cheeseburger and french fries into his McDonald's bag in order to toss it into the garbage bin.

"What?"

"Did you know turtles can breathe through their ass?"

CHAPTER 25

"Telling the world to eat shit and die," Cady said, back in the holding cell with Leahy, "has got to be a hell of an exhausting mantra to live by."

Leahy said nothing.

"You're an asshole," Cady continued, "we get that, but now you're an asshole with a Hobson's choice. You know Director Roland Jund of the Criminal Investigative Division?"

Leahy nodded slowly.

"Jund knows your superiors' superiors on a first-name basis. He's waiting on my word to call Fort Meade and to inform your superiors' superiors about the breach, to inform your superiors' superiors about what occurred this afternoon." Cady set his cell phone on the table in front of him. "If you think your superiors' superiors will go to bat for you against the Federal Bureau of Investigation, by all means tell Director Jund to eat shit and die. Please do. But if you think your superiors' superiors may have something else in mind, you may want to select an alternate route."

Leahy said nothing.

"What about your peers at TAO? I'm sure they've got your back."

Leahy said nothing.

"You enjoy mysteries, right?"

Leahy said nothing.

"You pointed us in Colin Aadalen's direction in regard to the demise of an unhelpful FDA administrator. If that's borne out," Cady continued, "it's not too great a leap to believe that Colin Aadalen would have taken out his own kid brother because the kid had caused his parents a lifetime of misery. And Aadalen's kid brother's death links us back to Senator Brockman."

Cady tapped the Contacts command on his phone app to display a list of numbers.

"Thanks for that Roark Larson tip, by the way," Cady said. "Unfortunately, I think you're spent and, frankly, what you've given us can't be used anyway, you know—fruit of the poisonous tree." Cady stared at Leahy. "I'm not without bias here. Since you have nothing more to offer, I'm partial toward you recommending Director Jund's *final meal*. I'm curious about the extent of his reaction."

Leahy said nothing.

"You will not be given overnight to think about this situation. You will not be given five minutes to think about this situation. You will agree in one second to letting us know everything that you know—about how we came to be here today—and you will become the most helpful son of a bitch on planet earth . . . or . . . or you can tell Director Jund exactly what to eat before he kicks the bucket."

Leahy said nothing.

Cady picked up his cell phone. "Can I count on you to tell Director Jund to eat shit and die?"

Leahy grimaced as though he'd passed a kidney stone. "I'll help."

"What's that?"

"I said I'd help."

"He was for the most part obliging in his own reptilian manner," Cady said. The two agents were back in Jund's office. "He says he's a true crime aficionado and got sucked up in the senator's murder, and did some freelance poking about. If we believe him, Leahy hacked his way into Aadalen's computer network not to take it down, but to peek about."

"So he flew past their security and antivirus software like a hot knife through butter, just like he did with our system?" Jund asked.

"He's not sharing any of TAO's secrets, so I'm getting the *Reader's Digest* condensed version, but he claims he got into Aadalen Pharmaceuticals with some Trojan horse of his own design. Some midlevel manager inside Aadalen Pharmaceuticals canceled out of what appeared to be a mundane error message, but instead triggered Leahy's program and—presto—he owns them. He used another program to cull through Colin Aadalen's files, spreadsheets, reports, e-mails, what have you, looking for keywords or 'drama,' which is Leahy's word for conflict. He said Aadalen was consistently harsh and unsympathetic regarding Brother TJ's plight in numerous e-mails sent to Father Marcus before Marcus had his stroke. No smoking gun, well, if you don't count

Colin wishing to *kick the kid's ass*, which we know he did at least once, as well as hoping his brother *would fucking OD*."

"Colin Aadalen blames his father's crippling stroke on the living hell his brother put his parents through . . . and decided it wouldn't go unanswered?" Jund said.

Cady shrugged. "Leahy's trawling program came back with two years of *drama* regarding how a chemist, Roark Larson, in FDA's Center for Drug Evaluation and Research had been dragging his feet, continually finding problems with Aadalen Pharmaceuticals' NDA—their New Drug Application—endlessly requesting more information to make a determination, questioning the drug's effectiveness." Cady looked at Preston. "Aadalen's blockbuster drug for Alzheimer's."

"Attorney Trutwin's Holy Grail."

"The drama surrounding Larson tapers off at Halloween, everybody's back to business, no one's screaming from the rooftops about their NDA at the FDA."

"And by year's end, Roark Larson is dead," Preston said. "A suicide."

"Leahy said he then came across Larson's obituary on the Internet and, like us, thought it was a suicide, but Leahy was turning his head and avoiding my eyes so I think he got into Montgomery County's network, verified it was a suicide, thought it smelled fishy, and left us that tip."

"None of this we can use," Preston said.

Cady shrugged. "Not in the courtroom sense."

"Leahy's pointed us in the right direction," Jund said. "We just need to find another route in."

"What do we do with Leahy?" Preston asked.

Cady knew exactly what Liz Preston would like to do with Douglass Anthony Leahy; an act that would entail throwing away a key. Cady held a different opinion, but he looked toward Jund for an answer.

"Unless we go back to carving images on cave walls, which I don't see happening anytime soon, we'll continue living in fear of a cyber Pearl Harbor, a digital 9-11.You can't pick up a newspaper these days without reading about China or the Russians hacking into our business or government systems," Jund said and leaned back in his chair. "Quite frankly, Liz, I hope our side has an army of Leahy pricks feeding this shit right back at them."

"Leahy breached our system, sir," Preston pushed.

"Yes, he did."

"He needs to be punished. He needs to be made an example of."

"If this were to come out, the bureau would get a hell of a black eye, Liz," Jund said. "Haven't we had enough of those lately?"

"So he gets to walk?" Preston countered. "Is that it?"

"We're cast as benevolent figures in Leahy's mind right now," Cady said, tossing in his two cents. "The last thing we want would be for Leahy to view us as malevolent figures, as the people who destroyed his life. We don't want a man with Leahy's skill set fixating on us as his destroyers. Your credit cards, Liz, would perpetually be maxed out. Roland would wake to find warrants for his arrest in twenty states. My paid-off Escape would be repoed by the dealer. Terri's resort would lose electricity; no deliveries would ever again be made. If they didn't put Leahy in a hole with bars on top," Cady said, looking at Preston, "our lives would become Dante's eighth circle of hell. It'd be a fulltime job trying to sort out the mess, with Leahy piling more on each of us every week. But right now we're seen as having pulled the thorn out of his paw when we could have screwed him big time. And he knows he's in our scope, top of the list if there's any more bullshit."

"It doesn't seem just."

"You know I wouldn't let him skate away scot-free, Liz," Jund said. "He's doing remedial service right now as we speak."

"Where is he?" Preston asked. She'd been working the Aadalen-slash-FDA angle and missed out on Jund's latest tactic.

"Leahy's giving Bert Inveen and his group a quick seminar on best practices." Inveen headed IATU in ESOC—the Information Assurance Technology Unit in the Enterprise Security Operations Center. "I told Bert we had him on loan from an alphabet agency for the day—all hush, hush—and I thought his guys could benefit from picking the guy's brain. I may get a free dinner out of this if Leahy presents well."

"Good luck with that," Cady volunteered.

"Bert's been in IT three decades. He speaks fluent geek. I had Drew make it clear to Leahy to phrase it as stuff his area currently monitors, to keep it theoretical but to cover new methods in safeguarding against external attacks, and that Bert's takeaway

had damn well better be how to plug any holes that
Leahy used to get in."

"Bert knows not to show off any of our security
measures?" Preston asked.

"I made clear that it's a one-way data dump,
but I'd be surprised if Bert would be able to shock
Leahy."

Preston nodded. Cady could tell that Liz wasn't
happy about the situation, but she lived in the real
world, and, like Cady, she'd been unhappy before.

Jund's phone rang. "Speak of the devil," he said,
glancing at caller ID and hitting speaker.

"Me want," Bert Inveen said in lieu of greetings.

"You no get," Jund replied.

"I've got some worthless meat sacks I'd toss
under the bus to get him, Rollie. What is he—NSA
or CIA?"

"Something like that."

"You'd have to kill me if you told me, huh?"

"If only he were mine to give, Bert, but some of
the agents that have been working closely with him,"
Jund said, looking from Cady to Preston, "mentioned
he's a bit difficult to work with . . . a malcontent."

"With what he could bring to my table, I could
care less if he's a dick," Inveen replied. "I owe you,
Rollie. I'd take you out for a drink tonight, but I think
my team's going to be here awhile, kicking around a
few of Mr. Alphabet's suggestions."

"Have fun," Jund said. "I'll send my guy to fetch
him."

Cady was out the door before Jund hung up.

CHAPTER 26

Day 7

"You're with the FBI?"

Cady saw it flash through Elliot Kettler's eyes—fight or flight. He'd seen it before and readied himself in case Kettler made a move. The agents had caught Kettler at the door to his office right as the man had returned from lunch. Cady wasn't expecting the chemist to throw down and start swinging fists with his secretary in the background and colleagues strolling the corridor, but at that instant in time, flight seemed very much on the table. This was the reason Cady and Preston had shown up at the US Food and Drug Administration's main campus in Silver Spring, Maryland, unannounced. Cady wanted to do a drive-by, catch Roark Larson's FDA replacement without advance warning, and gauge the man's reaction.

And based on Kettler's reaction, Leahy had been barking up the right tree.

"Come on in," Kettler said, fumbling open his door. "What can I do for you?"

"Roark was heartbroken," Kettler said, steering the conversation toward Roark Larson's depression. "He'd been through a divorce and I guess he couldn't live without her."

"You were friends with Mr. Larson?" Preston asked.

Preston had worked the phone earlier that morning, starting with the FDA's Office of Human Resources and then being transferred to an administrative assistant in the Center for Drug Evaluation and Research. The reason for Agent Preston's request for data had been hazy at best, something indistinguishable about filing the final review on Roark Larson's passing, the admin assistant had been helpful, providing Preston with information as to how Larson's workload had been divvied up among four CDER chemists—with Elliot Kettler receiving the Aadalen Pharmaceuticals' New Drug Application for Neurzamine, a medication that, purportedly, prevents beta-amyloid fragments from clumping into plaques—a major characteristic in the Alzheimer's disease brain abnormality. The admin wasn't sure how the CDER evaluators had split up Roark Larson's various assignments, but she told Liz it was likely left up to the chemists to arm wrestle, flip coins, or draw straws. No matter how they juggled it, Kettler wound up with Neurzamine.

"Not close friends, but he was a colleague and we've both worked here for years," Kettler answered. "Sometimes a group of us would grab food in the cafeteria and, to be honest with you, the last couple of times we ate there, Roark seemed distant. Withdrawn."

"You read his divorce record?" Cady stared across the desk at Kettler, a dollop of antagonism in his voice.

"Of course not."

"It paints a different picture than what you're selling." Cady added several dollops of antagonism. "The kids were grown and Larson gave her the boot."

Kettler stared at Cady, eyes wide. "I heard he left a note saying he couldn't live without his ex-wife."

"That was news to her. As well as to Larson's divorce attorney."

Preston placed a hand on Cady's forearm as though to hold him back. "We have our forensic specialists looking into the legitimacy of Mr. Larson's suicide note."

Kettler swallowed hard. "What are you saying?"

"You damn well knew Larson wanted more studies, you knew he pushed to issue Aadalen Pharmaceuticals a complete response letter not approving their NDA," Cady said, swinging for the fences, hoping to end the dance. "So why'd you spin on a dime and green light Neurzamine?"

Kettler looked at Preston, pleading for a lifeline, but she returned his gaze.

"Uh, Aadalen provided more information to each and every one of Roark's inquiries." Kettler couldn't get the words out fast enough. "The others on the review team were all good with the NDA."

Dammit, Cady thought. Looks like we'll be doing the dance after all.

"You caught his reaction when we showed up, right?" Cady asked on the ride back to DC.

"It was pretty obvious."

"If the police show up at your house one night, sure you're surprised and maybe you pray that one of the kids didn't take something to the next level, but you don't look like you're going to bolt for the backyard, jump the fence and race for the woods."

"In your work on the Medicare Fraud Strike Force, Drew, you're familiar with drug manufacturers paying doctors for speaking engagements in exotic locales, which can include first-class travel, meals at five-star restaurants, over-the-top gift bags, entertainment, what have you?"

Cady nodded. "The controversy is over whether this influences their *prescribing* habits. Some call these vacations and view them as a form of bribery."

"If a drug company has money to burn for that type of activity, what do you think they might do if their billion-dollar *blockbuster* drug gets hung up indefinitely at the FDA?"

Cady nodded again. "I think Aadalen got to Kettler. I think they bribed him to give Neurzamine the green light. And I think Kettler's bright enough to look at Roark Larson's *suicide* and put two and two together."

"Are you thinking what I'm thinking?"

Cady nodded a final time. "We squeeze Kettler . . . and Kettler spills."

CHAPTER 27

It was an open casket affair.

Though the senator had indeed seen better days, the funeral home had pulled off quality work and Taylor Brockman looked contentedly at rest. The work of his assassin was easily concealed by means of a navy blue Brioni suit, a starched white shirt, and a red silk tie as though the senator were set to speak at a Fourth of July celebration instead of headlining his own memorial service. Widow Brockman had, evidently, ruled out the senator's trademark gray suit in favor of his spending eternity clad in something more patriotic. Cady made a mental note, as he did at every visitation, to place in writing his desire for immediate incineration with no display stops along the route to the crematorium.

There had been a private vigil—a short prayer service for immediate friends and family at Saint Peter's on Capitol Hill—and, which Cady caught from whispered voices, the president had attended. This was followed by a public visitation which Cady and Preston and, based on the standing-room-only crowd mingling about the social hall, most of the politicos in congress had graced with their audience. Preston circled the church parking lot like a shark in search of prey, but ultimately settled for practicing her parallel parking skill in a microscopic opening down the street. The agents passed two network news vans as they hoofed it to Saint Peter's and Cady spotted a helicopter, which he assumed was network number three or a local affiliate. Later tonight the senator's remains would be flown to Richmond, Virginia, where the funeral mass would be held tomorrow afternoon at the Cathedral of the Sacred Heart, followed by burial at Mount Calvary Cemetery.

"Thank you for coming," a visibly exhausted Elaine Brockman said by rote when the agents made their way to the head of the line to pass on their condolences. Then Widow Brockman leaned forward so only they could hear, "I'd kill for a drink. I swear to God I've hugged everyone in DC, except for Senator and Mrs. Pritchard who are suspiciously absent."

Though it was standing-room only, Cady spotted Elaine Brockman's chief of staff, Dorie Searles, in a corner chair. The two agents bumped their way through the horde of mourners toward her, mumbling apologies whenever anyone got jostled too inhospitably.

"How's she holding up?" Preston asked after air kisses were divvied out.

"I hope she chose better shoes than I did," Searles said. "My feet are killing me. I think she's doing okay, though with all this activity, she hasn't had much time to process. I'm here for moral support, but I think Elaine'll need that more next week when the music stops. She's got another huge day tomorrow."

"How are you doing?" Preston asked.

"I'm fine," Searles said. "I got to meet the president earlier. I wanted to take a selfie, but thought it might not be appropriate. He mentioned you were zeroing in on a suspect and assured us that it wouldn't be long before an arrest was made. Is that true?"

Cady did his best not to grimace, suddenly dreading their upcoming meeting with Jund. "We're pursuing a person of interest, but there's nothing solid."

"Can we get you anything?" Preston asked, changing the subject. There were light refreshments available on a table a couple of hundred people away.

"Can you guard my chair?" Searles replied, openly grimacing. "I need to use the restroom."

CHAPTER 28

Day 8

Must be a bitch working at a Fortune 500.

The Canadian followed the new assignment to an early afternoon of golf at Willow Oaks Country Club on Monday afternoon, and then, after eighteen holes, shadowed him to the Omni Richmond Hotel and watched from a chair in the lobby as he obtained a room from the front desk—a bit odd since the assignment had a ten-bedroom Georgian style less than a half hour away in Westham. But that query was quickly answered. The Canadian waited two minutes and then followed the new assignment into Trevi's Lounge. The man was sitting at a corner table, smiling at a young blonde who was in no way, shape, manner, or form his wife.

The Canadian ordered a light beer at the bar, walked it back to a small table, sat so the assignment's table was in the line of vision, slapped an iPhone on the tabletop, and began clicking at applications. The Canadian caught the assignment slide the room card across the table. The Canadian also caught Blondie slide it into a pocket, stand, turn, leave Trevi's, and head into the hotel lobby and toward the elevator atrium. The Canadian caught the new assignment wave down the bartender for another malt whisky.

The Canadian had smiled. The assignment was giving Blondie plenty of time to get up to the room. No sense in making it easy on whatever detective the little woman at home mindin' the chillun would eventually hire in order to boost the string of digits in the divorce settlement.

But today was Thursday and the Canadian's new assignment, creature of habit that he was, led the Canadian back to Trevi's Lounge at the Omni Richmond Hotel. Most everything appeared the same—low light, less than half the tables were occupied at this pre-happy-hour hour—except, of course, the blonde. And while this new blonde was still in no way, shape, manner, or form the assignment's wife, she was not the blonde from Monday afternoon. Blondie II was perhaps a little older than Monday's version, with a little longer hair and a narrower face. And Blondie II was sporting a wedding ring of her very own.

The plot thickens, the Canadian thought—perhaps I'm not the only thrill freak in the bar.

On Monday the Canadian had watched as the assignment made short order of his second Scotch, checked his watch, and then cut across the lounge and into the hallway that led to the bar's restrooms. A few minutes later the assignment returned, dropped a twenty on his table, exited Trevi's on the hotel side and made his way toward the bank of elevators. An early evening tryst before heading home for dinner and a few barks at the rug rats. As the Canadian finished the beer an idea began to take shape. This tryst at the Omni didn't look like a first, and the assignment hadn't appeared anxious or concerned.

This appeared more to be a way of life.

On Monday the Canadian had walked down the bar's back hallway and opened the door to the men's room. Very posh. Ice in the urinals. A stack of hand towels on the marble countertop, and empty—not surprising since happy hour had yet to kick in and the lunch crowd was ancient history. The Canadian then left Trevi's, as had the assignment, through the entrance that led into the hotel. The Canadian grabbed a dark roast, Venti size, at the Starbucks nestled in the hotel's lobby and set about counting security cameras. The idea was almost tabled when the Canadian spotted a camera aimed at the hallway entrance into Trevi's Lounge, but was delighted to find no sign of a camera trained at Trevi's street entrance on East Carey. No doubt there were video cameras peppered hither and yon about the streets and boulevards of Richmond, but nothing that a hat and obnoxiously large sunglasses couldn't counter.

But today was Thursday and the assignment's handing off of the key card to married Blondie went as smooth as silk. After married Blondie made her exit, the assignment jiggled his whiskey glass, polished off the Scotch in one long swallow, stood up, and headed toward the restroom hallway.

Check.

The Canadian gave the assignment a twenty-second head start, and then followed him across the half-filled lounge—past a couple of lookers on bar stools, past a bored dad chugging Guinness while his three kids sucked down Shirley Temples, past a young couple sipping margaritas—and into the back hallway. The Canadian opened the men's room door, noted no bar flies milling about the sink.

Check.

The Canadian took a quick look back—no one coming.

Check.

The Canadian slipped quietly into the restroom and spotted the new assignment's back as he stood alone at the row of urinals that extended along one wall. The Canadian crouched to steal a quick peek under the two stalls opposite the urinals. Empty.

Check.

The Canadian jammed a rubber wedge beneath the door—at the point where it swung inward—stood, turned about, and gave the wedge a defining kick with the heel of a shoe. The Canadian and the new assignment would not be interrupted.

Check.

The assignment finished the process with a zip and a flush. He turned and headed toward the sink when he spotted the Canadian.

"What the hell are you doing here?" the assignment asked, surprised, a mild grin working its way across his features.

"I've come to warn you," the Canadian said, stepping forward. "You're in danger."

The smile melted and the assignment planted a foot in front, a boxing stance. "I'm in danger?"

The Canadian took another step forward. "Your name has been placed on a list."

"What does that even mean?"

"You know exactly what it means."

The assignment's countenance began an exodus of color, hair standing on the back of his neck. "Why are you telling me this?"

The Canadian took a final step forward, now face to face with the new assignment, now in the strike zone. "So I can get closer."

The razor sharp stiletto blade snapped into place and locked as the Canadian's fist began its violent ascent. The six-inch blade thrust upward, under the assignment's rib cage, piercing the heart, killing him instantly.

Colin Aadalen, CEO of Aadalen Pharmaceuticals, never had a chance.

Check.

The older Aadalen brother was hefty while alive; his dead weight now slumped forward. The Canadian grabbed a fistful of suit jacket under Aadalen's armpit and used the blade's handle to shove the man into the nearest stall and onto the toilet seat. A second later and the stiletto had returned to its hidden pocket, and the Canadian now held a folded note inside a handkerchief.

"Screw it," the Canadian said and shoved the note between Aadalen's gaping lips.

The Canadian spent another second with the handkerchief, wiping blood off a wrist, before that worked its way back to the hidden pocket. The Canadian did a quick spot check in the mirror, everything A-okay, and now it was time to . . . there was a shove at the bathroom door. Then another shove, and then a hard kick along the bottom.

The Canadian was at the entry in a heartbeat, the knuckles of one hand gently on the wood of the door.

"Hey!" a voice called from inches away. "Is someone in there!?"

A couple more raps followed. The Canadian bent down, ready to remove the wedge. If the man on the other side of the door were to take this obnoxious behavior to the next level, there would be immediate consequences.

"Goddammit!"

The Canadian heard the guy marching away, angered, grumbling, likely to bark at the bartender about the need to take a leak. In a half second, the Canadian yanked the wedge and was in the hallway heading back to the lounge, passing two women who were giggling and gossiping their way to the ladies' room. The Canadian spotted a guy in a golf shirt making gestures and giving the bartender an earful; the Canadian spotted a group entering the lounge from the hotel side as well as a couple of cheap suits walking in from the street entrance. It was closing in on happy hour.

There was an unmistakable smear of blood on the bathroom floor, and one of Aadalen's legs was askew, sticking out from under the stall. The next guy in to see a man about a horse will have one hell of a story to pass along to his drinking companions, the Canadian figured, as there was no way he wouldn't notice the dead man. The near miss added to the adrenaline rush and the Canadian's heart beat as though it were trying to break free. Carrying out an almost-public execution and coming close to doubling down on a potential witness set every nerve ending on fire. It was like kayaking the class VI rapids on the Deschutes River around Lava Island Falls. It was like cave diving Cenote Esqueleto—the Temple of Doom—beyond the Tulum Ruins in Mexico's Yucatan Peninsula.

It was a fucking rush.

PART THREE

EULOGY

CHAPTER 29

Cady stared into the toilet stall.

Colin Aadalen's dead brown eyes stared back at him. It was a harsh glare—accusatory—as though, considering Aadalen's current surroundings, he were demanding privacy. The Richmond Police Department had been making ready to remove Aadalen's body when Cady and Agent Preston arrived. RPD's forensic team had completed all that could be done on-site, photographs had been taken, and the medical examiner had performed his stint, and would provide more specified results after an autopsy had been performed. Cady asked for a minute before the body bag came in, but all it took was an initial glance to recognize that he wouldn't need to pore over the report from RPD's blood spatter analyst to tell what had occurred in the bar's restroom.

Colin Aadalen had been stabbed; one wound to the heart, and then he'd been shoved into the toilet stall and set upon the toilet seat. Blood had worked its way downhill onto Aadalen's lap, puddling between his thighs, some dripping into the toilet, some dripping onto the bathroom's tile floor. Cady read no clues in the blood; no shoeprint left in crimson, no palm prints on the stall door. Aadalen's killer had kept the wetwork contained, which meant Aadalen's killer knew exactly what he was doing.

But that was old news.

Cady already knew that TJ Aadalen and the late Senator Brockman had been dispatched by someone who knew exactly what he was doing, but doing it in a private place—in a dark car on a secluded street or behind locked doors on a quiet night—where he didn't have to fret over the thousand things that could easily go south was the opposite of what had occurred here. Cady wondered if Colin Aadalen had known his killer. Or was it just another patron passing by on the way to use the urinal only to twist into attack mode at the last possible second, when it was too late for Aadalen to do much of anything? Colin Aadalen would have been a hard man to take down had the muscular CEO seen it coming.

Taking a life inside Trevi's restroom in the late afternoon was ballsy.

Next level shit.

The agents had spent the afternoon with Director Jund at the Hoover Building when the call from Richmond PD had come in. They'd been plotting the best way to put the squeeze on Elliot Kettler, the FDA inspector who knew more, much more, than he was letting on. Leahy's illicit snooping pointed them at Colin Aadalen per files and e-mails on Aadalen's PC at Aadalen Pharmaceuticals. Before Aadalen became acting chief executive officer, before his father's stroke,

Leahy's *research* indicated that Colin Aadalen had been clearing obstacles along the road to Aadalen Pharmaceuticals' new Alzheimer's drug Neurzamine . . . one such obstacle had been Roark Larson. Kettler had no poker face and his reaction to Cady and Preston's unscheduled visit to the FDA's Silver Spring office was all the agents needed to know that something was rotten in the State of Maryland . . . and Virginia. Kettler was involved, not in Larson's murder per se; more likely he'd been paid off to pass the Neurzamine New Drug Application with no more of Larson's foot-dragging bullshit.

If that's how Colin Aadalen dealt with pesky FDA details, it's no great stretch of the imagination to see him aim that angst at his junkie kid brother, a kid brother who'd made his parents' lives a living hell. And whether he was really pissed off at the senator is irrelevant, Colin Aadalen had used a hitter—maybe a pro on loan from his new pal George Hierra—to take out Senator Brockman in order to muddy the water. A senator doesn't receive Secret Service protection unless he or she becomes a viable presidential candidate or travels to a foreign country on government business. A cartel hitter flies in from Mexico, takes out the senator, leaves a eulogy note at the scene of the crime, and is on a plane back home the next day.

"So Colin Aadalen has no qualms about murdering an FDA chemist over a drug application, it's just another cost of doing business," Director Jund said, summing up their collective thoughts. "How is that different from how George Hierra would handle a conflict? Colin Aadalen didn't hit it off with Hierra because of shared interests or because they're on opposite sides of the same coin. Colin Aadalen hit it off with Hierra because, just like George Hierra, Aadalen will kill for his business interests, Aadalen will kill for his family." Jund thought for another second. "Now would be a good time to divest your 401k of any stock in Aadalen Pharmaceuticals."

Neither Cady nor Preston ran to phone their broker.

But Cady had called Terri. The Medicare hearings had ended and he'd reserved a seat on a flight to Minneapolis that left in the morning. Terri had been delighted and dropped another none-too-delicate hint about how they may have to act like rabbits in order for the stork to make an appearance next spring. Terri wouldn't have to twist his arm . . . the things you did for love.

Cady cursed himself for lacking the subtlety to flip Elliot Kettler during their meeting at FDA head-quarters, but once Director Jund started talking to the man about conspiracy to commit murder, Cady gave the chemist all of three minutes to fall in line. And once Kettler flipped, Jund would have Aadalen Pharmaceuticals by the short hairs and the bureau's computer gurus could then pick up where Leahy left off. Sure, Cady figured, he might be checking out early—and there would no doubt be twists and turns and legal challenges along the way—but it was nothing that the director of CID and his admiral girl Friday couldn't conquer. Colin Aadalen, who likes to hang with gangsters, turns out to be the man behind the curtain, pushing buttons and pulling strings. It made perfect sense considering what they knew.

Until a phone call from Richmond PD had blown it all to hell.

CHAPTER 30

Cady stepped far around the blood trail leading into the toilet stall, entered the hallway, nodded at the ME and his two assistants standing next to a gurney. Colin Aadalen was all theirs now. He headed to the bar where Liz was chatting with the RPD lead detective named Walsh and a Trevi's Lounge bartender.

". . . said the door was locked," the youthful bartender named Steve something or other was informing Agent Preston and Detective Walsh as Cady approached. He was pointing at a lonely guy sipping bottled water at a table near the hotel entrance. "That made no sense because the restroom doors don't have locks. I jog back with him and push open the door. I look at him like he's crazy, which I've since apologized for, and I head back to the bar, but only make it a few steps when Barry," the bartender paused again to point at the guy with the water, "starts yelling 'Hey! Hey! Hey!' I come back wondering what now? Then I saw the *mess* on the floor."

"And that's when you ran for help?" Liz prompted.

"That's when I made a complete ass of myself. First, I screamed 'Stay Here!' an inch from Barry's face. He understood that I meant not to let anyone in the bathroom. Then," Steve said and shrugged, "I don't know, my brain was stuck on happy hour and how folks were going to be streaming in any second, so I race like an idiot to the street entrance, slam the door, and lock it." Steve shook his head. "Then I grab a chair from a nearby table, yank it over in front of the door as if I'm trying to barricade us from the zombie apocalypse or something, but the chair clunks over with a hell of a noise. And that's when I flew like a bat out of hell through the hotel entrance and to the front desk to call security." Steve shrugged again. "Not my best moment."

"Did you see anyone in the hallway when you were first heading to the men's room with Barry?" Cady asked.

The bartender shook his head. "Krissi and Melanie were ahead of us, but I don't think they saw anyone."

"They stated that they didn't recall, but they were involved in a conversation," clarified Detective Walsh. The agents had spoken with Walsh twice via cell phone during their mad dash from DC. And Walsh also had given them the nickel tour of Trevi's Lounge upon their arrival. The detective was a short man with a lived-in face, likely years younger than he appeared. "The girls already had a bit too much to drink and were not of much help."

"Krissi and Mel waitress at the Grille during the day, then come here and spend some tip money," the bartender said in defense of the two young women, which made Cady wonder which of the two he was seeing.

"Hotel security did a bang-up job," Walsh said. "They shut the place down and asked everyone that was here to stay until we arrived. They even sprung for drinks . . . non-alcoholic drinks. We took names and addresses before letting anyone leave, but no one saw anything solid."

"Did anybody mention seeing anyone who was hanging around," Cady asked, "but disappeared right before the bar got locked down?"

"There was a dad in here getting drinks with his kids so his wife could sleep up in their room. He said he got the stink-eye from some fellow. He took it to mean the guy was angry with him for bringing his children into the bar even though the kids were drinking Cokes. He just caught a glimpse of the guy glaring at him before he shushed the kids, but he said the man had brown hair, average height, dark suit, and an intense stare. Another witness, a lady who was sitting right here," Walsh pointed at the bar stool nearest them, "said she probably saw the same guy in the bar mirror and with the way he was scrutinizing everyone, she assumed he was hotel security. She was wrong on that—turned out he wasn't. We walked the two of them around the bar before we began releasing people, but both witnesses stated that the guy was no longer here."

"Does that description ring a bell?" Cady looked at Steve.

"This place gets nuts from happy hour until close. I see so many people day in and day out that they blend together," Steve replied. "I only remember the obnoxious drunks."

"You got addresses and phone numbers on the two witnesses?"

"Yup," Walsh said. "The guy with the kids is from Harrisonburg, but they just flew back from a London vacation, so they're sleeping off jet lag before they drive home tomorrow. The woman lives in the city." Walsh tapped a folder on the bar top with a knuckle. "Like I said, we've got everyone that was in here when security locked it down talked to and tagged, but I bet the killer was already gone, out the door before discovery, certainly before Steve returned from the front desk with hotel security."

"How long were you gone from the bar?" Preston asked the tender.

"Maybe three minutes," Steve said. "I should have called security and tried to lock down the room myself, but my brain was mush and all I could see was the blood on the floor and that guy's leg sticking out from the stall. Keith Wellman, one of the security guys, saw me running to the front desk and jogged over. Keith alerted Paul Dupree, the head of hotel security, as we came back here."

"You did well, kid," Walsh told the bartender and then dismissed him, telling Steve he needed to huddle in private with the agents from the FBI. After Steve moved to the end of the bar, Walsh spoke, "We're working the security video that has Trevi's entrance on the hotel side covered. We're getting access to two outside street cameras. Both long shots. Neither directly covers the street entrance to Trevi's, and one of which I guarantee will be worthless, but the other one should get sidewalk traffic which we can run by our two witnesses and see if they're able to peg the guy they saw."

"It's worth a shot," Cady said. "Can Liz and I get copies of the witness statements?"

Detective Walsh nodded and sent a uniform over to the hotel's front desk to make photocopies of all the interviews. Then he looked at Cady and Preston and said, "I suppose we should talk about what the ME fished out of the victim's mouth."

CHAPTER 31

*Colin Marcus Aadalen, age 42, longtime resident
of Richmond, VA, and the civic-minded CEO of
Aadalen Pharmaceuticals, passed away suddenly
on August 7th whilst having an extramarital affair
at the Omni Richmond Hotel. He was preceded
in death by his adoring brother, Thaddeus Jay.
He is survived by his loving wife, Jennifer, and
his children (William and Christine). Memorials
preferred to Hospice Care Plus.*

"It had been stuffed into his mouth—something
you don't see every day," Detective Walsh said. "Not
much wetness or saliva damage."

Cady and Preston read the typed note through a
transparent evidence bag.

"It reads more like an obituary than a eulogy,"
Preston said.

"It has a touch of wryness, like the senator's
eulogy, with references to an affair and donating
to a local hospice. It's having fun with itself." Cady
flagged bartender Steve back from the far side of the
bar. "Did you know the victim?"

"He was a regular, came in for drinks a couple times a week," Steve replied. "Great tipper."

"Was he ever with anyone?"

"It's like I told the detectives, he'd have a drink with someone, but then she'd head out and he'd hang around for a while."

"Did he always meet the same person?"

"No." Steve grinned. "There were about four or five hotties that the guy seemed to juggle."

"Yet they never left the bar together?" Preston asked.

"No," Steve replied. "The women would leave and he'd have another drink or a bite from the happy hour buffet before he'd go."

"What was your take on all this?" Cady asked.

"They don't pay me to have a take, but I found it odd that he never left with any of the women at the same time, not even once. They always seemed pretty affectionate when they were having drinks together."

Walsh dismissed the bartender a second time, and then spoke in a softer tone, "Colin Aadalen is not listed on the Omni's guest registry, but Omni, evidently, is Aadalen Pharmaceuticals' hotel of choice for its clientele coming in on business trips. Currently, nine rooms are booked under Aadalen Pharmaceuticals for business guests. I walked through the rooms with the front desk clerk and got the names of out-of-town clients for eight of the nine rooms. Get this, the front desk has Colin Aadalen picking up the key card for the ninth room, but, we checked, and Aadalen had no key card on his body. My hunch is that Aadalen's date goes up to the room ahead of him, so it's not obvious to any casual observers, and Aadalen follows her up ten minutes later."

"Did you check the ninth room?" Cady asked.

Walsh nodded and said, "It was empty, but the bed sheets had been flipped back, so someone had been in the room after housekeeping cleaned it this morning. I have a team up there right now, but—you know—fingerprints in a hotel room, although we are dusting the doorknob. The sheets didn't appear to have had any recent *activity* if you know what I mean, so my thought is that Aadalen's date went up per the little ruse they had going, got ready for Aadalen's arrival, and waited. After a half hour or so, she probably got dressed and came down looking for him, saw the police presence at Trevi's and hightailed it the hell out of here."

"You got Aadalen's cell phone, right?" Cady asked.

Walsh nodded again. "We'll run down any recent calls and check for texts. Maybe we'll get lucky on a print off the doorknob, but all that'll bring us is Aadalen's hook-up, not his killer. And we'll probably get her on the security video anyway, leaving Trevi's on the hotel side."

"Aadalen's girlfriend might have input regarding other faces she saw in the bar." Cady shrugged. "Maybe she'll do the right thing and step forward."

"I wouldn't hold my breath on her doing the right thing, especially if, like Aadalen, she's married. And if she catches the news, which she most certainly will, she'll realize that she could be mixed up in a murder investigation."

"So if the eulogy is correct about Aadalen having an affair," Preston said, "it means our UNSUB has done a bit of stalking." Liz looked at Cady, her eyes filled with questions. "It was a different stab wound this time, Drew, albeit still one thrust to the heart."

"Aadalen's a big boy. Our UNSUB would have to work quickly to keep Aadalen from fighting back or screaming. If bar patrons hear screams, our guy is caught," Cady said.

Walsh changed the subject. "I did what you said and had a squad car check in on Karl Sandin at his home in Lynchburg."

Cady had asked Walsh if he could have Lynchburg PD visit Sandin at his mobile home, to cover that base. With Cady and Preston's existing *theory* currently being hauled out of the bar in a body bag, Sandin got shuffled back to the top of the deck. The agents looked at Richmond's lead detective.

"Sandin was at home. All alone. Claims to have been there all day and there is no way he made it from Richmond to Lynchburg before the officers stopped by unless he has access to a helicopter," Walsh said. "The Lynchburg officers smelled liquor on his breath; they said he was swaying back and forth."

Cady shrugged.

"The reason I bring that up is because whenever someone calls in to report a drunk swerving about the road, we get an address off their license plate and send an officer to the drunk's house. More often than not the guy is blotto, but inevitably he tells the officer that it was after he got home that he began drinking, pounding shots of this or that. And the officer winds up leaving empty-handed because the drunk quashed their case—no DUI."

"The alcohol alibi," Cady said. "He got drunk at home, not before getting behind the wheel."

"We've even had hit-and-run drunks try to pull that off," Walsh replied. "'Officer, I had a near miss on the way home so I needed some shots of Jim Beam to calm my nerves.' Anyway, what I'm driving at is that if I ever get around to killing someone or causing a person's death, when the po-po comes, they'll find me inebriated for two reasons. The first being that my attorney can make the jury believe I'd been drunk all day and couldn't have carried out a goddamned thing. The second reason, and this is more important as the three of us well know, is to make it difficult or impossible for any investigator to get a read on me." Detective Walsh looked from Cady to Preston. "Sandin could be trying to gum up the read."

CHAPTER 32

Day 9

"Christ." Jund stuck his head into Agent Preston's office looking grim.

"What happened?" Liz asked.

"We're at day nine. Remember, they got John Wilkes Booth in twelve." Jund looked about Preston's office, his mind seemed elsewhere. "Check the news."

And with that the director of CID was gone.

"Any point in reminding him they knew it was Booth from the get-go?"

Preston shook her head and began tapping at her PC.

Cady browsed to the Drudge Report. If a breaking story was big, Drudge would have a link to it. The image at the top center of the page was what had to be a photoshopped image of a church lectern, only in this picture the podium top was dripping blood. Below the image, in uppercase black boldface read the headline: *The Summer of the Eulogist.*

"That's not good." Preston had snuck up beside him.

Cady clicked the Drudge headline, which linked to an article in the *Washington Post*. The article was twenty minutes old.

Brockman Killer Leaves Eulogies at Murder Scenes

By Kathleen Haggerty, The Washington Post
A note eulogizing the victim was left at the scenes of the stabbing deaths of Senator Taylor Brockman and Thaddeus Aadalen, a source inside the murder investigations has told the Washington Post. *Calls to the Richmond Police Department as to whether a eulogy had been left at yesterday's slaying of Colin Aadalen, CEO of Aadalen Pharmaceuticals, at the Omni Richmond Hotel have been met with "No comment."*

Preston hijacked control of Cady's mouse and back-arrowed to the Drudge Report and read the headline out loud, "'The Summer of the Eulogist.'"

"Quite frankly, Liz," Cady said, "I'm surprised it took this long to leak."

"Kettler's lawyered up." Jund stuck his head inside Agent Preston's office a second time and informed the agents. "But I've got the Z-man on it."

"Zeke Wallace?" Cady asked. He wanted to kick himself for botching the initial interview with Elliot Kettler, for pushing too hard, for overplaying the bad cop, for chasing the FDA chemist into the all-too-welcoming arms of a defense attorney.

"Yup," Jund replied. "Z's got Kettler at two. He'll be stopping by any minute for you to brief."

As far as Cady was concerned, Zeke Wallace was the bureau's top interrogator. Hailing from North Carolina, Wallace was a towering African American who'd played point guard for the Tar Heels until he blew out a knee, at which point he traded hoop dreams for the paper chase and wound up graduating from the UNC School of Law at the top of his class. There was something about Wallace—some odd magnetism or charisma—a broad grin, a jocular demeanor, and nonconfrontational style that made him perfect for interviewing suspects. It was difficult to decipher, but people instantaneously liked Wallace, and, more importantly, they wanted Wallace to like them in return.

A half hour into an interview with Wallace and the most hardened of suspects who heretofore had yet to say "Boo" to a string of investigators started opening up. *I hate to disappoint you, Zeke . . . but, yes, I did the hitchhiker. She was so despondent, Zeke, so downhearted and, yes, Zeke, that's my MO. I strangled her with a boot lace. I know that's not a good thing, Zeke, but I get so excited . . . aroused. It's a chemical reaction that I have no control over, Zeke. I'm sure you understand.*

Cady had even heard about defense attorneys who'd fallen under Wallace's peculiar spell, one going so far as to advise his client—*I don't think it's going to hurt anyone if you tell Zeke the location of the shallow grave, perhaps just the GPS coordinates.* It was a perplexing hypnosis you fell under after ten minutes in Wallace's presence. You craved Wallace's friendship, you wanted him to like you, to be your best pal . . . and you wanted to share your deepest, darkest secrets with the man. Zeke was your father confessor. And, as you served your life term in prison or awaited the injection, you blamed everyone—prosecutors, witnesses, the judge, the warden, family members, even yourself—but you didn't hold Wallace accountable. Hell, Zeke was just doing his job, and you didn't want Zeke to get in trouble.

A decade back Cady had personally experienced the Z-man's enchantment firsthand. He'd gone out for beers with the bureau interrogator. By the time his second drink arrived, Cady found himself informing Zeke of something Cady had done at age fourteen. There'd been a mobile puppet show sponsored by the local library, that is, a small truck pulling a puppet wagon drove around the neighborhood in the summer months and, once it had enough kids on bikes in tow, the puppet wagon would pull over at a park or school lot, slide open the side window on the wagon, and put on a fifteen-minute show. As a kid, Cady had himself attended many of the programs. But one afternoon, several years later, Cady and a few neighborhood teenagers raided their parents' refrigerators, lifted a dozen eggs or so, and ambushed the puppet show in midperformance. Cady and company hid behind a row of bushes atop a minor hill—the high ground—and rained eggs on the pack of children watching the marionettes. It was a slaughter. No child went unscathed. The puppeteer—some college girl trying to make a few bucks—dropped her puppets and stared out the stage window in shock, and that's when Cady unleashed his last egg. It hit the puppeteer smack in the forehead. The poor girl screamed, and Cady's crew did an about-face and ran like hell, leaving the sobbing, egg-peppered muddle behind them.

The crazy thing was they got away with it. Scot-free. No neighboring parents appeared at the Cady household demanding justice, no police stopped by to inform Cady's parents of what their son had done . . . nothing. But Cady felt like a guilty little shit, even back then. The echo of the college girl's shriek of horror stuck with him over the years. Cady still felt shame, and had never shared the story with anyone, but suddenly—after a single beer—he found himself spilling his guts to Zeke Wallace.

Wallace had chuckled at the time and told Cady, "Cut yourself some slack, you were just a dipshit kid."

And to this day, whenever Cady's thoughts returned to his having rained eggs down on a bunch of eight-year-olds watching a puppet show and hitting a college girl in the face, he pondered Wallace's words and felt better.

"The Z-man," Cady replied to Jund. "Perfect."

CHAPTER 33

"I just want to go back to bed."

"I'm sorry to wake you," Cady replied. He was on the phone with Jim Ballard, the father in Trevi's Lounge who may or may not have seen Colin Aadalen's killer. "I know you flew in from Europe yesterday morning."

"I hate jet lag, it's like I'm under water," Ballard said. "I spent all last evening with Detective Walsh looking at those videos."

Cady knew from Walsh that there'd been no hits off either the hotel side or the street side cameras. The mystery man appeared to have evaporated into thin air. But Cady wanted to connect with Ballard before he headed back with his family to Harrisonburg. "Sometimes after a good night's sleep, the mind settles, and a person remembers more detail."

"I wish I'd gotten a good night's sleep."

Cady heard kids banging about in the background and felt sorry for the jet-lagged patriarch. "Can you tell me about the man you saw, Mr. Ballard? Walk me through it and maybe something new will crop up."

"There's not much to share. I got the sense that someone was staring my way so I looked up and I see this nearby guy glaring at me. I assume he's pissed about the kids—they were acting apeshit—so I tell them to keep it down and I didn't look up again because I didn't want to get into some awful confrontation with the guy. It's like I told Walsh, I thought he was irate at my having kids in a bar while I'm having a beer. I didn't know he was casing the joint."

"Any specifics on age or height?" Cady said into the cell phone.

"Midthirties to midforties. Maybe my height. Five nine or five ten. Like I said, I saw him for a second and only remember him at all because he looked so pissed."

"You gauged his height because he was standing?"

"Yeah," Ballard replied. "I caught his eye when he was passing by."

"Was he heading somewhere?"

"I don't know—over to the bar, I suppose. I'm just glad he didn't stop at our table."

"Could he have been heading toward the restroom?"

"I have no idea," Ballard said. "Look, I wish I could be of more help, but like I keep saying, I only saw the guy for half a second. You should really talk to that lady. Maybe she got a better look at him."

"The Metro Richmond Zoo?"

"What?" Preston asked, peeking up from behind her PC.

"I've tried calling that other witness Walsh gave us—Mary Ellen Doats—the woman who may have seen our UNSUB, but I keep getting the Metro Richmond Zoo."

"Really?"

"I'm getting the same thing," Detective Walsh said over Preston's speakerphone. "I wanted her to come in at lunch and look at the video feed, see if we can get a hit, but I get that zoo. I'm sure the number is just a digit off."

"What's her story?" Cady asked.

"She was there to meet some girlfriends after work, only hotel security had shut the bar down before her friends showed up. She was trying to be helpful, but had to run and pick up her kid at daycare or face the wrath of her ex."

"What did she look like?" Preston asked.

"Petite. Late twenties, early thirties," Walsh replied. "A bit of a looker."

"It says her name is Mary Ellen Doats," Preston said, looking over Walsh's interview notes, "but what's this 'Marzy' thing?"

"She said her name is Mary Ellen Doats, but that her friends call her 'Marzy.'"

"Marzy Doats?" asked Preston.

"Yes."

"And the phone number Marzy Doats gave us is for the Metro Richmond Zoo?" Preston continued to probe.

"The number was probably mistranscribed."

"Mairzy doats and dozy doats and liddle lamzy divey," Preston said.

Cady stared at his colleague as though she'd sprouted a mustache.

"What?" Walsh volunteered over speakerphone.

"The nursery song," Preston said. "Mares eat oats and does eat oats and little lambs eat ivy."

A lengthy silence ensued, and then Walsh said, "You're telling me she gave us a nursery rhyme name based on animals and a phone number to the zoo?"

"You've got an address on her, right?" Preston asked.

"Just a second." The agents listened as the Richmond detective barked orders in the background and then he returned to the phone. "I've got someone running down her home address."

Cady had a thought. "You said she was small and a real looker?"

"Yes."

"Does Richmond have a problem with call girls working bars in some of the high-class hotels?"

"Oh, shit," Walsh responded. "Marzy Doats or whatever in hell her name is could fit that description. Rich travelers and handy rooms."

There was more muffled yelling, and then Walsh came back. "The address is a fake too. The apartment building she gave us exists, but not the apartment number. Just my luck—a goddamned hooker spots the killer."

"She's there to work Trevi's Lounge just as happy hour is about to kick in with a crowd of businessmen staying at the Omni," Cady said, pursuing his train of thought. "She picks up on the killer's vibe, notices him in the bar mirror, and probably thinks he's hotel security and that he's made her as a pro working the bar. So she doesn't mingle, she nurses her margarita and gives him no cause to approach her, but then this craziness breaks out and she notices the guy she pegged as security is no longer around. So she helps you as much as she can by providing a description of the man."

"And she fake IDs us because if we get her real ID, we'll figure out why she was at Trevi's," Walsh said.

"She may be on your books," Cady told the detective. "Check through the past couple of years—mug shots on those soliciting at hotel bars—and see if any officers recognize any faces."

"Of course there could be another option," Preston said.

Cady locked eyes with his colleague and guessed what Liz was about to say. "She's our killer."

CHAPTER 34

That goddamned bartender.

The Canadian had walked back to her seat at the bar, took a final sip of her strawberry margarita, and when the bartender and the annoyed, bladder-filled patron headed toward the back corridor, the Canadian fished a twenty out of her purse to cover her tab, slapped it down, and began heading toward the street-side exit. She heard the commotion from the restroom hallway and suddenly out shoots the bartender, sprinting for the street doorway like a headless chicken. For a second, the Canadian thought the barman was going to parkour a table. Then the guy locks the street door—her exit path—he even topples a chair in front it and then goes galloping off in the opposite direction, through the interior hotel entrance, and out of sight.

After a pregnant pause, everyone in the bar—including the Canadian—began chuckling at the Trevi's employee's bizarre performance. At this point, thirty sets of eyes would bear witness if the Canadian trotted over to the door, shoved the chair aside, unlocked the street door, and left the lounge. And, of course, the video camera would catch her if she exited on the hotel side. While the patrons shared in the comedic moment, the Canadian returned to her bar stool, sat down, and pocketed her twenty dollars.

There would be no tip today.

The Canadian overheard and then piggybacked on the semi-inebriated father's tale of some asshole who may have looked at him wrong in the last hour . . . or week . . . or month. Lending a hand to the detectives in a crime of her own making held a more subtle kind of thrill—more sugar high than heroin—but she kicked back, got lost in her new role as police witness, and enjoyed herself. There was minimal risk and, as it turned out, five minutes after being dismissed from Trevi's, the Canadian no longer had red hair or blue eyes.

The Canadian knew her whimsical Marzy Doats ID was forever burned, but once she retrieved her luggage—four seconds spent inside her Super 8 motel room, which she immediately vacated sans checking out—she had access to both the Johnson and Andrews passports from the compartment hidden in the bottom of her TravelPro Maxlite. The Canadian decided to bring the Johnson persona back into play for phase two of her new assignment and continue to save Andrews for the flight home.

And speaking of phase two of her new assignment, the Canadian changed lanes and steered her rental car toward the Lynchburg exit.

CHAPTER 35

Day 10

"The family is broken," Langdon Trutwin said.

Cady and Preston were back in the executive suite on the top floor of Aadalen Pharmaceuticals, this time piggybacking on Detective Walsh's investigation of Colin Aadalen's death. Walsh had his team of investigators taking statements from CEO Aadalen's immediate colleagues, that is, a smorgasbord of upper echelon executives—the COO, the CFO, a squadron of executive VPs, a troop of general managers, and a team of division directors, and, of course, all members of Aadalen Pharmaceuticals' Board of Directors.

The agents wanted time with Aadalen Pharmaceuticals' general counsel as per their earlier meeting; Langdon Trutwin appeared to be the one who knew how all the Legos stacked together. Trutwin hadn't shaved and, unlike on their previous visit, not every hair was in place. Grooming visibly took second place to personal and professional tragedy.

"Relapse may not be the correct term, nor regressed, but Marcus isn't talking anymore, or even attempting to, and Cathrin sits for hours and hours in a dark room with old photo albums." Trutwin gestured about his office with one arm. "Our work family is broken as well."

"Without Colin Aadalen as chief executive officer," Preston said, "what happens here?"

"I have been asked to step in as acting CEO, to tend the garden at Aadalen Pharmaceuticals until Colin's successor can be found. And I assure you mine will be the world's shortest reign as we shall begin our search as soon as the dust has settled." Trutwin looked hard at the agents. "Weeks have passed since TJ's murder. I would think a United States senator's death would light a fire under someone's ass. And now my other nephew. How long will it take for you to catch . . ." Trutwin looked disdainfully at the headline in the *Richmond Times-Dispatch* that lay on top of his desk, ". . . The Eulogist?"

"We're working twenty-four-hour days to coordinate with the separate investigations in each of the jurisdictions," Preston said diplomatically.

"Did you know Roark Larson at the Food and Drug Administration?" Cady added less diplomatically.

Trutwin's eyes centered on Cady. "I believe Larson was part of the CDER team working the New Drug Application for Neurzamine."

"So you knew Larson?"

"I knew of him," Trutwin corrected. "I wouldn't recognize him if we passed in the hallway. I also believe Larson was the poor gentleman who killed himself late last year."

"That death is being reexamined," Cady replied.

Aadalen Pharmaceuticals' general counsel shrugged in response.

"You probably knew Larson questioned the quality of your data. He was pushing for new clinical trials, more large-scale studies," Cady said. "Larson didn't want to file your NDA."

Trutwin continued staring at Cady for several seconds, and then broke into laughter. "Thank you for the chuckle, Agent Cady. After the events of the past day, I needed that. But no, my friend, here at Aadalen Pharmaceuticals we are not in the business of, what would you call it—*whacking?*—CDER members who have issues with our products." Trutwin turned his stare toward Preston and switched into lecture mode. "We play pat-a-cake with the FDA all year round. They want this, we give them this. They want that thing over there; we give them that thing over there. At any given time someone on a CDER team is jumping up and down over something. Are there delays? Absolutely. Are there millions of dollars wasted? Absolutely. Unfortunately that's how the game is played. But we'd be fools to do what you're suggesting, Agent Cady."

"Even when a blockbuster drug is on the table?"

Aadalen Pharmaceuticals' general counsel turned his full concentration back toward Agent Cady. "Kindly govern yourself accordingly, my friend," Trutwin said, exhausted but with grit in his eyes. "Don't start rumors where you know not of what you speak. Don't make me put on my lawyer hat and walk down to eighteen—which is where my Legal Department is located—and unleash the pit bulls. If scurrilous chatter like that becomes public, I'll know from where it came . . . and, don't mistake, there will be consequences."

"Because Colin Aadalen was a rich boy jerk-off who'd be more interested in buying a jet plane and starting his own mile-high club than running Aadalen Pharmaceuticals."

It was deep into the afternoon, the natives were restless, and the agents had the drive back to DC to consider, so Cady took board member Gavin Forstner while Liz questioned the other two board members who completed the triumvirate of the pissed off that the agents had witnessed on their previous trip to the pharmaceutical company's main campus. Forstner was a short man with an intense stare and, as far as Cady could tell, he didn't need to blink his eyes. They sat at a table in a conference room the size of a city block. Forstner took the seat at the head of the table as if he'd been born there.

"Didn't Aadalen get his MBA at Wharton?" Cady asked.

"If Colin wrote his own papers, I'll eat this table," Forstner replied. "Look, I feel awful about Colin's death, especially after the things that were said—the things I said—at the appointment gathering. But that was just a shot across the bow to let Aadalen know, in no uncertain terms, that we had our eye on him, and that there'd be an adult in the room whenever he stepped on his dick."

"Wouldn't Colin seek counsel from his father or Langdon Trutwin?"

"Have you seen his father lately?"

Cady nodded.

"It takes Marcus ten minutes to ask for coffee and you need an umbrella for all the spray. And Marcus was only marginal to begin with. Langdon's a gem, but he's been trying to retire for the past decade. He keeps talking about wanting time to water his lawn or some such horseshit."

Cady looked at Forstner a long second. "I was there when you stormed out of the prior board meeting—Colin's CEO appointment."

"I saw you."

"You were quite vocal."

"I said far worse in the actual meeting."

"You seemed adamant about ousting Colin Aadalen."

Forstner returned Cady's stare, still yet to blink. "I didn't make my nut being politically correct. I don't know how many employees I've fired over the years, both vocally and adamantly, and as far as I know, they're all still alive and no doubt hating my guts."

"But you had no power to fire Aadalen."

"No, I did not," Forstner said. "I'm a glorified bean counter, Agent Cady; I deal in balance sheets and cash flow, not murder. I may bark a hell of a lot and occasionally I bite, but—please—it's like I told that other detective, I'm not going to kill anyone."

Forstner's sentence lingered in the air for a minute.

"Do you know a man by the name of Roark Larson?"

Forstner thought for a second. "Doesn't he play shortstop for the Nationals?"

CHAPTER 36

"Elliot Kettler is on the precipice." Zeke Wallace sat in Liz Preston's guest chair, his long legs crossed. Wallace had set the chair sideways so he could look between the two agents as he updated them on his dealings with the FDA chemist. "I could see it in his eyes. He's still processing the shock of finding out his career is finite, but give it a day or two. He'll cut a deal."

"You got all that from his eyes?" Preston asked.

"I've been doing this since Cain killed Abel and tried to skate," Wallace said. "Kettler's verbals were all bullshit. Heavy breathing; the guy had his hand over his mouth half the time he spoke. And his head darted back and forth like a metronome whenever I'd ask a question. Textbook lying." Wallace began bouncing an imaginary basketball. "I just got off the phone with Kettler's attorney—some weak suck who I think is his brother-in-law—and mentioned you'd been pushing Roark Larson in your interviews at Aadalen Pharmaceuticals. There's a long silence and then he asks me if we can schedule a meeting first thing tomorrow morning. So the plan worked. We've scared Kettler into our arms. They've entered into *avoid prison* mode." Wallace tossed the imaginary basketball into the air. "He shoots. He scores."

"Do you think Kettler can give us Aadalen Pharmaceuticals?"

Wallace turned to Cady. "As I laid out how Kettler's helping us would in fact help himself, I read his nonverbals and got the feeling that, sure enough, he'd taken money. In these instances, it's not likely that he's meeting with Colin Aadalen or, quite frankly, anyone sitting on Aadalen's *formal* payroll. And very seldom does the bribe giver hand the bribe taker a business card, much less use his real name. But if Kettler did what he was instructed to—push through AP's NDA at the FDA—and got paid off for it, then we sic our forensic accountants on the bribe. Follow the money, someone once said." Wallace glanced at his watch. "It's almost eight and my dinner's getting cold. You two should head out as well. Big day tomorrow."

Wallace uncrossed his legs, stood, stretched, and walked to the doorway of Preston's office. The Z-man turned around and looked back at the agents. "Kettler will deal on the bribe. He'll probably say he took it out of fear of meeting a similar demise to that of Roark Larson. This works for us because from there it's a logical inference that if AP bribed Kettler to green-light Neurzamine, then AP took out Roark Larson who fought tooth and nail against green-lighting the New Drug Application."

"You think we'll get all that from Kettler tomorrow morning?" Preston asked.

Wallace shrugged. "He'll come around—he's a frightened FDA chemist for crying out loud. It's not as though he's hardcore." Wallace glanced in Cady's direction. "It's not as though he's some sick fuck who'd egg a puppet show."

"Puppet show?" Preston looked at Cady after Wallace left. "What did he mean by that?"

Cady looked away. "I have no idea."

CHAPTER 37

Day 11

"You got Tay's killer yet?" It was Elaine Brockman on the other end of the line.

"Not yet," Cady said, fumbling a packet of powdered cream into his first cup of coffee while keeping the phone at his ear. "We are pursuing several leads," Cady mumbled the boilerplate, "and I assure you that you'll be the first person we'll call with any news."

"It's got to be tied into that CEO's death," Widow Brockman replied. "Maybe Aadalen Pharmaceuticals has some kind of *Game of Thrones* thing going on over there. But that's not why I called. I'm being pressured by Governor DeMarco to fill Tay's senate seat until next year's election. DeMarco wants an answer by the end of the August recess at the absolute latest, and guess what? I think I'm going to say yes."

"What about the Pritchards and the baby?" Cady asked. "You were concerned about it turning into a circus."

"The Pritchards are back to lovey-dovey, at least for now. They plan to keep the baby. Senator Pritchard assured me he'd like the whole matter kept private, and that he planned to raise the child with Tanya and love it as though it were his own. So it may not turn into Ringling Brothers after all."

"I'll be damned," Cady said. "I didn't see that coming."

"I know," Widow Brockman said. "I hate to paraphrase from the *Grinch*, but perhaps all of this has made Holocaust Barbie's small heart grow three sizes."

"So what do you plan to do as senator?"

"Hell if I know," she replied. "Since I won't be running for reelection, maybe I can push a bill to make hotel chains like churches." Elaine Newell Brockman chuckled for a second. "You know, tax exempt."

"Good luck with all that."

"Her name is Karla Dieteman," Detective Walsh said, again on speakerphone. "She admits to having had a drink with Colin Aadalen at Trevi's Lounge, but said that was all that occurred, and that she wasn't seeing him romantically, and that she had to leave early to pick up something from work and then get to church in time to lead bible study. I should state that Karla Dieteman is indeed married—to some big-shot doctor—and has two children."

"Did Dieteman come in of her own accord?" Preston asked.

"Yes, but the news articles mentioned the video cameras at the Omni Richmond, so I'm betting she figured she'd best get her ass in voluntarily with half a story," Walsh replied. "The cameras put Dieteman in the elevator atrium after leaving the lounge and then have her exiting from the atrium nearly an hour later. She started to cry when I brought up the atrium video. I'm sure she's terrified of her name splashing up in the papers . . . of her husband finding out. You'd need to have three marriage counselors on retainer to weather shit like that. We can always brace Dieteman on this down the road if needed, but," Walsh continued, "for now, she doesn't recall any undue attention in the bar. She only had one drink with Aadalen before leaving for their hotel suite, which we know to be true. She said everything at Trevi's Lounge was mellow. She doesn't recall any irritated man casing the joint, à la Jim Ballard's description, or the *Marzy Doats* redhead at the bar."

"I guess Mrs. Dieteman's attention was elsewhere," Preston said.

"You get anything from the Aadalen executives?" Cady asked as they'd not had a chance to compare notes.

"It was a bust," Walsh replied. "No leads. Most think Aadalen sadly got sucked into whatever conspiracy killed his junkie brother and Senator Brockman. None seriously believe Gavin Forstner or the other disgruntled board members had anything to do with Colin's death. How about you?"

"We hope to call you back later today with some good news," Cady said, thinking of Wallace's meeting with Elliot Kettler.

"I could use some good news," the Richmond detective said.

"Hopefully within the hour."

The Z-man strode into Agent Preston's office at eight thirty on the dot, plunked down in the visitor's chair which had remained sideways since his visit the night before, cleared his throat, and then pronounced in the King's English as fluently and convincingly as any classically trained Shakespearean actor, "Fuck."

Cady felt the hair rise on the back of his neck. "Kettler?"

"He clammed up," Wallace said. "In fact he was a no show. No Kettler, no suck-ass brother-in-law attorney. Instead he's got new counsel—some Peter Lorre-looking m-effer."

Cady had never seen Zeke Wallace angry before. It did not bode well. "What did his new attorney say?"

"That Kettler has said all he's going to say," Wallace replied. "He gave me his card and said that going forward, all communication would be through him less a harassment charge be leveled."

"Kettler did an about-face in twelve hours," Preston said. "Our plan to chase him into your arms backfired."

"I didn't read Kettler wrong," said Wallace, digging about a pocket as though in search of his lost mojo. "Someone got to him."

"Either someone got to him or he's been sitting on a phone number," Cady said. "A phone number that until now he's been too afraid to call, not wanting to get in deeper with whoever bribed him."

Wallace stood, pulled a business card out of his pocket, and handed it off to Agent Preston. "That's Peter Lorre. Find out who he is and who he represents. That's a start."

Preston nodded and set it next to her computer.

"I'm sorry, Zeke," Cady said. "We shouldn't have tipped our cards until we had Kettler sewn up, but I assumed he'd run to us like a lost puppy. I thought he'd be hiding under a bed at a Hampton Inn until your meeting."

"He broke my six-year streak," Wallace said. "Goddammit." And on that note the bureau interrogator disappeared into the hallway, an angry salmon swimming upstream.

Cady felt trounced, as though he'd taken a prison yard shiv. This was the second time a strong lead had blown up in their faces. First they barked up the Colin Aadalen tree, only to have Aadalen move from prime suspect to the morgue. Kettler had seemed so promising only to crater at the eleventh hour, and though Kettler was still very much alive, they'd now have to dance with his new lawyer. The man from the FDA had been shored up.

"I'm sorry, Liz." Cady threw a hand in the air. "I guess I'm rusty at this."

"Don't be," Preston replied. "Any doubt I had about Aadalen Pharmaceuticals' involvement is long gone."

"I don't think she's in any danger, but she's got a Secret Service detail until this thing is over." Cady was talking about Elaine Brockman. "She told me it's driving her crazy because she's staying at Dorie

Searles's small condo. People stepping over each other, I guess."

Cady and Preston were having a nightcap in the lobby bar of the Holiday Inn where Cady, at this point, was all but homesteading his room. They had to get out of the Hoover Building, to think outside of the box that was Liz Preston's small office, after their long day of disappointment and dead ends. Cady was having a Heineken, Preston a merlot. They were brainstorming every aspect of the case, reviewing all players, trying to think of unseen *others*— those hidden in the shadows.

Cady had gotten off a phone call with Terri, bringing her up to date on their lack of progress on the case, and letting her know he wouldn't be coming home after all. Although August was Terri's crazy month at the resort, she wanted to attempt a breakout and join him in DC for the coming weekend. Cady told her no. First, for good or bad, he was superglued to this investigation and she'd barely see him. Second, Saturday was when the resort guests checked out and settled up before the new batch arrived. It was not a day to be panned off on the college kid who mowed the lawns or old-man Gary from next door.

Cady flagged the waitress for another Heineken.

"Elaine Brockman has met Marcus and Cathrin Aadalen at fundraising events over the years, but doesn't recall ever meeting Colin Aadalen," Cady continued. "She knew nothing about Thaddeus Aadalen's pardon until after the fact. And Elaine has never met or talked with Karl Sandin."

Agent Preston took a sip from her glass of red wine. "You know what tomorrow is, don't you?"

Cady stared at Preston.

"Day twelve."

Cady chuckled. "Bet you a Chinese dinner Jund brings up John Wilkes Booth."

Cady had forgotten how exactly it had evolved, but he and Preston had taken to placing side bets over trivial topics or negligible events. The winner was to receive a Chinese dinner at the restaurant of their choice. Although there had been a dinner or two at Wah Sing on Pennsylvania Avenue, most wagers went unclaimed and, quite frankly, Cady figured he owed Liz at least a week's worth of chow mein and spring rolls.

"Actually," Preston replied, "I was hoping to make that bet with you."

The agents had spent a half hour with Director Jund early that afternoon. He'd already been briefed by Zeke Wallace on the Elliot Kettler situation and he agreed that they needed to find a new way to *put the screws to* the FDA chemist even if that included stepping on the toes of Oliver Price—the Peter Lorre doppelganger who had marched into Wallace's office first thing that morning. Oliver Price, sure enough, was a hard-nosed criminal defense attorney with an extensive reputation for taking and—more often than not—winning high-profile cases in and about the District of Columbia. High-profile cases translated into high earnings, and both Cady and Preston wondered why Price would even pick up the phone when a small fish named Elliot Kettler called, much less take him onboard as a client.

Jund had been relatively subdued throughout the meeting, soft spoken and even steered clear of the piercing rants for which he was well known. But Cady and Preston knew him all too well, and even though they couldn't read eyes and nonverbal communications at Zeke Wallace's level, they got the sense that Director Jund was beginning to crave a blood sacrifice—preferably theirs.

Preston said, "I keep going back to how Karl Sandin is the connection between the Aadalens and Senator Brockman."

"They got nothing from the search warrant," Cady replied. "One of the detectives mentioned he thought Sandin was in the process of drinking himself to death."

"How about another road trip?"

CHAPTER 38

By the end of the second day of casing Karl Sandin's corner lot at his Lynchburg mobile home park, the Canadian came to believe this assignment would be charity work, that she'd be doing the guy a huge favor. Perhaps she should step from the tree line, saunter down the hill, and have a chat with the sad sack about life in general and his in specific. Perhaps Sandin would be amenable, even helpful, in hastening his own demise. Perhaps, the Canadian chuckled, he'd even kick in a few dinero for the full Kevorkian package.

There was a patch of woods on the hillside above Sandin's lot that allowed the Canadian to sit amongst the rosemary pine with a pair of binoculars. Of course she had to play hide-and-go-seek with a pack of trailer-trash teens who used the woodlands to smoke pot and drink beer. It wasn't a difficult game as she could smell their cannabis from several acres away.

On her first day of the stalk, the Canadian was able to witness her assignment being served with what had to be a search warrant. Two Lynchburg squad cars and a couple of unmarked appeared around two in the afternoon. A suit sat with Sandin at his picnic table and the two pushed a document back and forth. The Canadian didn't need to read lips to see what Sandin mouthed at the visiting detective: *Bullshit!*

Two suits and an officer then had gone inside Sandin's mobile home. Sandin tried to follow, but the suit in charge, the one who'd sat with him at the picnic table, recited a couple of paragraphs and pointed at a uniform who, evidently, was going to be Sandin's chaperone throughout the remainder of the process. Sandin made arm gestures, but the suit shook his head and went inside. Sandin marched to the opposite side of his home, his police officer-slash-chaperone five yards in tow with a hand near his holster, and then Sandin lowered his sweat-pants and—call the *Guinness Book of Records*—took the world's longest urination onto a bed of weeds. Sandin spent the next hour sitting despondently at his picnic table. The lead suit stepped out to talk to him now and again, but Sandin's sole response was a half-hearted raise of his middle finger.

Sandin's dwelling was a twelve-by-sixty Spirit mobile home from the midnineties. And though the Spirit miraculously contained three bedrooms, the Canadian did the math and was amazed that it took the police more than an hour to execute the war-rant. Seriously, how much of those 720 square feet was taken up by a refrigerator and oven, a kitchen table and chairs, beds and a sofa? The Lynchburg Police were thorough little buggers, yet all they hauled away was an outdated computer. The Canadian smiled at the bulk of Sandin's monitor and the clunkiness of his antiquated printer.

The Canadian continued to watch from the tree line as two plainclothes detectives did five minutes with Sandin's beat-to-shit Chevy pickup. After that task was complete, the head suit tried handing Sandin a piece of paper, but Sandin refused to take it. Instead Sandin turned about and retreated into his trailer home. As the officers packed the box of removed items, the lead suit approached Sandin's mobile, opened the screen door, and tossed the court paper inside, and then made his way to his unmarked.

A minute later the posse was a departing trail of dust.

Five minutes after that Sandin jumped into his Chevy and headed out. Twenty minutes later Sandin returned with a thirty pack of Rolling Rock and a bottle of something in a brown bag. A few minutes after that the Canadian called it a day. She threaded her way back to the dirt path on the other side of the hill, careful to avoid any assembly of toking teens, and down to where she'd parked her rental car in the gravel lot of an abandoned playground. From there she drove back to her motel.

It had been an entertaining stalk.

Today's stalk was more subdued. No repeat matinee of the local gendarmes rattling Karl Sandin's cage. The Canadian again left her car in the gravel lot of a forgotten playground, made her way into the woods, worked her way over the hill, hiking far around the

spot where she'd spied the group of teenagers chill-
axing the previous day. Once situated in a cluster of
pines from where she had a clear line of sight of her
assignment's trailer, the Canadian took out a book
on Australia's Great Barrier Reef, possibly an upcoming vacation spot, and the bag of goodies she'd liber-
ated from the breakfast buffet at the Quality Inn.

Sandin came outside at ten—same gray sweat-
pants, same black T-shirt. He smoked a cigarette,
twisted it out on his picnic table, and then put his
head in his hands for five minutes. Yup, the Canadian thought, this assignment would be a mercy killing indeed. At four thirty, Sandin jumped into his
Chevy and left the mobile park. Based on how he'd
not changed his clothing, the Canadian had a hunch
where her assignment was headed.

The Canadian quickly bagged her book, binocs,
and empty food bags, tucked her hair underneath
the baseball cap, and worked her way down to
where the trees thinned out. She stood still for three
minutes. She saw no sign of human activity, no eyes
that might stray in her direction. She then made a
beeline from the woods to the back side of Sandin's
manufactured home, near the spot where Sandin had
watered his weeds the day before. Once there the
Canadian slipped around the trailer home until she
stood at the front door. The pick gun was in her bag,
but wasn't needed. She'd hit the lottery—Sandin had
left his trailer home unlocked.

A split second later the Canadian was inside. She
saw why Sandin didn't feel the need to lock his door.
Pathetic. Flies floating about a garbage bin stacked
full with paper plates and chili cans, a rancid smell

from soup pots stacked in the sink—obviously the maid's month off. The Canadian did a quick recon of the mobile home's three miniature bedrooms. One bedroom contained a single foldout cot with a sleeping bag on top, likely a guestroom for all that company Sandin invited over. This bedroom also appeared to be where Sandin's empty beer cases came to die. The bathroom made an eloquent argument for having itself condemned. The second bedroom, perhaps the master, contained an unmade bed, greasy sheets, and underwear on the floor. The third bedroom, on the opposite side of the trailer home, was exactly what the Canadian had been looking for. It was stuffed with chairs the Goodwill would reject, folding tables from the seventies, fishing gear, an ignored vacuum and overlooked mop, and an assortment of other items that looked like leftover rubble from a garage sale. On the floor of the corner closet sat two shopping bags, which were ironically stuffed full with unopened house cleansers. She shoved the bags aside. The closet would serve as the perfect spot for the Canadian to nest and wait out the evening.

The Canadian made her way back to the kitchen, peeked outside—no sign of Sandin—and said *screw it*. She rushed to the bathroom, emptied her bladder, and used an elbow to flush Sandin's toilet—thankful that the flusher worked. The Canadian then hung back behind the kitchen blinds, at an angle where anyone approaching wouldn't spot her, and waited. Five minutes later Sandin's pickup pulled into his parking spot.

Her hunch had been correct. Sandin had replenished his liquid refreshment supply. By the time Sandin entered the trailer with his fifth of Jack Daniel's, the Canadian was safely hidden away in the corner closet of the unused bedroom. Sandin would have to work his way through this warehouse of forgotten bits and pieces and stand directly in front of the closet in order to spot her, but the Canadian took out the laundry cord just in case. The Canadian spent the next few hours listening to some ballgame Sandin had on his kitchen television, listening to Sandin drink and burp and fart and fry something that smelled like spam. She heard Sandin pop the tops of a half-dozen Rolling Rocks that he had to be using as chasers with his whiskey. She listened as Sandin took endless leaks in his petri dish of a bathroom. He may have flushed once. Toward ten o'clock, the Canadian swore she heard Sandin slur *I'm sorry* or something to that effect.

She figured her assignment was mumbling to the ghosts of lives long past.

After that, Sandin took a concluding piss and retired to his master bedroom. Five minutes later, though he'd left the TV on, which now had changed over to the late news, the Canadian heard Sandin begin to snore. He was loud enough to compete with his forgotten television. The Canadian slipped her fingers into her unpowdered surgical gloves and double-checked the noose on the laundry cord. She took off her tennis shoes and crept slowly out to Sandin's kitchen. She paused long enough to draw the blinds, kill the light above the sink, and turn the volume up a notch on the old television set Sandin kept on the countertop. She saw that her assignment had made remarkable progress on the bottle of Jack Daniel's. And six dead soldiers sat in the wreckage that was the sink.

Excellent. This assignment would be like candy from a baby.

The Canadian stood over the passed-out figure of Karl Sandin, still in his sweats and T-shirt, face half planted in a pillow, an arm hanging to the floor. She could almost feel Sandin's snoring vibrate in the plywood flooring beneath the worn carpet. The moon shone in through the open bedroom window. The Canadian readied the noose as she listened to her assignment's labored breathing. She wondered if Sandin suffered sleep apnea, although that was soon to be a moot point. Careful not to nudge his draping limb, the Canadian calculated the angle that would make most sense for what she had in mind.

She felt the sweet intoxicating uptick in her heart rate as the adrenal glands kicked in.

In the blink of an eye the Canadian had the noose over Sandin's head and was then on top of the man, her knees on his shoulders. The cord immediately taut around his neck, the slipknot behind Sandin's left ear, ever tightening as she wrenched it up and forward, toward the wall. Sandin made a hissing sound, a snake unearthed, and then he began to buck and twist. One hand shot up, and then his other, his fingers prying about the cord in a frantic attempt to loosen what was stealing his breath . . . choking him . . . killing him . . . but by then it was too late.

For another minute Sandin's body quivered. Then it was over.

The Canadian slid down off Sandin's back and stepped onto the floor. She used the cord to lift his bulk—Sandin now a deadweight marionette—and haul him off the single bed. The Canadian used one hand to twist him about by his shoulder in order to center him under the bedroom window. She punched out the screen with the palm of her free hand and tossed the excess cord out into the night. Then she used both hands to hoist Sandin upward until his ass hovered several inches above the floor. Now came the tricky part. The Canadian grunted like a Russian weightlifter as she took a half second to hold the cord with one hand while slamming the window down on the cord with her free hand.

Breathing hard, she stepped back, flipped on her penlight, and audited her work. Sandin's bladder had released, wetting himself, which was to be expected. His sweat bottoms had caught the bulk of the urine. There might be some wetness on his fitted bed sheet and mattress, so she tossed his bed quilt over it. Considering Sandin's state of inebriation, that wouldn't be telling were it even noticed at all. The Canadian took a minute with each of Sandin's hands to press his fingertips against the cord about his neck, about the slipknot, as well as against the cord hanging from the closed window.

She stood back a second time and took the scene in as a whole, like a patron admiring a museum piece. Sandin twisted slowly, a perverted wind chime, eyes bulging, lips bloated, and saliva dripping from a corner of his mouth. She wondered if the cord would hold until he was discovered, but realized that wouldn't matter as it could have snapped on its own long after he had hung himself. It was brilliant, the Canadian, somewhat of a perfectionist, thought. She wished she could take full credit, but she'd gotten the idea from a famous comic actor who had checked out in a similar fashion some years earlier.

The Canadian retrieved her backpack and shoes from the closet. She took the note from the folder in her backpack, brought it into the bedroom, and pressed Sandin's fingers against the paper, both front and back. She returned to the kitchen and placed it on the table. She paused for a second, then picked up the nearly empty fifth of Jack from atop the refrigerator and set it down on top of the note.

She spent another minute in Sandin's mobile home double- and triple-checking her work. Then she put on her tennis shoes, placed the backpack over her shoulders, slipped out of Sandin's trailer, and was at the tree line in thirty seconds. At this point she stripped off the surgical gloves, tossed them in the backpack with the rest of her gear, and again snapped on her penlight. The Canadian began to sprint through the forest, a panther at night— faster, and faster still. She felt her heart race and the adored rush flooded every fiber in her body.

She was invincible.

CHAPTER 39

Day 12

Cady knocked harder on the screen door of Karl Sandin's mobile home. After thirty seconds of silence in response, he opened the screen door and began banging his knuckles on the inside door. The doorbell of course was broken and Cady's rapping had evolved quickly from polite neighbor tempo to stern landlord to miffed FBI agent. Liz had picked up Cady at the Holiday Inn at five sharp in order to get a jump on any rush hour traffic, and they made it to Sandin's trailer house at the Forest Lane Mobile Home Park in Lynchburg by half past eight.

Preston had finished walking a circle around Sandin's home. "There's a rope hanging out one of the back windows."

Cady shrugged. "He's probably got a redneck clothes dryer rigged up in there." Cady looked at the used Chevy in Sandin's driveway. "He's just got the one vehicle, right?"

Preston nodded. "That's all the Virginia DMV has listed."

Cady touched the doorknob. "Liz?"

"What?"

"It's unlocked." He pushed it open a few inches. "Mr. Sandin," Cady shouted into the open trailer home. "It's FBI Agent Drew Cady here with Agent Elizabeth Preston. May we come in?"

Ten seconds. No answer.

"Mr. Sandin," Cady shouted again, louder now, "I am stepping into your mobile home to make sure you're okay."

Ten seconds. No answer.

Cady stepped into the kitchen entryway of Sandin's mobile home. Preston followed close behind, one hand on her holster.

"Jesus, Liz," Cady said, pointing at the empties in the sink and the almost-empty bottle of whiskey on the kitchen table. "The guy's sleeping it off."

Cady started down the short hallway that held several doors. He looked in Sandin's bathroom, and then looked back at Liz and shook his head. He peeked in the guestroom at the small mountain of beer cases, and then headed for what he figured was Sandin's bedroom.

Preston looked down at a note on the kitchen table and began to read.

A second later, the two agents spoke at the same time.

"Drew," Preston said.

"Oh, shit," said Cady.

I personally killed the little shit who stole my son.
He didn't even recognize me when he picked
me up on Charles Street or when I offered him
a hundred dollars for noggin, but I told him who

I was before I stabbed him in his fucking junkie heart.

I did have help with Senator Weasel Fuck and that other Aadalen prick. Amazing what money can buy these days. I had Colin Aadalen killed so his shit parents would see how it feels to be childless, for them to understand the purgatory my life has become.

Good luck trying to find my hired hand. As you can see, my lips are forever sealed.

"Okay," Director Jund said over speakerphone as Cady and Preston sat in her Prius. "This will take the pressure off. My phone will stop ringing."

"Bullshit," Cady replied. "This is a frame-up. It's the same thing they did to Roark Larson. It's the exact same script."

Lynchburg PD was all over the scene. The plain-clothes detectives who served the warrant two days prior were inside Sandin's trailer home. Uniforms were going door to door, trailer to trailer, asking tenants if they'd seen or heard anything unusual around Karl Sandin's lot in the past week. It was half past nine and the mobile park was a hive of activity. A group of trailer kids hovered on the periphery, watching the police. It was this week's excitement.

"You're not hearing me, Drew," Jund said. "We go noncommittal, that is, no comment on Karl Sandin. The press runs with Sandin, but we keep chipping away. And, in a week or two, we nail Aadalen

Pharmaceuticals to the wall, whether Kettler comes clean or you open something else."

Underneath a mountain of mixed emotion and over a decade of conflict, Cady, at the end of the day, trusted Roland Jund. "Got it."

"Did any of you guys see anybody who shouldn't be here yesterday?" Cady asked the group of Forest Lane mobile home kids. "Or in the past week?"

The gang of middle schoolers shook their heads in unison.

"Any cars that shouldn't be here?"

All but one of the early teenagers shook their heads again.

"There was a car—I think it was a Camry—over at Duck Pond," said a thin boy with acne peppered about his nose.

"Duck Pond?"

"It's a playground on the other side of the hill," acne boy said. "No pond and no ducks, but there's a swing set and a slide and a place for cars to park."

Eight minutes later Cady, Preston, acne boy, and acne boy's older sister were at Duck Pond. It was a gravel lot over the hill from the Forest Lane Mobile Home Park. A generation or two ago, the city had placed a small playground at Duck Pond and then completely forgot about it. The canvas seats on the swing sets were frayed, the slide rusty, and the merry-go-round immovable.

Cady pointed at the gravel and said, "That's where the Camry sat for the past couple of days?"

They nodded agreement.

"Did you ever see the driver?"

They shook their heads.

"You guys hang out in the woods?" Cady asked.

"It's summer," acne boy's sister said a little defensively, "there's no school."

"But you didn't see the driver?"

"Just the car."

"When did you last see the car?"

"It was starting to get dark last night and we were hacking around on the swings," acne boy said. "Maybe ten o'clock or so and it was still here."

"You'd have to be a local resident to know about this park, right?" Preston asked.

"I guess," acne sister said and both kids nodded.

"If I climbed over that hill," Cady said, "would I be able to see the mobile park?"

Both kids nodded again.

"Would people in the mobile park be able to see me?" Cady got the impression both kids were subject matter experts on hanging out on the hillside.

"Not if you're in the trees," acne said.

"What about Mr. Sandin's lot?"

"He's the last trailer at Forest Lane," acne said. "He'd be easy to watch."

"Did you get a number off the license plate?" Cady asked, holding his breath.

"I think I remember the first couple," acne replied, "but it had a Hertz sticker."

CHAPTER 40

"The Camry's still out," Detective Walsh shouted over the speakerphone. "It's due back today, but it's still out."

Cady was abusing Preston's Prius, going ninety miles an hour east on the Richmond Highway, while Liz sat in the passenger seat and worked her magic over the phone line. They had the teen siblings back at the mobile park in five minutes, with Liz on the horn to Walsh the entire way. Cady did another five with a round-faced detective named Jerry Brenchley, bringing the man up to speed on the rental car development. The Lynchburg detective had been the one who served Sandin with the search warrant earlier in the week and was telling Cady how Sandin seemed more angry and hung over than suicidal when Liz ran to them holding her phone in the air.

"They've got the Camry tied to Hertz Rent A Car at the Richmond International Airport. Walsh is headed there now."

"So are we," Cady said.

"The Camry's signed out to a woman named Patricia Johnson from Portland, Oregon," Walsh informed
them.

"It's a bullshit name and a bullshit address," Cady
spoke out loud as Preston held her cell phone in
front of the dashboard between them. "Don't spook
her with squad cars or she'll ditch the Camry and
we'll never see her again. Get your best guys working the return line. When the Camry pulls in, have a
fake customer box her in from behind with an SUV
or something."

"On it," the Richmond detective replied over
speakerphone. "My thought is to cuff her when she's
signing off on the return."

"Good idea," Cady said. "But put her down on
her ass. Hard. This woman kills people for a living.
She's good at it."

The Richmond detective had sirened it over to
the airport and commandeered the rent-a-car company. Cady sped past a motorcyclist and listened as
Walsh held a muffled conversation with someone at
Hertz. Walsh's voice appeared to grow in excitement,
but Cady couldn't make out the detective's words.

"Is she there?" Cady yelled. "Is she there?"

"No," Walsh replied, his voice flowing with enthusiasm. "But guess what? The guy here tells me
they've got some kind of tracking technology in case
one of their cars gets ripped off. They've got a GPS
tracking device that can give us the Camry's current
location."

Cady caught Preston's eye for a second and then
turned his attention back to the road. The Richmond

Highway had turned into 460E. The agents heard a muffled voice in the background.

"Of course I want it," the agents heard Walsh bellow.

The muffled voice spoke again.

"Yes, I'll get you an official police report so you can cover your ass," Walsh shouted at whom Cady took to be the manager of the rental car company.

More noise from the muffled voice.

"Oh for Christ's sake—I am police business. In fact, I'll have you arrested if you *don't* get me those goddamned coordinates."

A few seconds later Walsh was back on the line. "Okay, their tech here is working on it. He'll get the latitude and longitude from the GPS receiver and we'll sort out what that location means."

A minute went by before the agents heard a different muffled voice speaking in the background.

"The car's not turned on," they heard Walsh reply to the muffled voice. "Is that going to fuck us?"

More muffled talking, before Walsh returned. "Okay, gang, here's the scoop. The Camry is not currently being driven, but we've got the car's last-known position. Let me just map out the location and . . . holy shit."

"What?" the agents asked in unison.

"You two got to turn around," Walsh said. "The car's still in Lynchburg."

Cady hit the hazard lights and left-turn signal simultaneously and brought Liz's Prius down to twenty miles per hour on the highway's left shoulder in search of a patch of flat grass where he could cross the median without getting stuck or ripping out the car's undercarriage in order to reverse course and head back west on 460.

"Your insurance up to date?" Cady brought the car down into the median strip, did a broad U-turn across fifteen yards of dried grass, and popped up onto the left shoulder of 460W.

"Probably not for this," Preston replied, right hand in the Jesus strap above the passenger door, left hand on the dashboard, cell phone in lap.

Cady jammed the gas and merged into traffic. Twenty seconds later he had the Prius back up to ninety miles an hour.

Cady turned into the Lynchburg Quality Inn and began weaving through the rows of parked cars. Preston touched his arm and pointed at a gray Toyota.

"We've got eyes on the Camry," Cady said. Preston now held her cell phone below dashboard level in case a certain person glanced their way. Both Detective Walsh and Detective Brenchley were wired in. "It's in the second row in the south lot. Repeat, second row in south lot, halfway down."

"Roger that," Brenchley replied. "We're five minutes out."

Cady pulled into an empty space. "Jerry—we can't have squad cars pulling into the motel. If she sees a squad car, she'll disappear."

"There's a Denny's restaurant across the street," Preston said. "They plant one there?"

"You get that, Jerry?" Cady asked. "Put a squad at Denny's, mix it in with the other cars?"

"Makes sense," Brenchley said. "And the road behind the Quality Inn, a half block down, there's a

Hyatt. We can place another car there by where the valets park their cars."

"Okay, good," Cady said and collected his thoughts. "We're going to take her down in the parking lot. Let's hope her hands are tied up with luggage. When she reaches for the Camry, we give the word and all hands on deck. Remember, we want a massive show of force, so she doesn't get any ideas."

"Roger that," Brenchley said. "Darel and I will settle our unmarked in the east lot." Darel Ryan was one of the other Lynchburg plainclothes detectives who had been present at the Forest Lane Mobile Home Park crime scene that morning. "Our ETA is four minutes. Darel and I will be there in four minutes."

"Bad news, Agent Cady," Detective Walsh spoke for the first time in several minutes. The Richmond detective had been on the phone with the Quality Inn's day manager, Kathy Manning, clearing the brush for them. Ms. Manning had been helpful, agreeable . . . and scared.

The hair rose on the back of Cady's neck. "Let me have it."

"I had Kathy go into the system," Walsh said. "Patricia Johnson checked out over an hour ago."

"Did Manning check her out?" Cady asked.

"No," Walsh said. "Johnson checked out of her room—324—via that television thing they can do."

Cady looked at his watch. It was quarter to eleven. Check-out time was listed at 12:00 P.M., but Cady figured that most guests departed long before noon. He thought aloud. "She had a big night last night and a drive to Richmond today. The car rental's at the airport, so she must have a flight out. You run Patricia Johnson past Richmond International?"

"First thing I did," Walsh replied. "No Patricia Johnson from Portland, Oregon, listed on any flight."

"Of course not. It's a name that dies with the Quality Inn and the Hertz rental car," Cady said. He looked at Liz. "The last thing I do at a hotel is check out, so I'm thinking three options. First thought, she's out and she left the car and she's long gone and we're screwed. Second, the continental breakfast didn't quite cut it and she's within walking distance, grabbing a bite somewhere or getting a cup of designer coffee before the drive to Richmond." Cady paused. "Jerry—no squad car at Denny's. If they're at the restaurant, pull them out of there."

"They're not there yet," Brenchley replied. "I'll get them on the radio."

"Good."

"What's the third option?" Detective Walsh asked over the phone.

"What?"

"You mentioned three options."

"Yeah," Cady said. "I never use the TV check out. You get to avoid the front desk with that, right?"

"Correct," Preston said, seeing where Cady was going.

"She might still be in the room."

"What are we going to do?" Brenchley asked, adding, "Darel and I are pulling in."

Cady looked at Liz again. He felt a migraine coming on.

"You're burned, Jerry, from Sandin's search warrant. She spots you poking about and red flags go

up." Cady addressed Detective Ryan, "Were you with
Jerry and the warrant, Darel?"

"No."

"Okay, I need you in the lobby reading a magazine and looking all laid back, but keep an eye out
for—I don't know—an attractive thirty or thirty-five-
year-old who's all by herself. She's five two or maybe
five three. Right, Walsh?"

"Correct," Walsh confirmed. "Good looking, petite."

"And Jerry," Cady said, "I need you parked in the
south lot. You're going to be the trigger now. You're
Paul Revere. If she approaches the Camry, you call
the squad cars. Guns out, take no shit. Get her on
her ass, cuffs behind her back, okay?"

"Roger that," Brenchley said again.

"I'll head in now," Ryan said.

"Good," Cady replied. "Liz and I will be joining
you, but we don't know each other."

Cady then spoke to Walsh. "Tell Kathy Manning
we're coming in, but not to make a deal of it. Everything is rosy, okay? Just another day at the office."

"Can do," Walsh said. "What are you going to do?"

"We're going to see if she's still in her room,"
Cady said and looked at Preston. "Liz has always
wanted to be a maid."

CHAPTER 41

The Canadian had a restful morning.

Her flight was at six that evening and she could mosey her way to the Richmond airport with plenty of time to catch her flight back to Toronto. She got up at seven, watched the TV news for several minutes, and then did a quick reconnaissance as she walked down for the free breakfast—the coast was clear—and she carried her tray of goodies and the Lynchburg daily newspaper back up to her room. There was nothing in the paper or on the television about Karl Sandin. The man would likely not be found for days—perhaps not until Lynchburg PD returned the items seized in the search of his trailer—and, upon discovery, due to some distinctive work on her part, Karl Sandin's demise would be deemed a suicide.

The Canadian fell back asleep for another two hours.

When she awoke the second time, she got serious about heading out. First, she ate the rest of her breakfast. Second, she checked out using the invoice that had been slipped under her door along with the motel's television check-out system. Then the Canadian took the world's longest shower. After drying off, brushing both hair and teeth, and getting dressed, she tossed her clothes and ditty bag into her TravelPro Maxlite. She kept the envelope containing her Johnson and Andrews IDs on her person, inside her blazer pocket, and planned to jettison her Patricia Johnson ID once she used it to return the Camry to Hertz.

The Canadian walked about the hotel room to see if there was anything that she'd forgotten. All was good in the neighborhood. She extended the Maxlite's handle, opened the outside door, and rolled her luggage out onto the third-floor balcony walkway. She looked right. A maid two doors down was quietly auditing the shampoo bottles and soap bars on her cart. The Canadian looked left. A tall man carrying a coffee in each hand and an apple in his mouth was heading her way. She strode down the aisle, her luggage trailing like an old dog, the door to her room shutting of its own weight. Apple man nodded a quick *hello* in her direction as they squeezed past each other. Next up was a middle-aged man in a wrinkled sport jacket. He moved slowly toward her, his eyes scanning back and forth—quantifying, evaluating—taking everything in.

Cop eyes.

And if he's a cop, the thought blasted through the Canadian's mind like a stick of dynamite, then the other two on the walkway—apple man and the maid—were not who they appeared to be.

As the two closed the gap between themselves, the man forced himself to look away.

It was then the Canadian knew she was fucked.

Agent Liz Preston entered the lobby of the Quality Inn, stepped behind the front desk counter, marched into the back office and shut the door as though she were the district manager on-site to announce an impending closure. She was there to connect with Manager Kathy Manning, gear up in a maid outfit and Quality Inn apron, and in five minutes be pushing a cleaning-slash-restocking trolley past room 324 in quest of any sign as to whether the room had been vacated—open drapes and empty room, door left ajar—or still occupied—TV noise, do not disturb sign, whatnot.

Cady and Preston agreed that a front desk phone call to room 324 in order to ask if the room was available for maid service or for some other trumped-up reason would place the woman currently known as Patricia Johnson on red alert, which was the absolute last thing either of them wanted to do. Neither agent nor any of the detectives had ever heard of a hotel pestering guests prior to the posted check-out time in order to see if they've vacated their rooms.

If Liz did not notice any obvious signs of occupancy or vacancy, she would make a Broadway production out of knocking on the neighboring room—room 322—which manager Manning had assured them was empty as the family staying there had put in for a six A.M. wake-up call and had checked out and were on the road by six thirty. Liz would then do five minutes of vacuuming and thumping about before pushing her trolley on to room 324.

Then she'd give the door a light tap and say, "Maid service."

Cady wanted Marzy Doats or Patricia Johnson or whoever the hell the woman really was to be inside room 324 as that meant the takedown in the Quality Inn's parking lot was still on the table. But, Cady questioned, in the world of paid assassins, would it make more sense to simply walk away from a false persona—to walk away from a Marzy Doats or a Patricia Johnson—once the trigger had been pulled, leaving behind the rental car and whatever other loose ends? Were that the case . . . they'd be shit out of luck.

Cady didn't want to be left with an empty room and a wiped car.

Cady gave Preston a minute to approach Kathy Manning; he didn't want too much buzzing about the front desk going on in case *the woman* was herself poking about the lobby. Then he slid off his tie and slung it into the backseat of Preston's Prius. Cady unbuttoned the top two buttons of his dress shirt, ruffled his hair with some fingers, and strode into the Quality Inn's main entrance. He cut across the lobby, walked past Darel Ryan—who was sitting in an easy chair, studying a road atlas as though there were an upcoming quiz, and looking much the impatient father who had put space between himself and the kids if only for five minutes—and headed straight for the vending machines. He bought a Twizzlers, stuck it in the breast pocket of his suit jacket, and then glanced about the reception area: Detective Ryan still in his chair and a young couple checking out with the front desk clerk.

Cady heard a noise, walked a few feet down the central hallway, and peered inside what had to be the breakfast room. An unattended kid was trying to wrestle one of the remaining bagels into a toaster while another kid, probably an older brother, was sweeping together all the crumbs from an empty donut tray into one corner for easier consumption. Cady spotted a hand towel draped over the back of a chair at an abandoned table of used plates and spilled orange juice. Perfect. He slung the towel over a shoulder and headed to the breakfast bar. A vat of something Cady assumed was once oatmeal, a couple of plain bagels, and a fruit bowl of bananas and apples appeared to be the only survivors of the morning's feast. Cady grabbed a giant red apple and moved over to the bins of coffee. He emptied the rest of both bins, merging caffeinated and decaf into two of the largest Styrofoam cups he could find. The room truly was a mess. Perhaps when the morning's main event was over, and Sandin's killer was tucked safely in custody, Cady would inform Liz about the state of the breakfast bar as, in Preston's new motel maid role, she really should tidy up in here.

Cady walked back to the lobby. There was a second clerk behind the front desk, whom Cady took to be Quality Inn Day Manager Kathy Manning. And Agent Preston was now in a pair of black pants that almost fit, a white cotton shirt, and was nearly shrouded in a massive brown apron that sported the inn's logo on the front. Cady made a mental note to snap a portfolio of cell phone pictures of Liz in this getup before she got a chance to change back into her official wear. Liz was pushing a trolley loaded with soaps and lotions, shampoos and towels, toward the elevator. The cart also had a vacuum attached to its side. Preston glanced his way and held up three fingers for a brief moment.

Three minutes.

Cady and Darel Ryan stood at the edge of the stairwell on the northeast corner of the third floor and watched as Liz Preston pushed her service trolley in their direction from the northwest side of the Quality Inn's third floor. Cady wanted eyes on Preston at all times in case events went south. He wanted Detective Ryan with him for that same reason, but also to watch their six, to make sure that the female UNSUB wasn't—for whatever reason—coming up the staircase behind them. The motel rooms emptied out onto the balcony, an exterior hallway that led either to the elevator and staircase on the west side, from which Preston was heading, or to the east side staircase, where Cady and the Lynchburg detective stood, hidden from the street by fence boards and latticework. Cady peeked over the railing. A couple dozen feet below were a handful of remaining cars, those fortunate to have parked closest to the building the previous evening.

Cady then looked at Liz who now had her trolley parked in front of room 322. She was fumbling with the vacuum cord but the instant she caught Cady's eye, she knocked one of the miniature shampoo bottles off her cart. That was the agreed-upon signal.

The killer was still in room 324.

"Plan A," Cady said to Ryan, meaning the take-down would be in the parking lot. Ryan began relaying that back to Detective Brenchley over his cell phone when Cady, from his angle against the railing, noticed a shadow now where the door to room 324 had been.

"Oh, shit," Cady whispered, "she's coming out."

CHAPTER 42

Cady popped the apple in his mouth, picked up both cups of tepid hotel coffee that he'd placed on the railing edge, and headed in Preston's direction as a diminutive brunette in a lightweight blue blazer and white blouse pulled her luggage bag out from room 324 and onto the balcony corridor. Cady knew it'd be bad news for the occupant of 324 to spot him and Ryan loitering in the corner stairwell and hoped Ryan was on his game enough to either head down the stairwell or follow at a leisurely pace behind Cady. The brunette peeked over her shoulder as Liz counted the bottles of shampoo and lotion, and then headed in Cady's direction.

Preston spotted the Do Not Disturb sign hanging off the handle to room 324 and dropped a bottle of shampoo—the agreed-upon signal. A second later the door to 324 opened inward. Liz went blithely about her inventory, feeling a set of eyes crawl over her, and then the woman currently known as Patricia Johnson rolled her small piece of luggage away from

Preston, heading toward Cady and the Lynchburg detective.

Liz watched as Drew walked her way, hair disheveled and an apple in his mouth, somehow a towel was on his shoulder and he carried two heaping cups of coffee—Cady as a businessman hauling a cup of joe to a colleague in a nearby room. Drew paused long enough to acknowledge the faux Patricia Johnson with an apple grunt and nod, before his eyes danced downward for a quick glance at her chest—Cady as a businessman who knows the locations of all the strip bars in the cities he frequents.

As soon as their female UNSUB disappeared down the northeast stairwell, Cady, Preston, and Detective Ryan would zip down the northwest steps and be part of the team taking her down in the south parking lot. Now that they'd had eyes on her, there would no longer be a need for her to approach the rental Toyota. They could take the woman down in the parking lot lane, which would be safer as she'd have no cover in which to make a last stand.

Darel Ryan now headed in Preston's direction, lagging four rooms behind Cady. Unlike Drew, unfortunately, the Lynchburg detective radiated an apprehensive vibe, like a security guard in hot pursuit of a spotted shoplifter. Approaching Patricia Johnson, Ryan appeared to have caught himself but then veered off in the opposite direction, now taking interest in the outdoor carpeting of the balcony hallway, in the window frames and doorknobs. As Ryan pulled even with their UNSUB, the woman halted, released her luggage handle, and in whip-like sequence, leapt sideways and sucker punched the Lynchburg detective with the heel of her hand right smack into his left temple.

Cady was a dozen feet from Liz when he spotted her jaw drop. Preston had been peering over Cady's shoulder as he approached; all calm and collected, but an instant later it was as though Liz had been poked with a cattle prod. Cady whirled about, coffee splashing over his hands and suit pants, apple tumbling from his mouth.

Darel Ryan was on the balcony floor, unmoving, and the woman currently known as Patricia Johnson was charging Cady like a Pamplona bull.

The Canadian shot the Lynchburg cop her best birdbrain smile though he now appeared preoccupied with glancing everywhere but in her direction, courtesy be damned. If this were an ambush, the Canadian needed him out of the picture ASAP. As she approached the cop the Canadian relaxed her body as much as possible, taking a deep breath . . . the calm before the storm. She felt the familiar rush—electrifying—her nerve endings aflame. As she drew parallel to the man, the Canadian dropped her TravelPro's pull handle, whipped her hips sideways, and sent a right palm into the cop's left temple, causing his brain to rock against his skull lining, causing him to black out, causing him to drop like a cement bag—out for the count.

Next up was apple guy. Even with a towel draped over his shoulder, the Canadian thought she'd spotted a bulge in the man's suit jacket, but because of the coffees and apple and generally doofus look, she assumed the man was smuggling a bag of breakfast bar goodies back to his room just as she'd done earlier that morning. She'd assumed bagels wrapped in napkins or a wad of granola bars, not shoulder holster.

She'd assumed wrong.

For her lifespan to exceed the next several seconds, the Canadian had to take out this next cop as fast as she'd done the first one. She had an idea, and she rushed toward apple man with the lightning speed of a rabid linebacker.

Cady only had time to toss the contents of both Styrofoam cups in the woman's direction before she knocked into him. It might have changed the battle course had the java not been sitting out for five hours. It was useless and Sandin's killer came in close on his left side, she jammed both palms up into Cady's left breast, slamming him sideways, a moment of inertia as his back smashed up against the third-floor railing.

Then Cady threw an uppercut with his left fist— his good hand—but she'd dropped to a crouch, each of her hands now clutching the back of an ankle. Cady realized where this was headed but was powerless to escape as his attacker rocketed upward like a Fourth of July firework. Cady's world upended, his spine a teeter-totter on the balcony railing, and in a flash he went over, airborne, flipping, falling, proving Newton's laws of motion were valid at Quality

Inn Motels. The hood of a first generation Dodge Durango rose up to greet him.

In under five seconds the Canadian had taken out two ambushers. She checked her back—still clear—and wondered why more cops weren't pouring out from the woodwork. But she didn't have to wonder long . . . the maid was now sprinting her way.

Liz ripped at her apron, cursing herself for not placing her Glock 22 between a stack of towels for easy reach, instead rigging her holster at belt level beneath the cleaning garment. Shocked when Drew flipped ass-over-teakettle from the railing, she said screw it.

Agent Liz Preston went after the woman currently known as Patricia Johnson.

The Canadian was thinking ahead, about what needed to be done after she dispatched with the maid. The car was blown and likely *other cops* were lying in wait for her. The Canadian had to get across the street and put a couple hundred yards of distance between *them* and her. And she had to do that without delay. Fortunately this frontage road housed half a dozen hotels. Hotels had cabs.

And she needed to be in one within minutes.

The Canadian let the maid come inside, and then shot forward a classic throat strike. It got swept aside like a cobweb and the Canadian took an elbow strike in return. She stumbled backward, her cheekbone burning, but jumped into a fighting stance. The maid pressed forward, coming inside again, and the

Canadian went for speed, snapping a front kick off her left foot. It stabbed at air as the maid danced out of reach. The Canadian returned to stance when the maid bounced forward with a foot sweep. The Canadian jumped back, but the sweep was a fake, and the maid came in hard with a roundhouse kick to the head. The Canadian saw it coming at the last instant, tried to pull back, but still took a heel to the forehead. She bounced backward again, kept in the fighting stance, and looked at the maid as though for the first time.

What the hell, the Canadian thought, I need to be across town—stat!—and I'm fucking around with a female Bruce Lee.

Cady's legs hit the Dodge Durango's roof, his torso the windshield, and his face planted into the SUV's hood. Cady was stunned—a bird flying into a window, an athlete down on the field, but not unconscious. The air was knocked out of him and after what could have been a second or a thousand years, Cady did a slow push-up on the Durango's hood. There was a dent where his face had been, now puddling with blood.

His blood.

Cady wiggled his body and though he felt anything but, he realized he'd been lucky that the sports utility vehicle had broken his twenty-something-foot drop. He wasn't sure he'd have survived hitting concrete. Cady took till the end of time sliding off the old Durango, noting the owner would need a new windshield as the safety glass had spider-webbed. Cady felt nauseous, had trouble breathing—the air pounded out of him—and he spit a tablespoon of blood onto the SUV's front tire. Blood ran into his right eye and he wiped at it with a sleeve. He felt as though both upper thighs had been batted by a designated hitter in the bottom of the ninth, likely the pain had come from the top of the Durango's windshield frame. He was thinking in slow motion, but one word got him reaching for his holster.

Liz.

CHAPTER 43

The goddamned maid had thrust and parried the Canadian back to the spot where she'd taken down the first cop. The maid answered the Canadian's missed blows with strikes of her own, no game enders—not yet—but chipping away. It was just a matter of time. Two reasons kept the Canadian from turning around and bolting. First, she might not make the stairwell before the maid had her gun out from under her apron, or, second, the maid screams into her phone and the Canadian is surrounded by eight squad cars and it becomes Custer's Last Stand.

The Canadian was efficient in the martial arts, but, clearly, this fake maid—another cop? FBI?— forever advancing on her was better. The Canadian needed a game ender. She needed to get the stiletto out of her blazer pocket.

Unlike with karate, the Canadian was an expert with a blade.

The Canadian broke stance, whipping a hand inside her jacket, when the maid struck. It happened so fast, the Canadian missed the beautiful execution of the sidekick that put her down on her back.

Liz Preston was a fifth-degree black belt, and this woman was not in her league, like a sparring partner from a lower class. Liz kept her focus on the woman, knowing Detective Brenchley was seventy yards away, in the south lot, with his eyes on the Toyota Camry. Hopefully the detective would realize their recent radio silence meant bad news. He might not call in the cavalry, not wanting to scare away the woman known as Patricia Johnson, but if he would hustle over to see what the hell was going on, he could lend a helping hand. Preston hoped a guest, or perhaps motel manager Kathy Manning, heard Drew's tumble—the hellish thud of him landing on a car roof—and had called 911, which would be A-okay in her book.

Liz prayed Drew was alive. A second-floor drop would certainly include stitches and bruised ribs, but a fall from the third floor, from this high up . . . that enters broken neck and fractured skull territory. Though it seemed an eternity, it likely wasn't much more than a minute since he'd gone over the railing. She hadn't heard Drew call out since his fall . . . and that's what horrified her.

Drew can't be dead. He can't be.

It would kill her to tell Terri.

Liz tried dancing the woman into the prone body of Detective Ryan, hoping she'd trip over him, but the hired killer sidestepped the man. The woman then broke eye contact, started to twist, a hand coming down and . . . that's when Agent Liz Preston kicked her into next week.

Cady limped eastward in the parking lane. Glock out but pointing at the ground, he used a sleeve to wipe the blood from his eyes every few seconds. Cady's head throbbed in beat with his heart, but he squinted up at the third-floor balcony. He could tell a commotion was occurring on that level, but couldn't make out the specifics. An arm flung here, a kicking sound there. Cady knew Liz was a whatever-degree black belt and once Preston got rolling, the bitch that flung him over the railing was in a world of shit.

God his head hurt.

"What the hell?!"

Cady turned back from where he'd hobbled. An elderly man with a gray buzz cut and Burl Ives's beard stood on the sidewalk staring at the decades-old Durango. Cady figured it had to be the SUV's owner. The old man stared at his dented hood with the pooled blood, his broken windshield, and a crimson smear down the driver's side panel.

He then looked up at Cady, seeing him for the first time.

Without another word, the old man turned and fled. Cady again wiped the blood out of his eyes and figured he must cut a hell of a figure. Face dripping blood and holding a gun. Jesus Christ, Cady wondered if the old man would ever stop running.

He looked back up at the third-floor balcony, and there was Liz Preston staring down at him

The Canadian bounced sideways off the wall and then down on the floor. It was over. The maid stood above her, yanking the apron upward with a left hand, and drawing her gun with a right. She aimed the Glock at the Canadian's face.

"Don't move," the maid said. "Don't breathe."

"What the hell?!" the Canadian heard a man shout from the parking lot, likely admiring her recent handiwork.

The maid edged over to the railing, gun still aimed in the Canadian's general direction. She peeked back at the Canadian, and then peered over the railing into the parking lot below. The fake maid was concerned about the fate of the apple man. The fake maid was a hell of an adversary, but more Marquess of Queensberry rules than street fighter.

Perhaps the Canadian's game ender was still in play.

She drew both legs to her chest, rolled backward onto her shoulders, hands behind her head, and in the silent blink of an eye kipped-up to a standing position behind the cop maid. The Canadian swept the gun aside with a left hand, stepped inside the maid's proximity, her right shooting into her blazer pocket, retrieving the stiletto.

She brought the blade above the cop maid's neck.

"What the hell?!"

Preston edged to the handrail, giving the prone Patricia Johnson a final look before glancing over the rail. Yes! Drew stood below looking much the mess— like something that had crawled out of a horror movie, but very much alive.

Liz Preston broke into a smile.

Cady stared up at Liz. Thank God. He'd have smiled back, but figured he'd look like a jack-o'-lantern.

Then he saw something above Liz shine in the sun.

Then he saw a spray of crimson.

Cady began to scream.

Liz heard an almost unintelligible whoosh behind her, and then felt her gun hand being brushed aside.

And Liz knew she'd messed up.

Cady raised his Glock, eyes locked on Preston's, watching her features advance from glee to shock. He stumbled backward, trying to get an angle, but the bitch knew he was there and hung in close, using Liz for cover, sliding downward with Preston's body. The two agents from the Federal Bureau of Investigation kept eye contact until Liz sunk below the railing.

Then Cady spotted the woman—an eighth of a second, peeking back at him—and aimed for a quick shot, but she pulled back. He heard more than saw her bolt for the northeast stairwell, where Cady and Darel Ryan had stood minutes earlier and a lifetime ago.

Cady took off in that direction, clearing cars, leaping over the curb, and cutting across the sidewalk, only then realizing that the inhuman sound buzzing about his skull stemmed from him.

The woman must have taken entire flights at a time, and dropped over the railing on the last crisscross of steps. When Cady made the cut-through between the motel rooms and the lobby, she had cleared the gap, darted diagonally, was now nearing the southeast corner of the lobby building, making for the sidewalk on that side of the motel's entrance.

Cady had her at forty feet, her face turning his way as she dashed past the corner wall.

Cady shot twice, but she was gone, his bullets smashing stucco and trim. Cady spotted Kathy Manning watching him from the glass door that led inside to the breakfast bar and front desk, her face as white as his was scarlet.

Cady screamed "Ambulance now!" at the startled hotel manager and though his body screamed back at him in protest, he took the stairs three at a bound, up toward Liz.

CHAPTER 44

"Should we come now?"

"That's a big negatory," Detective Brenchley spoke into the police radio, mildly annoyed. Brenchley sat in the unmarked, eyes on the Toyota Camry two rows and forty yards away. He'd informed the parked squads minutes earlier on Detective Ryan's update that the perp was still in her room. "Remember we don't want to chase her away before she comes for the car."

"Dispatch got a call about a deranged man waving a gun in the Quality Inn's north lot," the officer replied over the two-way. "I think your element of surprise just went out the window."

"But Darel and the Feebs are on—"

Gunshots reverberated throughout the parking lot. "Oh, shit."

Fuck!

If that goddamned red-faced monster comes ripping around the corner, the Canadian knew she'd be dead. She'd caught a quick glimpse. It was the apple man—now surreal—blood dripping from gashes to his forehead, dripping from his nose, his lips, his chin. His face a crimson grimace of pain and hatred.

And the man was screaming, deep and guttural . . . his handgun aimed at her face.

Grateful for going with tennis shoes on a travel day, the Canadian shot across the walkway as though it were the Summer Olympics, tore past the lobby entrance, through the west parking lot and bat out of hell'ed it across eighty yards of dead lawn before turning a corner and cutting through another parking lot.

Police sirens pierced the air. The Canadian forced herself to pause long enough between a Honda Pilot and a pickup to tear off her blood-spattered blazer. She used the jacket's interior to wipe blood spray off her face and hands. She stole the envelope from the hidden pocket before she tossed the ruined blazer under the Honda SUV. This action may have saved her ass as a squad car flew past on the street in front of the lot.

The Canadian jogged through the remaining rows of cars, up onto the sidewalk, and then slowed to a quick stroll. Running at this point meant attention—it meant eyes—so she moved with the form of a retiree power walking a shopping mall. The Canadian kept west toward the nearest intersection. She kept her head down, her right eye stinging, watering, from some errant piece of shrapnelling grit when apple man blew a fist-sized hole out of the corner post of the Quality Inn's lobby building in the exact spot her face had been a blink earlier.

She'd been beyond lucky the round had not removed her skull.

Halfway through the intersection it occurred to her to resume breathing. Sirens blared, back behind her as well as off to her right. She continued straight ahead, putting several streets between her and the Quality Inn in as little time as possible. She then jaywalked across the street before the next block, sirens still deafening, cut around a building, and then cut across that street and jogged to the next intersection. Finally the Canadian saw what she wanted— a place to take a quick pause, a breather. She cut across the parking lot to the outside bench at a Macaroni Grill. She blinked her watering eye, glanced left and right, and listened to the cacophony of sirens and alarms. The Canadian was checking to see if any bystanders were pointing her way, if she had tripped anyone's radar.

So far so good.

She dabbed at her watering eye with a sleeve and . . . goddammit . . . she had a plum-sized splotch of blood near the top of her white blouse. The Canadian held a palm over the spot as though the national anthem were underway at a sporting event and walked another street and headed through another intersection. The sirens, though continuing to ring, were now a half mile away—a cop posse gathering at the Quality Inn.

She cut diagonally across a large parking lot, heading for the Embassy Suites.

Cady hurdled a now-moaning Darel Ryan and sank to his knees in the broadening puddle of blood surrounding Agent Preston. He slid a left hand under her neck, squeezing the wound, trying to stop the once gushing but now trickling blood flow. He grabbed an elbow and pulled Liz to him with his feeble right hand.

Cady held her close.

Blood dripped from Cady's face, adding to the pool he knelt in. He bit at broken lips, but it didn't stop the tears from streaming down. Vacant blue eyes stared up at him.

Liz had bled out.

FBI Special Agent Elizabeth Kay Preston was dead.

The Canadian did a quick three sixty and then entered the Embassy Suites as though she were a longtime resident and followed the signs to the nearest restroom. Thank god it was empty and she washed her hands, forearms, and face with endless squirts of the liquid soap. She then soaked both hands in warm water and ran them through her hair, pushing the style backward and creating a new one. After that the Canadian worked her right eye, rinsing it repeatedly with cool water and dabbing at it with paper towels until the stinging finally tapered off. The Canadian slowly surveyed herself in the mirror.

Not bad, but her eye was bloodshot.

She then took refuge in a toilet stall for a minute, catching her breath, slowing her breathing . . . thinking. It had to be the damned rental car that led them to her; they can track those fuckers like cell phones. But how? Did the cops return to Sandin's mobile home first thing this morning with more of their search warrant bullshit? Did they not buy the suicide? The death of a tenant would be a major event on a summer day for trailer-park trash, with neighbors milling about and police asking questions and . . . and then there were those pot-smoking kids.

She was sure those kids never saw her, but did one of those little fuckers take it upon himself to jot down her license plate? That was the only link that made sense. Goddammit! She should have switched plates, but she'd parked on the other side of that goddamned hill so no one would report seeing her car at the trailer park.

Goddammit!

The Canadian took the Sheryl Andrews passport and driver's license and credit card from the envelope and shoved them in a front pocket, and then she left the stall and shoved the envelope containing her Patricia Johnson IDs into the sanitary napkin receptacle.

"It's the craziest thing," the Canadian said to the gift shop clerk as she bought the blue T-shirt, matching windbreaker, ball cap, and sunglasses. "I was just sitting out by the pool and I got a bloody nose." She handed the clerk eighty dollars. "Can you call me a cab while I change into this?"

Five minutes later, the Canadian was in the backseat of a taxi, heading across town.

CHAPTER 45

Day 17

It rained hard the day of the funeral.

The church service at Holy Trinity had gone well, Terri thought, that is, as well as it can go for a life cut short . . . a life stolen. The attendance was a tribute to Elizabeth Preston's reputation, how high in esteem the fallen agent had been held; the pews were full, not an empty seat in the church. Terri struggled to keep it together since receiving the worst phone call of her life from her husband a few days earlier.

Terri thought the world of Elizabeth Preston, partly because she knew that Liz held Drew's best interests at heart. In fact Liz had been the only agent from the Federal Bureau of Investigation to fly out to attend their wedding the previous summer. Roland Jund, of course, had backed out at the last minute, just as Drew had bet Terri he would. The day before the wedding, while Drew was in town picking up his tux, Terri took Liz on a tour of Bass Lake in the pontoon boat. They'd brought along some fishing poles, but those fell by the wayside in favor of a bottle of merlot. When they'd polished off the wine, Liz had looked about the lake and then at Terri and said,

"This is what he needs, Terri. This is everything Drew needs."

Roland Jund's eulogy was class personified. The director of CID informed the mourners how "Alethia" was the Greek word for truth, which translated into "not forgetting." Jund informed the gathering of Preston's family, friends, and colleagues that Liz's life was a quest for *Alethia* and that Elizabeth Preston will *never be forgotten*.

Cady's eulogy was not as graceful.

"Liz Preston and I had nothing in common," Cady began. "We voted for different politicians, pursued different hobbies, and cheered on different teams. I ate meat and potatoes, Liz ate arugula." Cady looked out over the people filling the pews, his face a tetherball of stitches and bruising. "Though we had nothing in common, Liz was the best friend I ever had."

Cady stood motionless for several seconds, tears began dripping down his face and splotching his crisp white shirt. Terri left her seat, stepped around the closed casket and up to the podium next to Drew. She placed a hand on the small of his back.

The church was silent.

"I'm sorry, Liz," Cady said finally. "I am so, so sorry." He continued staring at the casket. "It should be me in that box instead of you."

Along with Preston's two brothers and some cousins, Jund and Cady were pallbearers. Once they slid the casket into the hearse, Terri watched Jund turn to Cady, both men oblivious to the pouring rain. The director of CID reached out and squeezed Drew's shoulder for a long, lingering instant. And though Terri was several yards away, and though the rain came down in buckets, and though no words had been said, Terri felt as though a message had been exchanged between the two men.

Terri suspected it was the same message she'd conveyed to her husband earlier that morning. Neither had slept, but they tossed and turned and went through the motions. Drew had been torn in two over Preston's death—he blamed himself—and the thirty-six stitches in the various cuts in his scalp and forehead, the twelve stitches inside his lip, the eighteen on his chin, his broken nose, bruised ribs, battered shoulders and forearms weren't helping to release his guilt. Drew's concussion had earned him an overnight at Central Lynchburg General. It was from Lynchburg General that Drew had made the phone call to her at Bass Lake. He'd been barely able to state what had transpired, as though voicing Preston's death would make it permanent.

In their hotel bed Terri had slid up close to Drew in the predawn hour and whispered into his ear. "You find her, Drew. Find her."

The rain made for a messy graveside service.

Terri stood under a nearby tree, waiting, using the umbrella her husband had refused. She would stand there in silence as the seasons passed if that's what her husband required. After a brief prayer, everyone else had hustled back to their cars in order to keep dry and left Mount Olivet, driving back to the church for a basement luncheon of ham sandwiches, pasta salads, coffee, and remembrance.

But Drew stood next to Elizabeth Preston's fresh grave, unmoving, a cemetery statue himself . . . a battered gargoyle . . . a tombstone.

PART FOUR

INTERMENT

CHAPTER 46

Day 18

Cady rapped on the door while simultaneously pressing the doorbell.

It was six o'clock in the morning, another day of rain—perhaps less harsh—and he knew the man was home. He had blocked the man's driveway with his rental car. Then peeked in the side garage door—where a dusty Nissan 370Z sat in the single-car garage—then strode to the front door.

The house was a nondescript rambler in Odenton, Maryland, a six-minute drive east of Fort Meade, which is where the homeowner worked. Cady got the feeling that the man was awake, was quite likely standing behind the door and hoping that the agent from the Federal Bureau of Investigation would give up, fuck off, and go his merry way.

Cady pounded harder.

"I know you're in there," Cady shouted. "Open the goddamned door or your neighbors are going to watch me kick it in."

Cady heard a dead bolt twist. A second later the door swung inward and a balding man stood before him wearing a blue robe that Cady suspected the man had slept in.

"You been watching the news?" Cady asked.

A nearly discernible nod.

"Then you know why I'm here," Cady said.

A now-discernible nod.

"You owe me a favor."

Leahy paused for a second, shrugged, and then stood aside to let the agent with the scarred face enter his home.

"You know you can't use any of this shit in court," Leahy said.

"Let me worry about that," Cady replied.

They were sitting on padded folding chairs in Leahy's unfinished basement. Cady had heard that older elephants instinctively head toward an elephant graveyard when it comes time to die. Using that logic, Leahy's basement was where old PCs, laptops, and monitors gathered when the time came to give up the ghost. It was a clutter of stacked CPUs, power strips, dissected hard drives, elderly modems, fans, long forgotten motherboards, connectors, and what had to be a mile or three of tangled cabling. Rather than a desk, Leahy had a string of sawhorses set in a straight row with sheets of plywood on top, each one nailed down to avoid accidents. On top of the plywood sat three monitors—two the size of drive-in theaters—with a keyboard and mouse parked in front.

"No one can find out I'm doing this for you," Leahy said, holding Cady's eye, "or I'll be bunking beds with Snowden in Moscow."

"They won't get it from me."

Leahy digested Cady's assurance and nodded. "You have to give me some time."

"What does that mean?" Cady asked. "A day? A week?"

"Come back tonight and we'll see if I've nailed anything by then," Leahy said. "Bring me six items from Taco Bell, doesn't matter which ones. And a twelve pack of those Cinnabon Delights, you know, the ones with frosting in the middle."

CHAPTER 47

Day 19

The Canadian couldn't sleep.

She gave up at quarter to four and switched on the coffee. She sat on a dining room chair, waiting on the French Roast, and stared out the wall of glass, watching as the city awoke. When the coffee finished brewing, she poured herself a mug, brought it back to the dining room table with her, and flipped open her laptop. The Canadian booted up Google Earth Pro, pecked at some keys, and—for the fifth time in two days—brought up a bird's eye view of a string of lake cabins in northern Minnesota . . . along Bass Lake . . . Sundown Point Resort.

Apple man had to die.

The Canadian had taken a circuitous escape route back to Toronto.

The cab at the Embassy Suites had taken her to a sports store in downtown Lynchburg where she purchased in cash a Trek 820 mountain bike, a helmet, a bicycle lock, beef jerky, two water bottles, a small-sized backpack, and a camping knife. She also worked with the shop's obliging owner to chart the best biking route for her to take in order to get to Farmville. Farmville was an hour drive east of Lynchburg. The Canadian rode out of the bike shop at one in the afternoon and was in Farmville by six, although, truth be told, she took a lengthy break at a restaurant in Brookneal for lunch, to refill her water bottles, and to make a pay phone call to cancel her evening flight out of Richmond International Airport. The flight had been set in her newest persona—Sheryl Andrews—the last of her three IDs, and the only one that hadn't yet been burned. Since the rental Camry pointed at the Richmond airport, the Canadian certainly didn't want any of the apple man's colleagues finding the name *Sheryl Andrews* on a list of people who inexplicably missed a flight.

Apple man was all the Canadian thought about as she sweated her way across the side roads, back roads, freeway overpasses, and dirt trails on her exodus to Farmville. If the apple man had been a quarter-second quicker, the Canadian's brains would have been blown out the back of her skull and splattered onto the dusty hoods and dirty windshields of nearby vehicles. If apple man had turned the corner instead of rushing back to the aid of his already-dead colleague, he could have cut her spine in half with two shots. His bloodstained face wore the wrath of hell as he held her in his gunsight . . . and that primordial scream . . . no way a man like that walks away from having been tossed off a third-floor balcony, no way a man like that walks away from what I did to his colleague . . . his partner . . . his friend. Sure, the Canadian had felt the addictive buzz—the adrenal high—in the thrill of the fight at the Quality

Inn in Lynchburg, but there was a much less familiar sensation involved as she locked eyes with apple
man.

Fear.

By the time the Canadian's bicycle entered the
Farmville city limits, she'd come to the simple conclusion that apple man had to die. A predator rec-
ognizes other predators and there was no way the
Canadian would allow herself to be hunted—hunted
or haunted—by him. There was no way she would
traipse about her daily life under that kind of fucking
threat.

It was not in her nature.

The Canadian stayed at a Days Inn in Farmville.
After checking in under her Sheryl Andrews ID, she
biked across the street and nibbled at a Subway
for two long hours. She wore her ball cap, read the
newspaper, and monitored the motel. If there was
ever a time to be paranoid, it was now, she'd figured.
The Canadian couldn't think of any way in which her
Sheryl Andrews ID had been burned. The Andrews ID
had never been in play, this was the first time it had
been used since its arrival from her forger savant in
Manila. Even if the Canadian's booking agent in Bern
had fucked her, the booking agent had no knowledge of her use of a counterfeiter in the Philippines.
Never the twain shall meet; it was safer that way for
all involved. A win-win situation.

Her Sheryl Andrews identity was golden. It had to
be if she was ever going to get out of this bind.

The Canadian woke early that next morning,
showered, and checked out. She rode the Trek 820 to
a CVS Pharmacy, picked up some pancake makeup,

and then pedaled across the street to a McDonald's. In the bathroom she dabbed makeup over the yellowing parts of her face, the fresh bruises from the maid-cop's blows. Then she drank a bottomless cup of coffee until a nearby hair salon opened.

The Canadian was able to talk herself into being seen by a stylist without an appointment—just a half-hour wait. She had her dark locks cut short. Though partial to men, the Canadian's new pixie cut could now land her first float in a gay rights parade. The short cut gave her face a fuller look, and she was no longer in the ballpark of resembling either of her burned Mary Ellen Doats or Patricia Johnson personas.

The Canadian thought about what the cops would get from her TravelPro Maxlite luggage. Dirty laundry and fingerprints. Sure, they'd trace the prints back to her days in the Canadian Armed Forces, and they'd discover her birth name—Willa Reddon—but Willa Reddon hadn't existed in more than fifteen years. The Canadian's mother had passed away from ovarian cancer when she was twelve. And the Canadian hadn't seen hide nor hair of her asshole father since she'd joined the Canadian army at age seventeen, back when he'd grabbed her one last time and she'd broken both of his arms. And many of his ribs.

She imagined the authorities would soon be paying dear old dad a visit—if they could locate him—but he'd be of no help.

Twenty-four hours after barely surviving the occurrence at the Quality Inn, the Canadian was on a Greyhound bus to Durham, North Carolina. And the next morning Sheryl Andrews was on a nonstop Air

Canada flight to Toronto out of the Raleigh-Durham International Airport.

Yup—her Andrews ID was golden. And within two hours of her arrival back in her home city, all of her Sheryl Andrews IDs had been shredded. And all shredded strips had been gathered into an envelope to make for easy flushing in the restrooms of a variety of fast-food restaurants peppered along the route of her afternoon jog.

In the week since her escape, the Canadian had been glued to the news. Fortunately the narrative played out per the template she'd set in motion. Grieving father Karl Sandin took bitter vengeance against a well-to-do family that Sandin believed had done him wrong and against a politician that Sandin believed had betrayed him. Sandin's suicide note had been leaked to the press, including his confession of having personally killed TJ Aadalen. The death at the Lynchburg Quality Inn was attributed to Sandin's silent partner—the hired assassin who had aided Sandin in his elimination of both Senator Taylor Brockman and Colin Aadalen, the new CEO of Aadalen Pharmaceuticals. The FBI, however, was more tight-lipped about the case. The bureau stated only that they were "extremely saddened by the sudden loss of a highly treasured member of our team," but offered "no further comment at this point in time as the case remains an ongoing investigation."

And though the Canadian learned about the woman she'd been forced to kill at the Lynchburg motel—FBI Special Agent Elizabeth Preston—and about the other local police detectives littered about the scene, the stories in the newspapers and on TV failed to reference the name of Preston's FBI-agent partner who'd also been present at the motel, even though he'd survived a third-floor plummet and had been the only one at the scene that morning to discharge a weapon.

That ate away at the Canadian. Finally, at midweek, she'd launched a browser and logged into the fake e-mail account. She entered a coded request and saved the e-mail in the Drafts folder. The e-mail message asked for a special favor and that in return for this favor, the Canadian would shave a point off the fee on her next assignment. She asked her agent in Bern to utilize his sources in order to bring her data on Agent Preston's partner—the man who'd been with her in Lynchburg that morning.

A day later the Canadian had her response in a coded dossier that was identical in format to the useful data passed along to her with each new work assignment. After decoding the information and committing it to memory, the Canadian deleted the e-mail text and then entered a one-sentence coded response informing the agent in Bern of a new e-mail account that had just been set up—this time in Yahoo. The Canadian saved this final e-mail in the Drafts folder and exited the fake account. After her agent deleted the e-mail draft, and then deleted it from the Trash folder, neither of them would ever return to the e-mail account, an account which within its short life cycle had never sent nor received an e-mail.

The FBI agent's name was Drew Cady and he'd had an active career, most of it spent in the FBI's Criminal Investigative Division, but he was now assigned to the Medicare Fraud Strike Force in Minneapolis.

Unfortunately the dossier failed to explain how Agent Cady wound up working the Senator Brockman case, but it did contain an address where Cady currently lived and, for the most part, worked out of . . . a resort owned by his wife in a pimple-size city in northern Minnesota called Cohasset. A brief section of the report highlighted Cady's time in CID, which removed any doubt from the Canadian's mind about her decision to take Cady out less she spend her future looking over her shoulder.

That morning the Canadian had placed an order with her man in Manila, a new batch of IDs would be heading her way within the week. That was good because the Labor Day Weekend was nearly upon them. She had no idea about Cady's role in the bureau's "ongoing investigation," but considering his recent wounds, the Canadian figured he'd be at home on Bass Lake licking them over the long holiday weekend.

And she'd be there to greet him.

Since the Canadian was her own client this go-round, she needn't worry about performing anything elaborate. No fires or drownings or rigged suicides to complicate matters this time.

What do the shrinks say? Confront your demons?

The Canadian figured she'd rent a boat, fake fish near Sundown Point Resort, and wait for Agent Cady to stroll out on one of the resort's many docks. And when Cady did—she'd confront her demons all right—she'd motor the boat over, let the man from the FBI get a good look at her in his final second of life and then say to him, "Remember me?" before planting two in his face . . . just like he'd tried to do to her.

CHAPTER 48

Day 20

*D*ear *FBI Tipline,*

It is impossible to watch TV these days without being bombarded with updates on the murders of Senator Taylor Brockman and the two Aadalen brothers. Although it appears that the person responsible for those heinous acts has confessed and committed suicide—and it's likely my tip has nothing to do with the case—I would be remiss if I didn't share my piece of information with you as it has been rattling about my brain ever since the untimely demise of Colin Aadalen, whom we all know was the chief executive officer of Aadalen Pharmaceuticals.

In June of this year I played eighteen holes at Hampshire Greens in Silver Spring, Maryland. My golfing partners had wives waiting with dinner, but I had time to kill so I went into the clubhouse and grabbed a stool at the bar. I struck up a conversation with a gentleman next to me and then began boring him about my new Mercedes E-Class that I'd bought that month. As it turned out, the gentleman was also interested in luxury cars and started bragging about how he'd gotten a "knockout deal" on his BMW X5. Turns out he'd bought it used off "some rich guy." It wasn't even a year old, had all the bells and whistles, and had only 4,000 on the odometer.

I'd priced BMWs before going with my E-Class so I knew the ballpark of what an X5 was worth, so I asked the gentleman what kind of deal he'd gotten. My drinking companion mumbled a price. I didn't want to hurt his feelings, but I had a couple of gin and tonics in me by this point and I mumbled something back about how he had paid practically what the X5 was worth, especially considering how, unlike other vehicles, BMWs hold their value once you drive them off the lot.

My new friend looked at me and said, "I used my cash stash."

I was confused. No one uses cash anymore and yanking nearly 60K out of the bank seems a bit of a hassle in these times so I slurred some question marks in his direction.

He winked at me and repeated, "I used my cash stash."

I let it lay. We had another drink and talked about golf and politics and work. We even exchanged business cards.

I'd hit my limit, but he begged me to stay and have one more with him, saying we'd each toast to our new cars. I figured what the hell and ordered a final gin and tonic. We tinked glasses to my Mercedes E-Class. I took a small sip, but my new friend tossed back his shot of vodka and waved the bartender over for another.

Then we toasted his BMW. He put away his final shot of vodka; at this point he was clearly feeling no pain. But, and this is the part that's been haunting me since the news of Colin Aadalen's death, my clubhouse companion lifted his beer chaser and announced, "To Aadalen Pharmaceuticals."

"Huh?" I asked.

"To Aadalen Pharmaceuticals," the man repeated.

Confused, but too buzzed or apathetic to sort it out, I raised my gin and tonic and said, "To Aadalen Pharmaceuticals."

I mentioned we had exchanged business cards. After hearing the recent news of Colin Aadalen's murder, I dug through the card drawer in my home office until I found the one my Hampshire Greens' drinking partner had handed me that June night.

His name is Elliot Kettler and he works at the Center for Drug Evaluation and Research in the US Food and Drug Administration.

You see, after reading about Colin Aadalen's murder in the Washington Post, *I recalled my evening spent overimbibing with a stranger in the clubhouse at Hampshire Greens. It struck me as odd how an FDA chemist would use a "cash stash" to buy a nearly new BMW. And though my drinking companion was several exits past blotto, it also struck me as odd to find us tossing back toasts to a random pharmaceutical company.*

I apologize for not including my name, but I'm in an executive position at a major financial institution and, quite frankly, I don't care to be dragged into a murder investigation because I had drinks with an alcoholic two months ago.

I've told you everything I know about that June night at Hampshire Greens. It may mean absolutely nothing . . . but do with it what you may . . .

"That never happened," Elliot Kettler protested. "And I'm not an alcoholic."

"Elliot," Oliver Price said, holding a palm up to his client, "no more. Say nothing. Don't move, don't breathe. This *man*," Price pointed across the table at Agent Zeke Wallace, "is not your friend."

"I can't help what comes across the tipline." Wallace looked as though his feelings had been shattered. The trio sat in a conference room in the Hoover Building. Wallace on one side of the table, Kettler and his lawyer the other side. Wallace pointed back at Price. "And when this came to my attention, I communicated through you per your stated request at our last meeting."

"Of course, the *infamous* tipline," Price said slowly. "Funny how this lead didn't come in through your online form, which could be tracked. It's also funny how this lead didn't call your tipline number, which could be recorded. No," Price said, rolling his eyes, "this lead is mailed in *anonymously*."

"Mailing has always been an option," Wallace replied. "But you're right; the anonymous nature tends to send up a red flag. Anonymous tips are oftentimes some jerk dicking with a despised colleague or a neighbor or an in-law. That's why I asked you to come in today. So we could clear this up and have you both on your way in five minutes."

Oliver Price tilted his head and returned Wallace's stare.

Wallace turned his gaze to Kettler. "Have you ever been to Hampshire Greens?"

Price placed his palm a second time in front of his client.

"You're not making this easy," Wallace said to Price.

Silence ensued.

Wallace shrugged. "As you wish. It was a rhetorical question anyway." Wallace looked at his yellow notepad. "You play golf at Hampshire an average of three times a month during the season, but I see that you were there four times this past June." Wallace flipped a page. "And by and large it appears that you end up in the clubhouse after eighteen holes."

Price's features reddened. Kettler's whitened.

"So my client plays golf at the course nearest his home," Price responded. "So what?"

"You may want to find another golf course," Wallace said, looking at Kettler. "I think you pissed someone off at Hampshire." Wallace flipped another page in his legal pad, read for a second, and then looked up. "I must admit that after reading that tip, I surfed the BMW X5 online and . . . holy shit . . . I'd give my left nut for that SUV, or I think BMW calls it an SAV—a Sport Activity Vehicle." Wallace shook his head and sighed. "But I'd never get it past my wife, though; it'd swallow our entire nest egg in one gulp. No college for the kiddies."

"Is this going anywhere?" Price asked.

"There's no need to be uncivil," Wallace said, again looking hurt. "Remember, I communicated through you per your stated request at our last meeting."

"Elliot and I would be forever grateful if you could possibly move the meeting along," Price replied. "We have a tee time at Hampshire Greens in an hour."

"Touché," Wallace said and chuckled. "I knew you had a sense of humor. Hey, anyone ever say you look like Peter Lorre?"

Price answered Wallace's query by glancing at his watch.

"He may have been a tad before your time." Wallace refocused on Kettler. "The quickest way to put this anonymous tipline lead and its allegation of a *cash stash* in the rearview mirror would be for you to boot up your bank account," Wallace said and spun his laptop to face the FDA chemist, "and show me the monthly payment for the X5 or the cash withdrawal from when you purchased the vehicle."

"My client will be doing no such thing," Price said, shifting about in his chair.

"But that'll put this specious accusation behind us and I'll buy you both a Pepsi on the way out," Wallace replied. "Look, Elliot, Oliver and I will turn around so we can't see your login or password."

"My client will be doing no such thing," Price repeated, again shifting in his chair, "without a court order or search warrant."

"A search warrant?" Wallace's grin lit up the room as he reached into the manila file beneath his yellow tablet. "Funny you should bring that up."

CHAPTER 49

"I'm back," Wallace informed the room. "The streak continues."

"We got Kettler?" Jund asked.

Cady and Wallace sat in the director's office, across from Jund. It was late afternoon and Wallace was ecstatic.

The bureau's interrogator nodded. "When I informed the two that we in fact had acquired a search warrant for Kettler's Silver Spring home, the chemist turned to jelly. His mouth was quivering like I just stole his lollipop." Wallace laughed. "I let them have the room to discuss the situation and went to use the restroom and grab a drink of water. I'm gone maybe five minutes—maybe five—but I hear a commotion on my way back. Kettler's outside the room, standing in the hallway now and yelling for me. 'Zeke,' Kettler's calling and pointing back in the room, 'Zeke, he wants me to take the fall. He wants me to take the fall.'"

Wallace chuckled again.

Cady wished he could partake in the interrogator's glee, but all he could think about was how he was sitting in the chair Liz had been in the last time they'd met in Jund's office.

"What happened then?" asked Jund.

"I separate them like I'm the principal at recess. I took Kettler aside and asked him if he wanted to fire Price. And Kettler screams 'Yes!' about eight times. So I get him into another conference room and tell him to call his brother-in-law or whoever the hell he now wants for counsel."

"What did you do with Price?"

"I walked him out of Hoover. We don't say a thing on the way down, but his nonverbals are all over the place, like water on a skillet. Price is starting to realize he may have fucked himself. In the lobby, as he's on his way out the revolving door, I say to him, 'Don't leave town,' just like that, as though I'm Marshal Dillon. Now I'm messing with his head because I'm still a little miffed at how our initial meeting played out. Yes," Wallace said, looked from Jund to Cady, "I am that small. Anyway Price gives me a vacant look and nods as though he's agreeing to stay in DC, but I can tell his thoughts are an ocean away."

"Are we able to walk back the bribe?" Jund asked. "Find Kettler's mystery man?"

"Mystery man met Kettler on the first day of a biologics symposium held at the Embassy Row Hotel early last December. Mystery man said his name was *Phil Anderson*," Wallace said, "perhaps a touch less generic than John Smith, I suppose. Surprisingly, the two wound up in most of the same lectures and by the end of the week they were as thick as thieves. In later weeks they met a few times for food or drinks, and it was at a lunch in mid-January that Phil Anderson put his cards on the table, asking Kettler how much it would cost for him to resume Roark Larson's work on Neurzamine at the FDA, but instead push through its NDA. Kettler claims he was scared shitless as he'd met Anderson before Larson's *alleged* suicide. In other words, Kettler's claiming he was terrorized into accepted the money."

"How'd he wind up with Oliver Price?"

"We just about had him on the line last week, but he called the number Anderson had given him and left a message. An hour later Anderson calls him back and tells Kettler to go meet with Price—all expenses paid."

"Can we track the phone to the mystery man?"

"Already on it but so far no pings," Cady replied. "It's likely a burner picked up for the mystery man to use only with Kettler. Quite frankly, I'd bet it sunk to the bottom of the Potomac five minutes after Oliver Price spoke to his source at Aadalen Pharmaceuticals."

"We need to brace Price," Jund said. "He's AP's hired gun, and we need to make disbarment the least of his concerns."

"That may take some time," Wallace said. "I had him on his heels, but Price'll cobble together some bullshit—say that he took Kettler on as a walk-in, say that Kettler was confused about the billing process."

"Stay on him," Jund said to Wallace and leaned back in his chair. "This was a good day's work, gentlemen." The director looked Cady's way. "Kettler's not the first idiot to be caught by bragging to a stranger."

"It was a rookie move by a rookie lawbreaker," Wallace said. "Shit like this was so much easier in our grandparents' generation. Back in the day, if grandpa pulls into the rest area only to find dead mobsters and a briefcase full of hundred-dollar bills, gramps runs it straight to the bank. Hell, the tellers would help him smear off the blood and give him a few free toasters. Nowadays, with drug cartels and terrorists, you have to hide the briefcase in your basement and use the cash for all your shopping needs."

"Kettler never should have bought that BMW."

"Actually," Wallace said, "buying used from a third party isn't such a bad idea. He just shouldn't have gotten blitzed and shot his mouth off. After Kettler sold his old car on craigslist, he only should have shuffled in ten or fifteen grand from the *cash stash* and bought a nice set of wheels but not something so in-your-face big dollars. Let's say some guy's selling a midlevel car that for all practical purposes is new, you show up and kick the tires, take it for a test drive, grumble a bit to shave off a few hundred, and then tell the guy you're going to the bank to get the cash and that you'll be back in an hour, but you go grab a beer instead to kill some time." Wallace thought for a second. "If anyone started questioning me about throwing around cash, I'd say it's my blackjack winnings. Come to think of it, I could go to the casino and sit at a progressive jackpot and feed the bribe money into the slot machine until I actually won something big."

"I can't believe I'm being dragged into this conversation, but I'd go the antique route," Jund said. "Buy high-end antiques with the cash, take pictures of them in different rooms of my house, and then turn around and sell them off. I'd say I inherited the American Colonial George III table from nana after the cancer got her, and the Philadelphia Sterling silverware from 1860 came from Aunt Gladys before she passed in '78. I'd mock up an Excel sheet for tax purposes and tell everyone I'm finding good homes for all my historic artifacts since I'm downsizing my nest now that the kids are gone."

"I see you've been giving that a lot of thought," Wallace said, "haven't you, Director?"

CHAPTER 50

"You know how they hunt ermine?" Leahy asked.

"What the hell's an ermine?" Cady asked back.

It was ten o'clock at night and the two stood in Leahy's kitchen. Cady sipped water from a cup he hoped had been washed at least once since the last presidential election. Leahy was on his eighth Mountain Dew of the day.

"It's a stoat, basically a short-tailed weasel," Leahy replied. "Anyway they scatter salt on the snow and then when the ermine comes out, it keeps licking away at the salt until the little fucker's tongue freezes to the ice."

"Charming."

"Not that I've been stewing over it, but that's how you caught me. I kept licking away at the salt and suddenly there you were."

"I think you were licking away at cheese fries."

"And now you've utilized that bullshit tipline to snare the chemist, to freeze his tongue to the ice," Leahy said, realizing that his cyber-procto exam on

286

all things Elliot Kettler would never blow back on him. "That's genius, Cady. That's goddamned genius."

"Kettler's small fry. He goes with Aadalen Pharmaceuticals' pattern of corruption, but I need the guy who set the pattern."

"Yeah, but Kettler's the turd in the punch bowl that screws the rest of them."

"They'll take on water," Cady said. "We'll get them on the bribe, but Aadalen Pharmaceuticals will deny Roark Larson's murder and that case will get mired down because Larson's suicide was staged so well. Probably by the same person who killed Liz. AP's PR team will jump up and down about how the charges are horribly wrong, and how they're working around the clock with law enforcement to ferret out the rogue at AP responsible for bribing Kettler, and how the ends never justify the means, but they'll also broadcast how they've got this brand new Alzheimer's drug that they need to get to market in order to relieve so much human suffering," Cady continued. "Hell, a year from now—after the fines have been paid and the stocks have rebounded and after some midlevel sacrificial lamb takes the hit on the payoff—they'll be back where they are today . . . and we'll never know who set it all in motion."

"Remember the speech you gave me at Hoover that first day?" Leahy crushed his empty soda can and tossed it in the sink. "About my superiors' superiors?"

Cady nodded.

"If my superiors' superiors catch wind of what I've been up to, there will be a cage in the ground with my nameplate on it," Leahy said. "That part's not bullshit."

"No matter what happens," Cady said, "I'll lead them away."

"Does anyone else know what we're doing?"

Cady shook his head.

"Director Jund?"

"He's not asking and I'm not telling," Cady replied. "Like I told you—anything happens—I'll lead them away."

Leahy stared at Cady as though he were driving past a four-car pileup. "Jesus Christ, Cady—the Samson option. You're going to take it all down even if a block of stone lands on your own head."

"I have no idea what you're talking about."

"We should hit the computers," Leahy said, staring at Cady for another second. "Let's go find your next pillar."

CHAPTER 51

Day 23

"Get down here now." Detective Walsh's voice over the phone sounded like if he'd been in the room, he'd have grabbed Cady by the lapels.

"What the hell's going on?" Cady replied into his cell.

"Something came in that may blow this fucker wide open."

"What's that?"

"A whistleblower."

"I'll be there in two hours."

"Make it one."

"Holy Christ," Jund said. When Cady told the director that Richmond PD had a game changer, Jund had his administrative assistant cancel all afternoon meetings and came along for the ride. "All this showed up in your mail?"

Agent Cady, Director Jund, Detective Walsh, Richmond Police Chief Alfred Lanham and a prosecuting attorney named Ted Shaner sat in a closed conference room for privacy.

The Richmond detective nodded. "Inside an Aadalen Pharmaceuticals' envelope no less."

"Anyone with a printer could rig that address logo on an envelope," Cady said.

"It was mailed from Richmond," Walsh replied.

"Visiting a post office is not an impossible feat."

"Don't shit on the parade," Chief Lanham piped in. "Read the goddamned documents."

Director Jund handed Cady six transparent evidence bags. Three contained documents, another contained a screenshot of a server accessed by top executives only, with one particular folder open and its list of corresponding files on full display, one contained the envelope in which the documents were mailed, and the last one, which Cady read first, was the cover page.

Dear Detective Walsh,

I work in the IT department at Aadalen Pharmaceuticals. As you are most certainly aware, my employer has been in a state of crisis since our Chief Executive Officer Colin Aadalen was murdered in a downtown Richmond bar two weeks ago. Yesterday we found out that the Food and Drug Administration's Center for Drug Evaluation and Research has rescinded our New Drug Application for Neurzamine. In my eighteen years at Aadalen Pharmaceuticals I have never heard of the FDA withdrawing a passed NDA, but today's headline in the New York Times *screams about a CDER official having been paid off by AP. AP's stock price is in free-fall and my colleagues and I are left wondering if any of us will have jobs this time next week. With that framework in mind, I did something I would never before have contemplated. In our IT department, I have access and the ability to acquire additional access to areas outside of my domain. I am also aware of the various private servers utilized by executive leadership (screenshot of one such server, including files and subfolders, is enclosed).*

I have also enclosed two sheets from a single Microsoft Excel file that I came across while inappropriately accessing one of the executive drives (exact location noted in screenshot). The name of the Excel file is disexledge.xlsx (file noted in screenshot). Though no title exists on the spreadsheet itself, I infer from the file name that it is a discretionary expense ledger, and that it tracks the costs for nonessential items or services of some nature. The separate sheets along the bottom of the Excel document are labeled per four alphanumeric characters—the first two digits indicating a fiscal quarter and the last two digits indicating its corresponding year.

Though column headers are absent, each quarterly sheet contains what appears to be a column of bank transaction numbers with corresponding columns for dates and amounts. There is a fourth column that only exhibits data in a handful of rows. The sporadic fourth row data appears to be two capital letters that may or may not relate to a person's initials and that may or may

*not coincide with the transactions and dates
contained in the other columns. For example, the
initials RL appear in a row that correlates with
a December transaction in the sheet covering the
fourth quarter from last year (note first sheet) and
the initials EK appear in a row associated with
a February transaction in the first quarter sheet
for this year (note second sheet). Perhaps your
forensic accountants can make heads or tails out
of this data as well as identify what executive
leadership hands it passed through.*

*The third document discusses the plan of
succession after Colin Aadalen's death, detailing
the transition of power. No great shakes there
as, even in tragedy, Aadalen Pharmaceuticals
must move forward. That was my thought until
I went into the document's properties and noted
that its creation date and time stamp were set for
the afternoon of Colin Aadalen's death. That is,
this succession/transition document was created
several hours before Aadalen's murder in the
Omni Richmond Hotel bar.*

*Although I'm not an attorney, I assume what
I have done would, at a minimum, result in
the termination of my employment at Aadalen
Pharmaceuticals. I imagine it could likely
involve my being subject to lawsuits as well as
potential criminal proceedings, which is why I
am submitting these documents anonymously. I
apologize and understand how my hacking may
not be admissible evidence to be utilized in court,*

but perhaps, Detective Walsh, your verification of the evidence I'm presenting to you will be admissible in court as well as lead to additional evidence.

Sincerely,
AP IT

"This allows us to seize their computers," Shaner said. The prosecuting attorney had premature gray hair that likely helped whenever he stood before juries. "I'll have a court order by the end of day."

"We've been living at Aadalen Pharmaceuticals since Kettler came clean," Jund told the gathering. "Acting CEO Langdon Trutwin has been most amenable, getting us answers to all our questions, walking us through org charts, pointing us at Human Resources and Security. The man's in CYA mode; he's hoping to weather the storm and keep the company together, but, after this . . . I don't think all the king's horses would have much luck."

"I don't know," Cady said. "How can an anonymous informant be credible? It could be an employee with a vendetta."

"We get handed a break on a goddamned platter and you're all sunlight and pixie dust." Chief Lanham looked moments away from testing his Taser gun on Special Agent Cady.

"Drew," Jund said, his eyes lingering on Cady for several seconds. "This is great news no matter how it was obtained."

"I'm just playing devil's advocate."

"We got probable cause and reasonable suspicion from the Supremes in Illinois versus Gates
and," prosecuting attorney Shaner took a moment to
search his memory, "Alabama versus White. We cor-
roborate that information"—Shaner pointed at the
evidence bags in Cady's hands—"and I have Aadalen
Pharmaceuticals' tit in my wringer. I'll get a grand
jury to indict and we can put this fucker to rest."

CHAPTER 52

Day 24

"You're awfully quiet," the prosecuting attorney noted.

"I'm taking it all in, trying to *be* in the moment." As acting CEO of Aadalen Pharmaceuticals it was now officially his office, but Langdon Trutwin sat in the same spot on the leather couch where he'd sat when Agents Cady and Preston had first come to visit Colin Aadalen. Trutwin wore a dark gray suit and cobalt-blue tie, his silver hair complemented a perfect tan, and though ten minutes earlier he'd been served a court order granting Richmond PD access to his PC, Trutwin didn't appear to have a care in the world. He had a left leg draped over his knee and an arm atop the back of the sofa. One didn't become general counsel at a Fortune 500 if one turned wobbly at the drop of a hat. "I've never had a speeding ticket much less been accused of murder before."

Cady leaned against a wall, arms crossed, taking it all in himself. A CFE—computer forensic examiner—from the FBI sat with his counterpart from Richmond PD at Trutwin's desk, both hunched over Trutwin's

computer, both staring intently at Trutwin's monitor. Director Jund stood behind the computer gurus,
peering down, as though he were a subject-matter
expert himself. Detective Walsh sat as far away from
Trutwin as the office sofa would permit. Ted Shaner
stood before the acting CEO.

"I'd have thought you'd have had more to say,"
Prosecutor Shaner replied.

"Is that what you'd advise a client to do? Prattle
on endlessly to the authorities?" Trutwin looked up
at Shaner. "Tsk-Tsk-Tsk."

"I would think you would be taking this more
seriously."

"You're disappointed because both my first and
second reaction to this French farce was laughter.
Quite frankly, part of me feels as though I'm being put
on, as though this is an elaborate April Fools' prank
by some impish members of the board of directors,
yet you think I should be taking this more seriously?
Perhaps I should overpower you and make a break
for my car, run off to live in the mountains, eating
fish and wild berries." Trutwin uncrossed his leg.
"I apologize, Mr. Shaner, but having been immersed
in the study of law for more than five decades, I've
moved on to plotting recourse."

"Plotting recourse?"

"I've bent over backward this past week to work
hand-in-hand with the Federal Bureau of Investigation over allegations that some cretin at Aadalen
Pharmaceuticals was dim enough to bribe the FDA.
On its face it's a cockamamie scheme—and I'm the
person paid, and paid well, to kick anyone's ass who
presents cockamamie schemes—but we're a gigantic

company with a lot of moving parts, so I have been an open book with the FBI. I've gone out of my way to cooperate, no matter how absurd I've found many of their requests. Meanwhile our reputation has been dragged through the mud, our stock has been flushed twice down the toilet, and our very future in the pharmaceutical industry is uncertain, and beyond the truly tragic events that have plagued us this past month, beyond all of that, I understand that Neurzamine—a wonder drug that would alleviate suffering on an unheard of scale, that would save lives—has been yanked from the market. Neurzamine's death is the homicide that no one seems to care about." Trutwin leaned back on the sofa. "So, yes, Mr. Shaner, I am most certainly plotting recourse."

"Good luck with that," Shaner replied. "A whistleblower finds incriminating evidence on your personal computer and *you're* plotting recourse."

"I'm not sure your terminology is correct. Can an anonymous and malicious hacker be called a whistleblower?" Trutwin scratched at a cheek. "And if an anonymous and malicious hacker can break into a computer system, I assume that same anonymous and malicious hacker can add his or her own files or tamper with existing documents within that network system."

Shaner pointed at the forensic examiners. "They'll be able to educate a jury on the life cycle of a document, and whether it's been tampered with or not."

"Assuming all this makes it to a jury." Trutwin chuckled softly. "They cover the exclusionary rule at that online law school you attended? Hearsay . . .

prejudicial evidence . . . illegally obtained evidence . . . any of those terms ring a bell?"

Shaner responded to Trutwin's taunts by turning about, marching toward the floor-to-ceiling windows, and gazing outside. Cady watched the two computer experts, who were now quietly whispering.

"Agent Cady," Trutwin said.

Cady turned his attention toward Aadalen Pharmaceuticals' chief executive officer.

"It's the silent ones that frighten me," Trutwin continued, "and you've yet to say a single word."

"I'm just here to see what they find," Cady replied.

"Are you really?" Trutwin said. "When you last visited, my friend, I recall requesting that you *kindly govern yourself accordingly.* I'm not so sure you've been doing that."

Cady refused to take the bait and turned his attention back toward the computer forensic examiners who were now looking about the executive office and nodding their heads.

CHAPTER 53

"I like my villains with a little less champagne," Jund said.

They were now in Prosecutor Shaner's office. Police Chief Lanham and Director Jund commandeered the seats across the desk from Shaner as though they were visiting dignitaries. Walsh and another Richmond detective named Stubbe took cushioned armchairs along one wall, and Cady rolled a chair in from an adjacent conference room.

"Trutwin's a slick one all right," Walsh replied.

"The man's making bond as we speak, which must set some kind of record." Shaner squeezed at a stress ball and laid out the road map. "We'll see him again tomorrow at his first appearance, which is where the judge sets the case for the preliminary hearing and will likely take place in two or three weeks. The prelim will be a minitrial over whether the evidence supports our charge against Trutwin, whether there's *probable cause* that Trutwin committed the offense charged. That's why between now and the preliminary hearing, everyone works overtime to shore up the evidence in case the exclusionary rules swing Trutwin's way." Shaner added restless leg syndrome to his squeeze ball repertoire. "At this stage we pray the case is sent on to Circuit Court—where I can prima facie case it with the grand jury. And if those eight souls decide there's enough evidence, if those eight souls decide we've hit the standard of probable cause—they'll return an indictment. Clearly Langdon Trutwin's going to plead not guilty at the arraignment and that, my friends, means we fasten our seat belts for a jury trial."

"Don't sweat the early stage," Jund, a juris doctor himself, replied. "I've heard tell you state guys can indict a ham sandwich."

"Grand juries are prosecutor-friendly, some call them a rubber stamp," Shaner said with a squeeze of the ball and tap of the foot. "The level of proof needed for an indictment is not nearly as high as we're going to need for a conviction, but remember, we're talking about a man who's been general counsel at Aadalen Pharmaceuticals since I was in the fifth grade. We're talking about a man who knows the justices on the Supreme Court of Virginia on a first-name basis—they dine and golf together. We're talking about a man who has the governor on speed dial." Squeeze ball, foot tap. "And I guarantee you that if it comes to trial—if we squeak by the prelim—we'll need a *substantial* amount of proof to get a conviction. Substantial. What we have now won't cut it. And you can bet Trutwin will be there at every juncture and twist in the road. The man will most certainly fight us at the hearing. The man will also demand to present evidence at the grand jury." Squeeze ball, foot tap. "The son of a bitch is going to fight us every step of the way. He's going to be a thorn in my side from here on out, big time." Squeeze ball, foot tap.

"You will have our full cooperation," Director Jund said, looking from the prosecutor to Cady, and then back at Shaner. "*Mi casa es su casa.*"

Shaner nodded. "Like I said, everyone in this room needs to give me anything they've got as soon as they've got it, because Trutwin's going to try for a toss under the Fourth Amendment. And if the judge agrees, decides our search was *somehow* illegal—we're fucked—the evidence gets suppressed and our case flies out the window. Trutwin's going to push prejudicial evidence. Trutwin will try to get our proof excluded, he'll say its probative value is undermined by the threat of unfair prejudice or misleading the jury." Shaner's ball squeeze and foot tap returned in play. "Trutwin's going to muddy the water, he's going to create an avalanche of reasonable doubt in order to skate. Who is this anonymous and malicious informant who cracked into the executive network drive at Aadalen Pharmaceuticals? What are his or her motives for doing such? How do we know this anonymous shadow didn't tinker with the data on that network drive? What kind of judicial system do we live in where I'm not entitled to question my accuser?" Shaner's ball squeeze and foot tap built to a crescendo. "Or . . . or if Trutwin doesn't get evidence tossed, he blames the dead man. 'The Excel sheet of discretionary payoffs was Colin Aadalen's document,' he'll say. 'I glanced at it a couple of times out of curiosity, but I figured my nephew was probably pricing ski chalets in France.'"

"You may want to audit his credit card purchases over the last year or two," Cady said, "see if he's made any *unique* purchases. Our financial analysts are tracking the account numbers and should have something for us by the prelim. Perhaps we can tie any trips he may have taken overseas to the country where this bank account exists. Grand Caymans? Switzerland? Wherever."

"That works for airline flights," Chief Lanham said, "but for other purchases, doesn't Visa or whatever card just list a date, store, and total amount?"

"You can contact most major stores with the card number and date of purchase," Cady replied. "The store can then look up past purchases made on that account."

Agent Cady knew something that the others in attendance did not. Trutwin's credit cards already had been vetted by the man from the NSA's Office of Tailored Access Operations and, except for the periodic purchase of a disposable cell phone or two, Trutwin's personal expenses had been given a clean bill of health. However, the purchase dates on the throwaway phones more or less lined up with at least half of the dates for the transactions listed on the Excel sheet from the executive network drive. His latest pay-as-you-go cell phone purchase came the day after Senator Brockman's murder. Sure, it was circumstantial evidence, but it would cause Langdon Trutwin a modicum of discomfort as he attempted to clarify to twelve angry men how he'd purchased these throwaways to be used as gifts or placed in the glove compartments of his vehicles in case of breakdowns on the Virginia highways, but that he kept misplacing them and that these throwaway cell phones were most certainly at no time ever utilized to orchestrate, say, an extramarital affair or murder-for-hire endeavor.

Cady had only met the prosecuting attorney the previous day, but it was palpable that much of the air had been let out of his tires after his brief tête-â-tête with Trutwin in Trutwin's corner office at Aadalen Pharmaceuticals. This new evidence regarding the burner phones might serve to get Prosecuting Attorney Ted Shaner back up on his feet, to put the calcium back in his vertebrae. Who knows—the prosecutor might even let go of the stress ball. Cady liked the man and was glad Shaner was sweating the *big* stuff.

The man was no fool.

Cady felt his cell phone vibrate. He slipped it from his pocket and noted the caller ID. He stood and stepped quietly to the door, making sure to shut it on his way out. Cady walked several yards before answering the call.

"I got her, Cady." Leahy was jubilant. "I got Reddon."

CHAPTER 54

Day 28

"I'd like to request the use of a firearm," Cady said.

"You're here as an observer only," Toronto Chief of Police Mark Sayers replied. "Your role is to identify Willa Reddon once our ETF has taken her down."

Director Jund sat across from Sayers in the chief's office in the Toronto Police Headquarters on College Street. In a chair next to Jund sat Deputy Chief Jim Everling. Everling was in charge of Specialized Operations Command and, as such, worked hand-in-hand with ETF—the Emergency Task Force. Cady remained standing as he was about to depart for the fifty-five-story skyscraper in which Willa Reddon aka Patricia Johnson aka Marzy Doats had been tracked by the cyber agents in the FBI's Cyber Division.

Cady and Jund had landed at Toronto Pearson late the previous evening. A little more than six hours later, at first light, the two were meeting with Chief Sayers and Deputy Chief Everling at an upscale coffee shop a stone's throw from police headquarters. The chief and deputy chief looked as though they could be related—both midsize, wiry, midfifties with receding hairlines and politician handshakes.

Jund had been on the horn with one or both of them for much of the past two days and, upon meeting in person, it was like a mini family reunion . . . when schmoozers meet schmoozers.

Cady sipped at his dark roast and listened until it was time for them to migrate to the chief's office and meet with ETF.

Sayers had a big office, which worked out okay because the back half of the room currently housed a team of nine gentlemen in street clothes. The men stood quietly holding duffel bags. They had arrived early from their Don Mills station in the North York district of the city and looked as though they'd be equally comfortable playing rugby as they would fighting on whatever passed for the latest front line in Afghanistan. The men were members of the Emergency Task Force—the tactical unit of the Toronto Police Service or TPS. Their gear remained in their bags as it wouldn't be terribly wise to have them storm Reddon's condominium dressed as what they were—the Canadian equivalent of Special Weapons and Tactics or SWAT.

"Reddon has seen my face and if anything goes wrong, I'd hate to be naked."

"But you'll be in the van," Deputy Chief Everling said.

"I went over the plan with Staff Sergeant Hartman." Cady glanced at the ETF leader and walked to the first-floor blueprint, one of many taped to the chief's wall. "I am to come in the condo's rear security-only entrance. When the sergeant radios me an all clear, I walk head down the eight feet from this security door," Cady pointed at the diagram, "to the door to the southern stairwell. That'll take me all of two seconds. Then I hike up the steps until I'm a couple flights above Reddon's place—her suite being on the twenty-second floor." Cady pointed at the neighboring blueprint of Reddon's unit. "I wait in the upper stairwell until the sergeant lets me know that Reddon has been taken into custody. At that point I enter the twenty-second floor from the stairwell and jog to Reddon's condo to confirm her identity—that she is in fact the woman who attacked us in Lynchburg."

The takedown had been planned for when Willa Reddon was at the door of her suite, if possible, out of concern for whatever firepower she may have hidden inside her unit. No sense in granting Reddon even the slimmest of possibilities of accessing any heavy artillery she may have stashed there.

"Special Agent Cady is one of my finest," Director Jund said, staring from the Toronto chief of police and then to his deputy chief. "He will not abuse the privilege."

Police Chief Sayers shrugged. Deputy Chief Everling looked at Sergeant Hartman and nodded. Hartman zipped open his gear bag, stirred about its innards for a second, fished out a holstered Glock 19, walked over, and handed it to Agent Cady.

"Don't make me regret this," Hartman said. The sergeant—six four, two-twenty, no smile lines—was a man who any rational human being would do anything and everything to shelter from disappointment.

Cady nodded and checked the magazine.

"Remember, men," Sergeant Hartman addressed his fellow ETF officers, "per their Intel," he motioned at Director Jund and Cady, "she has made a career out of being paid beaucoup bucks to off people. Reddon's been doing this for years—likely since her discharge from the Canadian army—and she's skilled at it. That's not something we bump into every day, so watch your six." Hartman glanced at Cady, then ordered, "Let's roll."

"There's some kind of murder-for-hire hub in Bern, Switzerland," Leahy had told him as soon as Cady had arrived following his mad drive from Prosecutor Shaner's Richmond office to the hacking wizard's home in Odenton. "It's run in a similar manner that allowed us to track terrorists five or six years back, you know, following the money trail. One of the spokes out from our hub in Bern goes to a numbered bank account in Lebanon where it sits for about two seconds before being split evenly among numbered accounts in Singapore, Luxembourg, and another account back in Switzerland. Now the numbered accounts in Luxembourg and Switzerland, for the most part, sit dormant—gathering interest—but the account in Singapore acts as a kind of clearinghouse with yet another spoke that points us to someone nesting in Canada. You see, on the fifth of every month, 20,000 dollars—Canadian— are deposited into the Royal Bank of Canada."

Cady's jaw had dropped to his rib cage.

"And here's a breadcrumb trail for you to slip your financial analysts . . . to get them jump-started." Leahy had handed Cady a small piece of paper.

"Tell me you've got an address," had been the first words out of Cady's mouth.

Leahy had grinned from ear to ear.

CHAPTER 55

The condominium suite on the twenty-second floor was registered in the name of one Sierra Melichar, yet another alias utilized by Willa Reddon to help keep prying eyes misdirected. Sergeant Hartman had spent the previous afternoon networking with Cadence Security, the firm that handled safety measures at Reddon's high-rise. The security firm had paged the condo's onsite guards back to Cadence's office suite for an emergency ad hoc meeting, swapping the sentries out with temps, so the sergeant could question the guards about their service at the condominium high-rise without arousing suspicion. Though no one knew *Sierra Melichar* by name, the morning guard from the lobby desk recognized the image Hartman passed around Cadence's conference room that he'd gotten off Melichar's driver's license.

"I think she works later in the day," the complex's first-shift lobby guard had informed Hartman, "because she goes out jogging after rush hour on most mornings. She takes a monster jog, like, maybe an hour and a half," the guard had said, and looked again at the picture. "Her hair's not that long anymore."

And a plan was born.

ETF had a tenth man already on site, awaiting the group. The tenth man was sporting the standard gray suit jacket worn by all of Cadence Security's team of protectors-for-hire. He sat sipping coffee next to the morning sentinel who was the man who had shared the pertinent tip with Hartman. ETF's tenth man was, for all observable purposes, a new employee in training.

ETF could take Willa Reddon down on the street as she began her morning jaunt, but there would be no onlooker hustle and bustle in the twenty-second floor hallway outside Reddon's doorway upon her return home. It made good-enough sense and Cady would have been more than happy to grant his approval had Hartman asked, but Cady got the feeling that the real reason ETF wanted to grab Reddon in the hallway was because the burly men on Hartman's team wouldn't fancy any cell phone video—taken by some busybody passersby highlighting them forcing a pint-sized woman to the cement sidewalk—going viral on YouTube.

Quite frankly, had the ETF sergeant requested Cady's input, Cady would have strongly lobbied for taking Reddon into custody outside her unit upon her return from her late-morning trot. Of course Cady knew something that nobody else in Chief Sayers's office that morning knew. Leahy had discovered two things of additional interest on Reddon's laptop. First, her Google Earth history pointed toward a certain rustic resort in northern Minnesota and, second,

Reddon had been fanatical about tracking her work-out, itemizing the miles run on her morning jogs as well as listing the calories she burned by sprinting up the twenty-two flights of steps on the way back to her condo at the finish of most workouts.

And Cady would be there to greet her.

"There's something else you need to know," Leahy had told him, looking down and glancing sideways about the table.

"What's that?" Cady had asked.

"There was a recent transaction from her Singapore account to a numbered account in the Philippines. I just got around to tearing into that and it appears that there's a man in Manila who's making a big nut in counterfeit documentation, you know, passports and credit cards, driver's licenses—a one-stop shop, that kind of thing."

"A forger," Cady had replied. "He supplies Reddon with her IDs."

Leahy had nodded and said, "A lot of what he does is created with some state of the art imaging software and, as I dug deeper, I saw that he had begun work on a new set of IDs once the Singapore transaction was complete."

"It's her, right?"

Leahy had nodded again and said, "This is huge. I've rigged a program to run at TAO that'll make it look like I tripped over Manila while running another net. TAO can then dig into this guy's files and catch a lot of big-shot fuckwads. Maybe terrorists, maybe other killers like Reddon."

Cady had nodded his approval.

Leahy had kept looking about the room, avoiding eye contact.

"What aren't you telling me?" Cady had probed.

"This new ID of Reddon's," Leahy had said. "She's booked on a plane to Minneapolis the Thursday before Labor Day Weekend."

CHAPTER 56

The restraining order added insult to injury.

Langdon Trutwin—former CEO and general counsel of Aadalen Pharmaceuticals—leaned back in the teakwood lounge atop his back patio, took another sip from his mint julep, and reviewed the events of the day. After an exhausting back and forth regarding the pros and cons of his providing testimony in the preliminary hearing, his team of criminal defense attorneys had broken early for lunch. The consensus was that it would never come to that, that Trutwin's lawyers would be able to convince the judge that Richmond PD's search of the executive network drive at Aadalen Pharmaceuticals was, in fact, illegal, and that its highly suspect evidence based on a highly suspect anonymous informant needed to be suppressed from the pending case.

Trutwin's wife, not wanting to face either neighbors or the gossiping hens at church, had gone on an extended visit to her sister's in Roanoke. Hard to blame Margaret, though, treated as royalty one week, suited for a leper colony the next. However, the real reason Margaret bugged out for Roanoke was quite simple . . . she knew his moods. No matter how calm and collected, judicious, and self-effacing Trutwin appeared on the surface—for outsiders to consume . . . Margaret knew his moods. And right now, with the restraining order barring him from access to any Aadalen Pharmaceuticals' locations or facilities sitting on the table next to him, he was in a foul mood.

A cancerous mood.

A malignantly cancerous mood.

Trutwin had punched back at law enforcement, of course. Hard. He knew he had to use PR to help define the issue, to set the narrative lest he be run over by it. A longtime reporter friend at channel eleven had granted Trutwin a *friendly* interview, chock-full of softballs, allowing Trutwin to inform the viewing audience that: "It's two parts Orwell, one part Kafka, and entirely Lewis Carroll. The Richmond police along with their counterparts at the Federal Bureau of Investigation swoop down on Aadalen Pharmaceuticals to inform me that our network system has been compromised, and that it has been breached by a person or persons unknown. I'm trying to digest this information when suddenly I'm arrested based on breached documents that, evidently, implicate me in all manners of fantasy. I find myself in detention for crimes another man has already confessed to. It's pure Kafkaesque. In fact, the same authorities continue to search for the young female who aided Karl Sandin with his kill list. Now my eyesight may not be twenty-twenty," Trutwin had spoken into the microphone while pointing at his glasses for emphasis, "but the last time I looked in the mirror, I didn't appear to be a young woman."

The interview had come across so erudite and cutting that one of the cable networks—which always enjoy a good skirmish—had run with it as well. Let's see if Richmond Police Chief Alfred Lanham and CID Director Roland Jund need to use entire tubes of Preparation H to unwedge that from between their buttocks, Trutwin had thought. He would make them look like laughing stocks at the preliminary hearing.

They would rue the fucking day.

Trutwin's arrest, as surreal as it had been, had immediately led to his . . . ouster . . . for lack of a better word. Cathrin Aadalen had seized the reins at AP, which made perfect sense, and her first move as acting CEO had been to throw Aadalen Pharmaceuticals on the mercy of the apparatchiks at the Food and Drug Administration. It was a bright move— the only sensible move—on Cathrin's part. It was essentially the same route, albeit less subtle, that he'd been taking. Evidently, Cathrin's second official action was to have Trutwin served with this restraining order. It cut deep, but he couldn't blame Cathrin for that chess move. In fact, were their shoes on different feet and Trutwin still in a position to advise Cathrin, he'd have counseled her to do just that.

Trutwin had to give Cathrin credit, which wasn't difficult as the woman had more intellect in her little finger than both of her sons and her invalid husband ever had amassed. It had been all but impossible for Trutwin to believe that Marcus and Colin and Thaddeus Jay were the direct descendants of Melvyn Aadalen. Melvyn Aadalen had been crafty, cagey, intuitive, and always—always—three steps ahead of the next-brightest guy in the room. Melvyn Aadalen had spotted something similar in a young Langdon Trutwin all those decades and decades back, fast-tracking Trutwin through Legal and stepping on more than a few toes to appoint Trutwin as general counsel before Melvyn's leukemia took its final toll. Melvyn Aadalen had invited Trutwin to all family events, made him feel at home . . . treated Trutwin like a son.

And Trutwin loved the man.

And Trutwin had spent decades repaying him by shepherding Melvyn's biological son toward selecting the soundest of marketing decisions and business options which, with a stubborn egoist like Marcus in the early years, was often like Sisyphus rolling the boulder uphill. When Marcus went down with a stroke and Colin Aadalen appeared at bat . . . it became a bridge too far. Trutwin had listened to Gavin Forstner rattle off rationale after rationale in the assorted board meetings and, though he agreed with every point Forstner had raised, he was forced to shake his head and mutter, "He'll learn, Gavin. Colin will learn."

But Trutwin knew Colin, had known the spoiled muscle-bound shit since the day he was born, and what Langdon Trutwin knew for certain was this— Colin Aadalen would never learn. Colin Aadalen didn't give a rat's ass about the pharmaceutical industry. Colin Aadalen only cared about Colin Aadalen. Well, that and screwing anything and everything female that came within groping range. For the love of god, Trutwin thought, Colin Aadalen had begun hanging

out and having drinks with a major leaguer in the
Los Zetas cartel.

Marcus, against Trutwin's wishes and behind
Trutwin's back, had shared certain facts of life with
Colin several years earlier. Marcus had shared with
his first born facts about how the business world at
large truly worked, about how impediments may—
as a very last resort—be removed from the corporate roadway. Worse yet, Marcus had shared certain
specifics with Colin about how these *arrangements*
were initiated. But what Marcus failed to empha-
size to his son was how these steps were only utilized in third-world countries where corruption was
a way of life—like Argentina or Venezuela—and not
back home in the United States for Christ's sake. You
don't shit where you eat. So if hanging out with a
full-blown gangster wasn't bad enough, Colin, impatient dunderhead that he was, had gone behind Trutwin's back and ordered a professional hit on Roark
Larson.

What else was there to say?

God forgive me, Melvyn, Trutwin had thought at
the time, but your idiot grandkid has got to go.

Just then opportunity had knocked and knocked
hard. An opportunity that would take Colin Aadalen
out as though he were the morning trash and have it
all point at Karl Sandin—the most ideal patsy since
Lee Harvey Oswald.

Opportunity knocked and Trutwin made the
arrangements.

CHAPTER 57

"The coast is clear."

It wasn't Sergeant Hartman's voice on Cady's cell phone. Cady figured it was ETF's tenth man posing as a lobby guard who had just given him the verbal thumbs up. Sure enough, Cady slipped out from the back security door and walked five paces to where a man Cady's size in a Cadence Security sport jacket stood holding the door to the southern stairwell open for him to enter. He winked as Cady slipped past.

Tenants needed to use their proximity ID card— prox card—to make the elevators run or access stairwells. Tenants could drop the prox card in their wallets or purses or attach it to a key chain and, as they waved it in front of the card reader, the radio frequency identification technology—a transponder chip in the prox card—took care of the rest. Conceivably, ETF could work with Cadence Security to track Reddon's movements once inside the high-rise, but all roads led to Reddon's condominium unit on the twenty-second floor.

Cady ascended the steps two at a time.

The ride over in the ETF van had been awkward.
Cady was the kid in gym class who nobody wanted
to pick for their team. It didn't matter. Cady understood. He sat off to one side and listened to the
squad of specialists banter about baseball and girls.

Cops were cops, no matter what country.

The morning guard and his *employee in training*
had contacted Willa Reddon's left-side neighbors—
retired couple Bob and Dorsey Lewis—as soon as
Reddon had left the building for her morning work-
out and requested that they come down to the lobby
immediately as a safety precaution. The couple was
met at the elevator and hustled through the same
back security door that Cady would later use to
head to the stairwell. Sergeant Hartman had been in
the lead van and by the time Cady's crew arrived,
the ETF leader was briefing a red-faced Bob and a
wide-eyed Dorsey.

The sergeant was a persuasive man and a minute
later the elderly couple agreed to let the ETF men
use their condominium.

After hearing about Lynchburg, Hartman wasn't
going to provide Reddon with so much as a hiccup to
cause her to start second-guessing the state of affairs.
There would be no handymen working an errant light
fixture, no cleaning staff pushing a vacuum, and, for
God's sake, no team of painters slapping an unnec-
essary coat of paint on the corridor wall. The ETF
leader rigged an under-door camera system at the
bottom of the Lewises' entranceway. ETF now had a
visual of any person approaching from either side of

the twenty-second floor hallway. By the time Reddon was close enough to wonder what a black nickel was doing at the base of her neighbor's door, it would be too late.

"Oliver Price is having an affair," Leahy had told Cady in their last visit. "And he takes pictures. He's got a wad of jpegs on his PC."

Cady had shrugged.

"Price is married," Leahy had followed up. "If that Richmond DA is peeing his pants over Trutwin's hearing, we could turn Price like we did Kettler. If the DA gets Price—it's over—and Trutwin can kiss the baby."

Cady had thought for a second.

"You want to see the pictures?"

Cady shook his head and had said, "Let's see if we get anything from Toronto first. Willa Reddon may have something stashed away in a hidey hole that we can use."

They had been standing in Leahy's kitchen and Cady pointed at the bag he'd placed on the table. "I picked you up a double dose of those Cinnabon Delights you like."

Leahy had ignored the dessert. "We should think about doing this on an ongoing basis. Think about what we've accomplished so far," Leahy had said. "Think about the other cases we could break wide open."

"Who's flirting with the Samson option now?" Cady had said. "Did you forget about the cage in the ground with your nameplate on it?"

"You and me working together," Leahy had responded, excited. "Nobody would ever catch us."

"I don't know that world." Cady had smiled and shaken his head. *"I'd not even realize I'd screwed up until there were two nameplates in the ground."*

The two men had stood silent, staring at the floor for several seconds.

"You know something, Leahy?" Cady had walked to the front door, but turned in the doorframe to face the computer savant. *"You're not as big an asshole as you lead everyone to believe."*

CHAPTER 58

Trutwin took another sip of his mint julep and then set it down atop the restraining order on the table next to him. It figures, he thought, my downfall stems from Colin adding initials that any two-year-old could decipher to an otherwise nebulous spreadsheet. Of course Trutwin had himself to fault for beginning work on a transition document before there was a reason for a transition to exist. But both of those documents could be easily explained and Trutwin would be more than ready if the decision came down for him to testify at the preliminary hearing. First—blame the deceased—the spreadsheet was Colin Aadalen's work. Trutwin would tell the judge that he'd certainly been into the document a few times: trying to make heads or tails out of the damned thing, trying to figure out what it signified, and had even made a mental note to ask Colin, but didn't get around to it before Colin's sudden demise. As for the transition document, it was originally my retirement speech, Trutwin would tell the court. Some kind words and a few witticisms for my company colleagues of all these years, but, after the shock of Colin's death, I turned it into a transition-succession document.

Trutwin knew he'd hold his own under any kind of fire, but felt strongly that it wouldn't ever come to that. His dream team put the odds at sixty-forty that, considering how they planned to hammer home the anonymous nature of the tip from an anonymous hacker with malicious intentions, that the documents would get dumped and the case against him would collapse.

Then . . . of course . . . recourse.

He hoped he wouldn't have to butt heads too hard against Cathrin. He imagined that once the charges were tossed out the window and he'd made the rounds on some of the local news channels asking where he could go to get his reputation back, a sizable check would be cut from AP in his name. He hoped Cathrin wouldn't fight it. She would have had a long conversation with Marcus—that drooling fool—and know that, over several decades, less-than-pleasant arrangements had been set in motion for the sake of their company. And if they began hurling accusations back and forth . . . it would amount to a policy of MAD—mutual assured destruction. But if Cathrin blamed Trutwin for the death of both her boys, something of that nature had a tendency to put an end to any judicious thought.

That was one of several wild cards in the deck. And for Trutwin, that was the saddest part.

A second wild card in the deck was the torch Trutwin had been carrying for so many years that it had become a part of him as though it were the very nose on his face. Langdon Trutwin had been in love with Cathrin Aadalen since that first day he laid eyes on her, back when Marcus had brought her home from Northwestern University over Christmas break to meet the family and let everyone know they were engaged to be married. Trutwin remembered that afternoon as though it were yesterday. After the holiday feast, Trutwin had to leave the dining room as he'd had trouble taking his eyes off her. He took sanctuary on a lower step in the curved staircase as other guests mingled about the living room, chatting and drinking eggnog. Someone tickled ivory on the Steinway grand and, eventually, Cathrin entered the room, spotted him on the stairway, and headed toward him.

His heart beat so fast he thought it'd quit.

"Is this step taken?" Cathrin had asked with a glistening smile that Trutwin knew could belong only to an angel.

"I believe it may be reserved for later this evening," Trutwin had said, "but until then, it's all yours."

After Cathrin had settled on the step, Trutwin had said, "Welcome to the family."

She had looked at him for a long second. "I think it's going to be a wild ride."

"That it will," Trutwin had told her. "That it will."

And that was what had kept Trutwin's mood foul—a tumor of malevolent cancer. It wasn't his arrest on such a flimsy bag of charges or the efforts by some in the media to drag his name through the mud. It was the loss of status in the hazel eyes of the only person he'd ever truly cared about.

Trutwin had been the one Cathrin called when
Marcus strayed . . . and Marcus had strayed. Trutwin had been the one Cathrin called when trouble
with TJ arose. Trutwin had been the one Cathrin had
relied on for the sense of caring she never received
from a vacant and vacuous Marcus. He had been the
one Cathrin turned to. But, outside of a quick hug or
peck on the cheek, he'd never laid a finger on her.
His feelings had never been consummated. He loved
Cathrin from afar . . . platonic . . . like a starstruck
schoolboy discovering poetry in English class. He
could never tell Cathrin how he felt, because . . .
well . . . that's not something men do.

But Cathrin likely knew, sensed it, as women do.

And though Margaret knew his moods, she never
suspected where his thoughts may roam whenever
they made love.

So Trutwin sat alone with his cancerous thoughts.
It wasn't the bind he was in, as Trutwin certainly did
take that seriously . . . it was that the only love of
his life would never again look in his eyes in fond-
ness, with friendship, with affection, with hopeful
reliance. Cathrin would look at him with revulsion.
With hatred. And Cathrin would never speak to him
with anything but spite.

Trutwin took a long last sip of his mint julep, finishing the drink, and began contemplating the third
wild card in the deck . . . Special Agent Drew Cady.

There was something brewing behind those
poker-player eyes of his. Cady's partner had been
killed—most unfortunate, indeed—and yet there he
was, Trutwin thought, in my Aadalen Pharmaceuticals' office acting like a bit player, a fly on the wall,

a disinterested third party. Yes, Agent Cady standing there, quietly feigning the half-wit, when in reality he's being too clever by half. Suddenly, the FBI steals Elliot Kettler as a cooperating witness. Suddenly, the FBI and Richmond PD show up to seize Trutwin's computer, Trutwin's files.

Trutwin didn't buy that his network drive had been internally hacked. He didn't buy that for a New York second. Trutwin had briefly considered those devious bastards at Roche or Johnson & Johnson—spotting a chance to take down AP—but Trutwin was well aware that the FBI had a division that specialized in combating cyber threats, so . . . ?

A veteran FBI agent almost certainly would know of someone who may be of after-hours assistance.

All roads led back to Special Agent Cady.

A flash of movement from the rose bushes in the back garden caught his eye. Trutwin rarely saw deer, but rabbits, chipmunks, and the occasional woodchuck would wreak havoc with his landscape plants. Any other day and Trutwin would have gone in search of his pellet gun, but today he didn't move a muscle. Somehow Trutwin doubted his home would be making Richmond's public tour for garden week this season.

Even though the air was on, he'd left the sliding glass door to the back patio open and Trutwin swore he heard the front doorbell ring. He wasn't meeting with his attorneys again until tomorrow and any of them would have called first had something important cropped up. Remarkably, Trutwin's social calendar was wide open and, he glanced again at the restraining order underneath his empty mint julep glass on the side table, Trutwin had no place of employment to attend. Margaret might return home from Roanoke at any time, but she'd use her key to get in, not ring the bell. Trutwin hoped it wasn't Margaret; it'd be best for her to stay out of the way until all of this unpleasantness was put to rest. Trutwin heard the doorbell again and then listened as the security guard he'd hired—an overgrown bruiser named Donovan or Donaldson—marched from his kitchen perch toward the front atrium.

Trutwin wondered who it could be.

CHAPTER 59

The Canadian felt the hair rise on the back of her neck as she cut across the lobby toward the building's front row of entry doors. Someone was staring at her. Her right hand hovered behind her, edging close to the hidden pocket sewn into the back of her gym shorts. She shot a quick glance at the lobby desk. Sure enough. Of the two security guards seated behind the counter, one was new and he sat there gawking at her, a big, dopey grin on his face. In the quarter-second their eyes connected, he gave her a friendly nod of the head.

Sometimes she got that from men.

The Canadian didn't respond in kind. Instead she exited the high-rise and a half second later was heading down the sidewalk at a solid clip. The Canadian turned on University Avenue, figuring that today she'd start out by heading past King Station and toward Saint Lawrence Market in the Old Toronto district, get her blood flowing, and sort through the details of her upcoming excursion.

The Canadian would fly into the Minneapolis-Saint Paul International Airport where she would pick up a rental car. She would then make two stops on her road trip to Grand Rapids, Minnesota. The first stop would be at an REI store five minutes from the airport, where she'd pick up a passable lock knife. The Canadian's second layover would be in a Perkins's parking lot off I-94 where she would be handed a Lunds & Byerlys reusable shopping bag by a man wearing a Green Bay Packers jersey.

Inside the reusable shopping bag would be a shoebox. Inside the shoebox would be a Beretta 92FS, two magazines, two boxes of ammo, and a custom silencer. The Canadian, per her routine, would arrive at Perkins two hours early, circle the neighborhood—get the lay and feel of the land—and, if anything felt the least bit *hinky*, she'd drive away and find another handgun later.

Standard operating procedure.

Once in Grand Rapids she'd stop at a Walmart and purchase the cheapest fishing gear available. The gear would be for appearances only. Then she'd check into her cabin at Pincherry Grove Resort, which was across the far side of Bass Lake from Sundown Point Resort . . . Special Agent Cady's resort. It would be Labor Day Weekend and Bass Lake would be bursting at the seams with activity—one last summer fling before school began and the weather turned cool. Pincherry Grove rented boats and the Canadian would spring for their most powerful motor.

All the long-term forecasts—warm and sunny.

Perfect killing weather.

The Canadian had dismissed approaching Cady while he was prancing about one of the resort's docks. Too many witnesses, too many other boats, too many cell phones. A dockside stunt in front of vacationers would likely lead to a tsunami of squad cars flooding Pincherry Grove as she docked up and attempted to head out. No, this would require her highest amount of subtlety and finesse. The Canadian had all but memorized the Google satellite photos of Sundown Point Resort. She knew the barnlike structure where the rental motors were housed. She knew the playground where the kids played. She knew Sundown Point's office—how it faced the lake—how it was the place where visiting fishermen went to purchase minnows or night crawlers, or their children went to purchase candy or ice cream. It was the place the guests went to settle their accounts at week's end before jumping into vehicles and heading back to the real world.

And it was the place where the Canadian would slay her demon.

Sundown Point's office had a wall of windows that faced Bass Lake, with a fair-sized deck outside its entry door that was likely used predominantly by Cady or his wife to sit in lawn chairs, watch the lake, or read a book, and let the visitors know that someone was available if they needed any fishing tackle or wanted to settle their bills. She imagined Cady or his wife would be hovering about the lake-side office and outer deck, certainly within a stone's throw, for much of the holiday weekend. The Canadian also was aware of a small dock with a sitting bench placed on the west side of the resort next to where the fishermen backed their boats into the lake. It was hidden from Sundown Point's office by about thirty yards and a strip of white birch and pine. It would be the perfect spot for the Canadian to dock her speedboat before ambling up the short redwood steps onto the office's outer deck.

With any luck she might find Cady napping in a deck chair.

The Canadian would use her binoculars to case Sundown Point from her rental boat, which would be one of the numerous crafts hidden in plain sight in the overcrowded lake traffic of the holiday weekend. The Canadian would wait patiently until she spotted Cady perched on the deck or sitting in the resort's office, and then she'd glide her small ship to the hidden west-side dock. She'd wear a bright sundress, a pair of oversized sunglasses, and a wide brim sun hat, fitting in perfectly with the endless parade of visiting tourists that marches through a northern Minnesota resort each and every season.

The perfect scenario would be to catch Cady dozing in a deck chair with his legs sprawled up on the railing. The Canadian would wait in the tree line until no customers were milling about, and then she'd wander up, slowly and nonthreateningly, until she stood near his side. Then, as he turned lazily in her direction, she'd pull the 92FS with attached silencer from the folds of her sundress and remove her sun hat and glasses with her free hand. The Canadian would watch as the recognition dawned on Cady's features. Then she'd shoot him twice in the face.

Because that's what one did to excise demons.

The Canadian hoped she wouldn't have to do the wife, but, as is always the case, the situation would dictate what measures would be required.

If everything went as planned, and with a little luck, Cady would not be discovered until she was back at Pincherry Grove. And by the time the sirens screeched toward Sundown Point Resort, the Canadian would be miles away in her rental car, heading toward Madison, Wisconsin, where on the Tuesday following Labor Day, she would begin the first leg of her journey back to Toronto from the Dan County Regional Airport.

The Canadian jogged Lake Shore Boulevard for a block or two, and then turned back. She'd save the Martin Goodman Trail for another day, for a day that she wanted to open all cylinders and run for miles. By the time she got back to the high-rise, the guard with the dopey smile was being shown something on the computer screen by the regular lobby guard. He didn't glance her way, probably too self-conscious at how she'd shut him down, but it got the Canadian thinking about how long it had been since she'd been with anyone. Her chosen profession placed certain limitations on retaining a *normal* social life. Of course she'd never start anything with a dopey security guard, but it got her thinking about celebrating having cleansed herself of her demons once she hit Madison. Perhaps there'd be someone marginally attractive in the hotel bar.

An added benefit of her chosen profession was that the Canadian didn't have to worry about her safety when entering strange hotel rooms with men she'd just met.

The Canadian hit the elevator call button, considering blowing off the stairs as she did every day, but thought about getting old and then carded her way into the south stairwell.

The Canadian already was covered in a sheen of sweat; the steps turned that sheen into drips. Her shirt and jogging shorts, now clammy, would get tossed into the laundry first thing and then, second thing, she'd take a lengthy shower. As she passed the entry door to the fifteenth floor, the Canadian reached behind and underneath her damp T-shirt, slid her hand inside the back waistband of her jogging shorts, and slipped the stiletto out from the elastic bands in the cushioned pocket she'd hand sewn.

Don't leave home without it.

The Canadian went full bore on the remaining fourteen flights—two flights per floor. She twisted about the railing on the final set of steps and . . . there, on the landing above, stood the man she'd last seen at a budget motel in Lynchburg, Virginia.

There stood her demon. His Glock 19 aimed at her center mass.

"I couldn't wait till Labor Day," Cady said.

CHAPTER 60

Cady saw Willa Reddon's eyes dart left, toward the flight she'd just ascended, and shook his head. "They're everywhere. Plainclothes at all exits, ETF team at your neighbor's home, set to take you down at your doorway."

Reddon stared at Cady. "Maybe that's bullshit. Maybe it's just you."

"Did you notice a new security guard in the lobby?" Cady said. "What are the odds of a new guard and me on the same day?"

"I could run."

"I'm pretty good with this." Cady kept the borrowed Glock at center mass. "If you run, I'll shoot you in the leg."

Reddon thought for a second and said, "How did you find me?"

"Some genius came across your money stream."

Reddon thought for another second. "How the hell did they do that?"

Cady shrugged. "I didn't take that class."

"So what happens now?"

"Extradition, trial—potential death penalty, but you know how those drag out. Perhaps life in a federal penitentiary," Cady replied. "You're thirty-six, right? So a life term could mean a half century in a cage with strangers."

"That doesn't sound like fun."

"What have you got in your hand?" Cady asked.

"This." Reddon held up her right hand, pressing the release with her thumb and the nearly four-inch blade sprung from the tip of the stiletto and locked in place.

"I'd appreciate it if you'd place that on the floor."

"Why am I still alive?" Reddon asked, knife hand still in the air.

"Because you're under arrest."

"I could have done a half-dozen things to disable your partner, you know, but I stabbed her in the neck."

"I know."

"I killed her right in front of your eyes . . . and you're arresting me?"

"Personally, I'd like to knock your teeth down your throat."

Reddon continued to stare up at Cady. "Why don't you try?"

"Things didn't fare too well our last go-round."

"No," the Canadian said, "they did not."

"The woman you killed—Elizabeth Preston—she and I would often disagree, and then we'd try to find a happy middle ground. Were Liz still alive, she'd insist I take you into custody so you could face trial, so that the system could take its course. Now that may not be exactly what I want, but the more I think about it—the more I realize that you're like me. Fifty years in a cage with strangers is much worse than death."

Reddon chewed on that, and then asked, "Why isn't ETF here by now?"

"I imagine they're wondering what's taking you so long. They've probably sent the normal guard past the swimming pool or the workout room to get a visual."

Reddon nodded. A plan was forming—not the greatest of plans but considering the options on the table, it wasn't half bad. The Canadian was skilled in hand-to-hand combat, but her knife throwing skills were . . . adequate. Unfortunately she held the knife by the handle. This was unfortunate because she gauged that it would take one and a half spins to nail Special Agent Cady. This was also unfortunate because she doubted Cady would spot her the seconds needed to switch her grip and hold the blade over her head like a circus performer.

But as an act of misdirection—a distraction—something to send Cady herky-jerky as she came for him . . . that could work . . . it had potential. If the Canadian played this perfectly, the agent from the Federal Bureau of Investigation would find himself plunging over a different type of railing this go-round. The Canadian felt the familiar adrenaline rush kick in—the exhilarating joy of the hunt and the junkie thrill that defined her. Everything melted from focus except for Agent Cady at the landing above her.

"If you try anything with that blade," Cady said, ignoring the now-vibrating phone in his breast pocket,

"I will kneecap you, and then you can do your fifty years on crutches."

With a heavy sigh, the Canadian dropped both hands toward the floor in capitulation. She took a step forward, her left foot now atop the first step, blade still in hand, tip pointed at the floor.

"Don't move," Cady said.

"But I'm surrendering," Reddon replied, taking another half-step forward.

"Then drop the—"

Reddon's right wrist flicked upward—a towel snap—the stiletto flying at Cady's center mass. And behind the airborne knife flew Reddon, a harpy escaping hell, rocketing up four steps at a time, readying a palm strike to the nose to take Cady out of commission before taking him out of existence. Cady jerked right, the switchblade handle bouncing off his left shoulder and she was on him, springing up off a left foot, Cady lowering his gun, her palm flying upward.

An explosion.

Then the Canadian dropping to the landing cement, support cut out from under her, the palm strike glancing hard off Cady's cheekbone.

Cady leapt backward and up a couple of steps of the next flight. He touched his cheek and said, "I told you not to move."

The Canadian sat on the landing, sinking into shock. Her left knee was ruined, a splatter of crimson coloring the gray landing. She reached for the stiletto and stared up at Cady.

Cady aimed the Glock 19 at Reddon's other kneecap. "Looks like it'll be fifty years in a wheelchair."

His phone buzzed again, and he knew he couldn't ignore it. Keeping his gun trained on Reddon, Cady fished his cell phone out with an awkward left hand and clicked it on with a thumb. He listened to Sergeant Hartman for several seconds.

"That was me," Cady replied. "Reddon's here. She's in the stairwell."

Cady clicked off and stared at Reddon. "They're coming."

He could hear them in the hallway, maybe Reddon could too.

The Canadian stared at Cady and forced herself to focus.

Thoughts of surgeries and courtroom trials and a lifetime of confinement raced through her mind like lightning across a darkened sky. She gripped the handle of the stiletto in her right fist and wondered if it was the shock sinking in or her adrenal glands secreting copious amounts of adrenaline in this final moment of extreme danger.

Either way, the Canadian felt the speed-like rush one last time as she jammed the stiletto blade deep into her right eye socket.

Cady watched as Reddon ended her life in front of him. Something flashed across her face before she did it, a smirk of some kind, but then it was over and Hartman's team spilled into the stairwell.

Cady thought of Liz. He somehow doubted she'd consider this a *happy middle ground.*

CHAPTER 61

Day 30

Canada was not happy with Special Agent Cady.

Back in the chief's office, Hartman got deep inside Cady's proximity and volunteered a dozen seconds of disjointed profanity. Cady assumed most of it had to do with his lineage. Cady stepped back from the ETF sergeant—unlike he'd done in his first and only meeting with Colin Aadalen in what seemed like years ago—and let Director Jund do the talking.

It was what the man was good at.

After several minutes of listening to Jund's nouns and verbs, adjectives and prepositions, Chief Sayers had heard enough and told Hartman to stand down. "The woman was a paid assassin, Sergeant;" the chief had said, "she was never going to surrender willingly."

"But this prick played us," Hartman had objected.

"Stand down," Chief Sayers barked again.

Cady felt great relief when United flight 3408 finally had cleared for takeoff at Toronto Pearson. In-flight coffee never had tasted so good.

Cady was now back at his TV-tray-sized perch in Agent Preston's office, filling out reports and wrapping up loose ends. He knew Liz wouldn't have cared had he sat behind her desk, but there was no way in hell he could bring himself to do that. It was eight thirty in the morning. Cady's plane to Minneapolis left at five . . . but he had miles to go before then.

Miles to go.

Jund appeared in the open doorframe. He glanced at Preston's empty chair before turning his attention to Cady. "Langdon Trutwin's gone," Jund said. "It appears he's in the wind."

"You're kidding?"

The director shook his head. "His wife came home to an empty house. No notes or phone messages. His bodyguard's gone as well."

"How long has it been?" Cady asked. "Could be he took a short trip to clear his mind—went fishing or something."

"His car is at the house and he's blown off a couple of meetings with his attorneys."

Cady's mind spun. They'd found nothing in Willa Reddon's condominium suite that pointed Trutwin's way. The preliminary hearing was two weeks out and Cady remained hesitant about Leahy's scheme of using the pictures from Oliver Price's extramarital trysts—the defense attorney's X-rated selfies found on his PC—to flip Price their way. Not only would that leave a bad taste in Cady's mouth, but it had the very real possibility of blowing up in their faces.

"Trutwin didn't strike me as a runner," Cady said.

"It might help our cause if he did run," Jund said and shrugged. "You know how this plays out, Drew—we'll find him eventually."

Cady nodded, lost in thought.

"You ready to go?" Jund asked.

"Give me five minutes."

Cady shut his laptop and stared at Liz Preston's empty desk. Cady wouldn't be returning to Agent Preston's office, and he figured the next time he was back in town, her office would be assigned to another agent. Cady swallowed his emotions, shoved the laptop into his briefcase, and went in search of Jund.

Cady didn't want to be late.

CHAPTER 62

"Don't you dare call me *Senator*," Elaine Brockman scolded.

Cady nodded. There'd been a private swearing-in ceremony at the governor's Executive Mansion in Richmond while Cady and Jund had been in Canada. The vice president had flown in to administer the oath, but other than that—and considering the circumstances—it had been a small affair: Governor DeMarco; his wife, the First Lady of the Commonwealth; some Virginian dignitaries; a handful of related Brockmans; and Dorie Searles.

Cady sat at a high-back chair in the living room of the Brockmans' Woodley Park residence, where it all had begun. He'd called the senator's widow earlier, and Mrs. Brockman mentioned she'd be in Woodley packing boxes of Taylor's clothes for Goodwill.

"I didn't get a chance to tell you how deeply saddened I am about your partner," Elaine Brockman said. "Dorie and I attended the funeral, but didn't get a chance to express our condolences. We didn't want to get in the way."

Cady nodded again.

"When's your flight?" Brockman sat on the sofa across from him.

Cady checked his watch. "I need to head out soon."

"Has the resort been in your wife's family a long time?"

Cady shook his head. "She started running it a few years back. Before that Terri was a teacher."

"There's no more honorable a profession than that."

"She taught grade school. Loved the kids. They wanted her to teach junior high, but Terri said they couldn't pay her enough for that."

Brockman smiled and said, "Middle school teachers should get combat pay."

"Terri believes even the sane kids are insane at that age," Cady replied. "And she's right. I did something in eighth grade that still makes me cringe."

"Do tell."

"I had this first-year English teacher named Nancy Nabors, right out of college," Cady said. "I don't think she returned the following fall."

"You drove her out?"

Cady shrugged. "I got to her class early one day, in the middle of passing time. No one else was in the room. They had a cabinet by one wall with games stacked on top, Monopoly, Life, stuff like that for when we had a free hour. The cabinet had a built-in sink, so I took the cover off the Monopoly game, filled the box with water, put the cover back on, and stacked it on top of the other games."

"You *were* a little shit."

Cady nodded. "If I told Terri about this, even all these years later, she'd force me to hunt down Ms. Nabors and apologize face to face."

"And rightly so," Brockman concurred.

"I snuck out of the classroom after vandalizing the game and then made a big production of returning a second or two before the bell rang. Ms. Nabors starts in with her lesson plan, but then notices there's a pond of water leaking from somewhere on the cabinet. She walks over and lifts the top off the Monopoly game and turns white. All the pieces are floating, the money is soaked. Thank god my seat was on the opposite side of the room."

Mrs. Brockman looked at Cady and shook her head.

"I was hoping that Ms. Nabors wouldn't notice it until a different hour," Cady said. "I'm starting to sweat now—shifting in my seat—as Ms. Nabors stares into that waterlogged Monopoly box. Anyway there was a guy in the class named Scott Isaacson. Isaacson was a big guy who'd hit you in the mouth if you looked at him wrong; he was always in trouble."

Brockman nodded and placed her cup of green tea on a table coaster.

"Anyway Isaacson sat next to the cabinet, so Ms. Nabors asked, 'Did you do this, Scott?'"

"What did he say?"

"Isaacson looked at her and said, 'Fuck you. Did not.'"

Brockman stared at Cady.

"And Isaacson got sent to the office." Cady thought for a second. "It's been twenty-five years, so I don't remember if he got booted from the class or just suspended for a few days. Either way, the investigation into the wrecked Monopoly game ended right then and there. I no longer had reason to fear. In everyone's mind, Isaacson was the culprit . . . and Isaacson wound up doing the time."

"It sounds like you owe him an apology as well."

"Probably."

"Hopefully you learned something."

"I did. I've been thinking quite a bit about Ms. Nabors and Scott Isaacson lately."

"Pangs of guilt?"

"Actually," Cady replied, "about how the two of them tie into this case."

"What are you talking about?"

"I've been wondering if someone much smarter than an eighth grader knew that murdering your husband would tear open a can of worms and have us chasing one Scott Isaacson after another?"

Elaine Brockman held Cady's eye a long moment and said, "First I'm led to believe that Karl Sandin killed Tay, and then I'm told it was Langdon Trutwin. Are you now informing me it wasn't Trutwin who had my husband killed?"

Cady nodded. "Langdon Trutwin was behind the coup at Aadalen Pharmaceuticals. He took advantage of current events and paid a professional to have Colin Aadalen murdered in the same manner as your husband—in the same manner as Colin's brother, TJ—a stab wound to the heart with a eulogy note left at the scene. Trutwin also paid the same killer to take out Karl Sandin, to make Sandin's death appear a suicide, to make Sandin the fall guy," Cady said. "You see Liz and I found ourselves bouncing into walls and banging into cupboards, like pinballs . . . until an Isaacson fell out of the woodwork."

"So if Trutwin didn't kill my husband, like they're saying in the media . . . then who did?"

"The woman in Canada—Langdon Trutwin's hired assassin—was maybe five foot two, a little taller than my wife." Cady shook his head and continued, "That kept eating away at me. No way can she be the six-one impersonator in the picture from your front door security camera. Even five-inch heels put her at five seven, and a wig puts her at five eight. She'd have had to wear stilts to pull off the illusion of being your husband."

"But the imposter only needed two seconds to get in, so if there's no one on the street, height's not really an issue."

"That image has been examined nearly as much as the Zapruder film. Analysts much smarter than I used the doorframe as a point of reference and, by measuring that, they were able to place the imposter at nearly six one. Not as tall as your husband, but could pass for him from a house or two away. There are other factors involved—scalpel versus switch-blade, obits versus eulogies—but it ultimately boils down to height. Quite frankly, Mrs. Brockman, your husband's killer came within five inches of pulling it off."

Elaine Brockman leaned forward. "Who murdered my husband, Agent Cady?"

"Someone five nine or five ten. Someone who knew there'd be a few skeletons and a handful of 'Fuck Yous' in your husband's closet—a Scott Isaac-son or two in the woodwork on which we'd bite and bite hard. And someone well-versed in the art of the scalpel."

Cady took the program from Taylor Brockman's funeral from the breast pocket in his suit jacket and placed it on the coffee table between them. "You did a first-class job on this, very thorough in listing the individuals important in both your and your husband's lives. Respectful in including their honorific titles—governor, attorney general, secretary of state," Cady said. "I even noticed that Ms. Searles is referenced as Doctor Dorie Searles."

CHAPTER 63

"You have got to be kidding me."

The two stared across the room at each other for several seconds.

"I realize it's an honorary title, there to be respectful, like how you address someone with a doctorate degree as 'Doctor.'"

"That's what it is," Brockman responded. "Dorie's an addiction specialist for Christ's sake, not an MD."

Cady nodded and said, "It got me thinking about what you told us, about how Searles got her start in nursing but went back to school before she could do any *permanent damage*. I did a little digging and you'll never guess what Searles did to pay the bills while attending night school for her doctor of psychology degree."

Widow Brockman didn't volunteer an answer.

"She worked as a scrub nurse, helping surgeons in the operating room."

Brockman reached for the phone on the side table. "Dorie killing Tay? You're out of your fucking mind."

Cady shrugged. "Guess what else, Elaine? Searles is five ten. Not obnoxiously tall for a female, but add a pair of boots and a wig—six one."

Brockman tapped in a string of numbers, and then glared at Cady. "I think you'd best go back to running a resort, building campfires for the kiddies."

Cady sat patiently.

After about thirty seconds, Elaine Brockman barked into the receiver, "Call me back ASAP!" Brockman then shot Cady a boardroom stare, harsh, as though she'd just decided to deny severance.

"If you're calling *Dr. Searles*," Cady said, "she may be indisposed."

"What have you done to her?"

"I'm not sure if she's still at Hoover or if they've processed her to MPD," Cady replied, checking his watch. MPD was the Metropolitan Police Department for the District of Columbia.

"Don't fuck with me, Agent Cady," Brockman said, her face a fierce red. "I will own your goddamned resort."

"Remember Dorie's discussion on curing addiction?"

Brockman refused the bait.

"Turns out Dorie can't use herself as an example of someone beating dependency."

No bait was taken.

"Turns out her kleptomania never really went away."

No bait.

"I'm sure she kept it in check over the years, but it stayed with her. And you'll never guess what we found inside one of her Russian nesting dolls."

"Fuck you," Brockman spoke in a deep murmur, a locomotive letting off steam.

"Souvenirs are such a rookie mistake, but with her history . . . completely understandable." Cady's eyes never left the new senator. "We suspected she's the one in the photo. Her height fits the description. And Searles was already in town, not how you led us to believe she flew in with you from Virginia."

"I didn't lead you to believe a goddamned thing."

Cady shrugged again. "Searles got physical when I opened the display case. Nesting dolls, the first place I looked—you know—*a hole in one*. Director Jund himself had to pull her off me."

Brockman looked down.

"Remember that ring? The one in the hallway portrait? The one your husband had made for himself when he first won the senate seat? You told me about it—sterling silver with the senate seal on top. The senator wasn't wearing the ring and you never listed it as missing."

"My husband had just been murdered and I forget to reference some silly-ass ring?"

"I can buy that. It's just a vanity ring in a house of more expensive goodies. But it's kind of an interesting token for a husband to hand over to his wife's *lover*, wouldn't you agree?"

Brockman raised her head. Her eyes were moist. "Dorie could have picked that up on any occasion."

"I imagine she could have, but after our tousle in her office—after the senator's ring tumbled out of one of the smaller dolls—Searles had a change in demeanor. It was as though someone flicked a switch."

Cady had sat on a metal chair in the corner of the interrogation room at the Hoover Building and watched as Zeke Wallace lived up to his reputation. Wallace's streak continued as Dorie Searles flowed like the Snake River after a flood. If anything, Wallace worked to ebb the flow of information, to slow Searles down and keep her focused as he played out the rope with which she was actively hanging herself. Cady kept quiet, offering Wallace a handwritten question now and again, whenever an issue occurred to him. Although Wallace still had been going strong, covering minor logistics, Cady had everything he needed to know and left the room as Brockman's chief of staff and personal addiction therapist was nearing the end of her first box of Kleenex.

"That woman you mentioned from your therapy session, the mousy one whose husband had her sterilized," Cady continued. "Searles told us you were talking about yourself."

CHAPTER 64

Cady watched Brockman as she sat on the leather sofa in silence.

Wallace had spent an hour at Hoover probing motive. In response, Searles painted a bleak picture of Senator and Mrs. Brockman—a tapestry of dysfunction . . . a dead marriage. As though lecturing causation to family members of an addicted teen, Searles framed it in terms of a high school allegory. Taylor had been football captain and homecoming king; he'd run with the in crowd since grade school, but to get his hands on the Newell Hotel fortune— to get his claws on the dowry—Taylor had to marry the ugly duckling. Like most sociopaths, Tay Brockman could be charming—and he aimed that charm at Elaine Newell. Both barrels. This was all very new for Elaine as very few boys had ever glanced in her direction.

Of course Elaine Newell fell and fell hard.

But once married, Taylor Brockman began to treat Elaine as the object of his resentment. After a year of marriage, Taylor couldn't contain his little cruelties.

In retrospect, Searles had informed Wallace, Holocaust Barbie would have been the perfect match for a man of Senator Brockman's appetites. Searles also surmised that Taylor's vindictive streak, his petty malice, was in fact aimed at Elaine's father—whom Taylor feared—and Elaine's mother, whom Taylor loathed. There were the sexual humiliations—the sharing; there was the withdrawal of affection that kicked in as soon as the wedding vows had been spoken. There were manipulations . . . guilt trips . . . incessant psychological and emotional abuse.

And there was a lone act of physical abuse.

An unforgivable act.

After one of many *sharing* sessions that Taylor Brockman had subjected his young wife to, Elaine became pregnant. Not confident of the true father, and blaming Elaine for her *carelessness*, Taylor set up the abortion. An old frat buddy of Taylor's had gone on to medical school and had become the Brockman family physician. Taylor had his doctor friend terminate the pregnancy—off books, of course—but while Elaine was under anesthesia, Taylor had his doctor friend perform an additional procedure.

Taylor had his doctor friend perform a tubal ligation.

Taylor's doctor used the monopolar coagulation method, that is, Elaine Newell Brockman's fallopian tubes were burned shut, leaving Elaine oblivious to the fact that any chance at biological motherhood had just been stolen from her. The scar from the incision was explained away as a laparoscopy required in order to find a suspected cyst, but, Elaine, not to fear, Taylor's doctor had assured her—everything checked out A-okay.

Making Elaine barren was Taylor Brockman's ultimate *fuck you* to his schoolmarm wife and insufferable in-laws.

Then five years ago—nearing the end of Brockman's first term in the United States Senate—Taylor's doctor friend, and the Brockman family physician, passed away from stage IVB liver cancer. Taylor's doctor friend knew the stats; he grabbed the pain meds but refused treatment, and went quickly into that good night. A few months after his passing, Elaine found herself a different practitioner to perform her annual checkup—a female physician this time.

And one can only imagine Elaine's shock, Searles had informed them in the interrogation room, when Elaine Newell Brockman found out what Taylor Brockman and his doctor friend had done to her all those years earlier.

Elaine Brockman broke the stillness. "Do I look like a mouse to you?"

"I believe the woman that you described disappeared forever in a doctor's examination room . . . when the truth spilled out."

Cady figured Taylor Brockman had signed his own death warrant when he'd ordered a tubal ligation without his wife's knowledge in some kind of warped and heartless power trip all those years ago. Cady also figured that Taylor Brockman got a half decade reprieve as his devastated wife fought her way out of an alcoholic haze.

"I was twenty-seven when Tay had that particular piece of butchery performed on me," Brockman said more to the living room than to Agent Cady. "I was forty when I learned what the son of a bitch had done."

"You could have had the procedure reversed."

"I was intoxicated by noon on weekdays, but even then I knew one thing for damn sure. I knew I'd not be bringing any more Taylor Brockmans into the world."

"Searles told us something else, said you were in DC on Newell Suites business seven weeks ago. She said you fell ill and came here to Woodley Park to rest. She told us you barely made it to the bathroom before throwing up—a spot of food poisoning or the stomach flu—and how as you kneeled over the toilet, you spotted something at the bottom of the trash bin."

Elaine Newell Brockman appeared on the verge of tears.

"You spotted a pregnancy test—a test that showed positive," Cady said. "Searles told us the two of you had talked about a world without your husband on numerous occasions—which she initially took to mean divorce—but that you spoke of nothing else since your discovery that afternoon."

"It appears that Dorie's breaching doctor-patient privilege."

"I suspect that losing her license is the least of her concerns," Cady replied. "Searles said discovering your husband had impregnated another woman was the last straw—the final injustice—and that the years of bitterness and resentment took a lethal turn. Searles also told us that, over time, the two of you had become *more* than friends. And Searles confessed to a couple of other things."

Elaine sat quietly on the couch.

"Searles told us killing TJ ripped her up inside. She wanted to leave the kid alone—that he had his own demons to contend with—but you kept at her, kept pushing that TJ was the lynchpin that would lead the investigation down a rabbit hole." Searles told them how Elaine had peppered her husband with questions about the Aadalens, discovered TJ's predicament, and figured out how best to use it to their advantage. The killing in TJ's Porsche Boxster had been a tag-team effort as Elaine sat nearby, in a dark car, scanning the street for any pesky interlopers. "In the end, Searles killed TJ for you . . . and it broke her heart."

Elaine stared toward the entryway and said nothing.

"She didn't express the same amount of regret over your husband." Searles came clean on killing the senator, but told Wallace that Elaine had greased the skids from the inside; Elaine had provided a key to the brownstone, Elaine had hidden duct tape, several scalpels, a LadySmith revolver—in case the senator was less than compliant—and the eulogy in a handbag under the kitchen sink. And though the senator slept like a bear in winter, Elaine had spiked his Glenlivet, which Brockman sipped nightly, with a mild sedative on her last trip to town to ensure his hibernation would make him additionally pliable in those dawning seconds of consciousness as the

senator woke to realize that an unexpected visitor
had come calling. "Or any regret at all."

A single tear appeared in the corner of Brockman's
eye. "God how I loved Tay, and I went along with his
every whim . . . unconditionally . . . because that's
what one did—don't you know?—that's what one did
to save their marriage. I had wondered why I wasn't
able to get pregnant—to bear Tay's children—and all
those years I thought it was on me, and thought I
was to blame when our sex life drizzled into noth-
ingness. Tay knew I'd scheduled an appointment
with a new physician, but the years had flown past
and the indifferent bastard had forgotten what he'd
had done to me—it registered so little on his Geiger
counter—such nonchalant malevolence. Yes, Agent
Cady, I was reborn in that examination room, and I
assure you I came home a changed woman. I con-
fronted the lying bastard. Tay feigned shock. He then
pretended we'd both come to that decision—that I'd
consented—that the sterilization had been carried
out for my own benefit, my emotional well-being . . .
my mental health."

"What happened then?"

"The mouse was no longer frightened of her
shadow and I began slapping Tay as hard as I could—
repeatedly—daring him to strike back. Soon after I
took the Chesapeake house and he stayed here."

The two sat again in silence. Brockman dabbed at
her eyes with a knuckle.

"Dorie knew the horror I'd been through, she
knew of my husband's . . . *ill will*. Our counseling sessions had taken on an odd feeling this past
year—inappropriate, I guess—but I discounted my

intuition as Dr. Searles continued to help me maintain my sobriety. Dorie often told me that she'd do *anything* for me, Dorie would say that repeatedly, but, oh, dear God, I never thought that she'd . . ." Her eyes turned cold and still. "I demand my right to have an attorney present."

"Searles will take a wheel when you toss her under the bus," Cady said, "and a good lawyer could sell that spiel. It might be an uphill battle, though, as Dorie's done her share of *eulogizing* since the nesting doll." Cady stared back at the new senator from the Commonwealth of Virginia. "Mostly about you."

Cady rubbed at a temple. He should have known better than to expect some kind of closure, but there was one last thing to say. "What you set in motion—the watch you wound—led to the death of one of the finest individuals I've ever known."

Cady then stood, walked to the entrance hall and opened the doorway. CID Director Roland Jund entered the foyer, several suits followed in his wake. A black sedan and an MPD squad car sat curbside, two uniforms stood on the sidewalk.

Elaine Newell Brockman's ride had arrived.

"Have a nice day, Senator," Cady said and left the brownstone.

EPILOGUE

Cady sat next to Elizabeth Preston's grave.

"Terri said I should just tell you what I'd say if you were here in person, Liz. No matter how much I look like an ass."

But what would I say, Cady thought to himself?

I'd tell you that I got Reddon, Liz, but perhaps you're already aware of that. I'd tell you that we got Dorie Searles and Elaine Brockman, too, the duo who started the whole ball rolling. I'd say that Langdon Trutwin's in the wind. I'd say that Roland feels good about that because we were all sweating bullets over the preliminary hearing, and that Roland believes that Trutwin knew the other boot—a boot we've yet to discover—was going to come down on his head, because, otherwise, it would have been a hell of a court battle with a likely outcome that Trutwin would have walked, especially with the water soon to be muddied by the arrests of Dorie Searles and Elaine Brockman in the murders of Senator Brockman and TJ Aadalen. And I'd also tell you, Liz, that if Langdon Trutwin is out there, Roland will find him.

If he's out there . . .

And I know you'd look at me in that detached manner of yours and query, "If he's out there?"

And I'd say, "Liz, remember."

Remember how Jorge "George" Hierra and Colin Aadalen hit it off? Someone who didn't need a damned thing from him was now Hierra's friend—buying him dinner and drinks, taking him out for golf—opposite sides of the same coin and all that.

A unique camaraderie, indeed.

What do you suppose would happen in Hierra's line of work, Liz, if someone killed off a trusted colleague or friend of his? Los Zetas has never appeared to be on the forgiving or forgetting edge of the great divide.

No, thought Cady, *I don't think Roland Jund will ever find Langdon Trutwin. I don't think the world will ever again hear from Langdon Trutwin or his bodyguard.*

Cady kissed his fingers and touched them to the top of Liz Preston's tombstone. Then he headed back to his rental car, hoping he'd make Reagan National in time for his flight.

ACKNOWLEDGMENTS

I would like to thank Judith Shepard, Martin Shepard, and Barbara Anderson at The Permanent Press for their kind words, encouragement, and meticulous editing; my father, Bruce W. Burton, for his numerous reviews; and my wife, Cindy—without whom I would truly be homeless.